The Nanny With The Nice List

K. Sterling

To Charles Greimsman for being the most caring, clever, and patient editor I've ever worked with. You make every book feel like a fun, loving collaboration and you put just as much of your heart into these stories as I do. I'm so grateful to have you on my writing dream team.

And to the human first aid kit that patches me up and heals me when I'm barely hanging on. Thank you from the bottom of my heart to Reese Ryan, Leigh Carron, Roshni, Melissa, Sue, and my amazing PA, Lindsey Middlemiss.

Finally, to Kalob Dàniel. Thank you for being the most supportive and generous muse an author could ever hope for. Your friendship and kindness touched my heart when I was just starting this series and your talent and creativity have inspired me to fill this world with braver, brighter, and kinder heroes like you.

The 'Nanny' with the Nice List

with the

by K. Sterling
illustrations by @i.nashkolna

The *Nanny* with the *Nice List* Playlist

Christmas All Over Again	Tom Petty and the Heartbreakers
It's Beginning To Look A Lot Like Christmas	Michael Bublé
Mr. Heatmiser	Big Bad Voodoo Daddy
White Christmas	Dean Martin
Sleigh Ride	The Ronettes
Last Christmas	Wham!
The 12 Days of Christmas	Straight No Chaser
Blue Christmas	Elvis Presley
Holly Jolly Christmas	Michael Bublé
Father Christmas	The Kinks
Elf's Lament	Barenaked Ladies, Michael Bublé
Christmas In Hollis	Run-D.M.C.
God Rest Ye Merry Gentlemen	Barenaked Ladies, Sarah McLachlan

Content Warnings:

Dear Reader,

This book is intended to be a heartwarming holiday romcom, but Gavin Selby's past includes moments that may be difficult for some readers. Specifically, an act of **homophobic parental abuse and abandonment of a child**. Thankfully, we only need to revisit that part of Gavin's and Briarwood Terrace's origins briefly in Chapter 1. After that, Dash comes to the rescue with the sweetest, sexiest holiday adventure I could dream up for Gavin.

There are also brief mentions of:
    * The death of a parent during surgery and from an illness, and a parent receiving end-of-life care.
    * Sports-related injuries, including post-concussion syndrome, depression, anxiety, and panic attacks.
    * Loss of a job.

Please be aware and take extra care if you are sensitive to parental homophobia and abuse because no reader should ever be harmed in the making of a book.

Love and happy reading,

K. Sterling

Prologue

I t all began with an ill-timed trip to the restroom. Dash had stopped by Briarwood Terrace to leave his resumé and have a word with Reid Marshall about joining the newly formed Marshall Agency. His work history was particularly light and Dash was hoping a basket of his famous orange and cranberry muffins would inspire Reid to give him a chance despite his lack of childcare experience. The doorman had buzzed Dash in and said that Reid's roommate, Gavin, had only just arrived.

The door to unit number 4 was cracked when Dash came around the corner. He let himself in, tapping and announcing himself quietly, but the living room and kitchen were dark. Dash heard Gavin talking loudly, then spotted him pacing on the other side of the kitchen windows with his phone.

Whatever the conversation was about, Gavin didn't look happy. He was flailing and had knocked over a chair in the courtyard. And instead of being hung on the proper hooks with care, Gavin's overcoat and briefcase were on the floor by the door. Not wanting to interrupt or disturb anything, Dash quietly picked up Gavin's things and left the resumé and the muffins on the kitchen table. He was backing away, intending to leave before he was detected, but Dash *really* had to pee.

He ducked into the hallway and used Reid's bathroom and Dash was set to make his escape when he heard a strangled expletive in the kitchen. Dash was stunned to hear something so loud and *angry* in Briarwood Terrace and from Gavin, of all people. Of course, Dash had heard Reid and Gavin swear before. They were more worldly and hardened than Dash was at just shy of thirty. But the gentlemen of Briarwood Terrace had long been the backbone of their little group and Dash couldn't recall either Reid or Gavin having a temper or losing their cool. And Dash couldn't recall either of them saying an unkind word to or about anyone, they were both so level-headed and mature.

"Son of a motherfucking whore!" Gavin spat, causing Dash to jump when something slapped against a counter or the work table.

Dash tiptoed closer and peeked around the wall, his eyes widening as Gavin's arms pumped and he punched at the air wildly. He'd removed his coat and his tie had been yanked loose, revealing an all-new Gavin Dash had never encountered. Gone was the sedate and dour accountant who rarely spoke above a dry rumble. Dash stared in awe and a touch of lust as Gavin's perfectly proper shirt stretched around his well-defined shoulders and revealed a narrow waist and a tight, but firm backside in his tailored trousers.

Dash had thought Gavin was rather handsome, in a nerdy professor kind of way, yet too aloof and far too serious for them to have much in common. But Gavin was *hot* as he swept his hands through his hair, his long, elegant fingers twisting in frustration and leaving his neat ash blond coif in sexy disarray. "You petty, miserable sack of shit, I hope you—!" Gavin pulled the refrigerator door open. *"Fuck!"* He yelled as he slammed it shut, making Dash jump again. "Where is my fucking teacup?" Gavin gasped shakily, turning and looking lost and devastated.

Dash had become a regular at the Gilded Era townhouse after his best friend and platonic soulmate, Penny Lane Tucker, had joined Reid Marshall's new agency. Reid and his younger brother, Fin, had been friends with Penny and her older brother, Penn, for just about as long as Dash had known the Tucker siblings.

Hanging out with Penny, Fin, and Riley had truly been an escape from the pressures of being both Swift Griffin's son and the heir to the Mooney football dynasty. Dash's friends simply forgot that his father was a football legend or did not care. The fact that the Tuckers, along with nearly all of their friends were queer and performing arts nerds probably had something to do with that.

Which was why it was such a shock to hear Gavin cussing and fuming like he'd just come off the field after a crushing defeat. The nurturing calm of Briarwood Terrace had been disrupted. It had been over a decade since Dash had walked away from a promising football career, but he was momentarily transported back to the locker room as he watched Gavin ranting and railing in the kitchen.

Dash stayed behind the wall, eavesdropping and waiting for a name or a reason, but Gavin seemed to blame himself more than whoever had wronged him.

"Reid can't find out about this!" Gavin fretted as he paced. "I have to fix this before anyone finds out."

Oh, no!

Dash covered his mouth, realizing he was now in joint possession of a secret. He *hated* secrets, but he trusted that Gavin had a very good reason for wanting to keep whatever this was to himself. And Dash found that he wanted to gain Gavin's trust and help him.

For purely altruistic reasons, of course. It had nothing to do with the fact that Dash was curious to see what Gavin looked like under his impeccably tailored suit. Or what else the uptight accountant was capable of once he had ripped off said suit...

Apparently, there was far more to Gavin Selby than Dash —and most of the world—had assumed. And Dash had a feeling that something *big* was going on. He didn't know what that something was, but he suspected it had the potential to upend the peace at Briarwood Terrace and put the Marshall Agency at risk. Most importantly, Dash's gut told him that Gavin was in trouble and needed help.

Dash had been looking for ways to prove he could be useful despite never having worked as a nanny. But now, he had a new reason for becoming indispensable to Reid: he had to get closer to Gavin and figure out how to save him.

Chapter One

T wo-and-a-half years later...

Most people—incorrectly—thought of the clarinet as a soft and somber instrument. Some might even suggest that it was a boring one. They would also be incorrect. The King of Swing, Benny Goodman, had played the clarinet and the versatile, single-reed woodwind had set the course of Gavin Selby's life as a child and it had saved him.

He always experienced a profound sense of gratitude whenever he took his contrabass clarinet out of its case and propped it on its stand for his sacred Saturday ritual. Gavin took great care as he shaved, laid out the day's suit, sat in his T-shirt, boxers, and socks, and picked up his instrument. Gavin's clarinet was a larger, deeper, pedal relative of the various Selmer jazz models the King of Swing preferred. But Gavin felt centered and balanced whenever he lovingly polished its nickel-plated keys and assumed a proper playing posture. And Gavin's heart fluttered whenever he set his lips to the reed and the mouthpiece and played his first note of the morning.

Gavin never would have moved to his uncle Henry's home at Briarwood Terrace when he was six, to attend Saint Ann's in Brooklyn, if it hadn't been for the "boring" instrument. His parents were delighted to have *something* to brag about the otherwise dull and unremarkable heir to the Selby financial empire. As a result, Gavin was sent to New York to learn from the best music teachers, in hopes that he would one day attend Juilliard. Of course, his parents couldn't be bothered with raising a child themselves and had remained at the Selby family estate, Heathcote, in Scarsdale, entrusting Gavin's maternal uncle Henry to oversee his care and education.

That had backfired on Gavin's parents because Uncle Henry was a wonderful older man who had loved Gavin like a son. Henry did his best to give Gavin a *normal* childhood and enjoyed thumbing his nose at the uptight Selbys whenever he could. Henry and Gavin's father didn't get along *at all*, but his parents weren't interested in relocating to Manhattan or raising their son, so they looked the other way. Thanks to Henry, Gavin had flourished in the city without his parents.

Then, during his sophomore year of college, Gavin was abruptly summoned home to Heathcote. He dutifully traveled to Scarsdale and presented himself in his father's study for what would be one of the most appalling and humiliating moments of his life.

"You know Hillary Lauder," Edward Selby began, but Gavin shook his head.

"Not personally, sir," he said, only to receive a dismissive wave. Gavin did his best not to shrink as the powerful financier and real estate mogul's eyes tightened behind his glasses, inspecting and assessing. Edward was tall, lean, and dour, and there was no mistaking that Gavin was his offspring as they came face-to-face over a Persian Kirman rug.

"No matter," Edward continued. "She's taking classes in the city now and it's time the two of you started going about."

"Going about? I'm sure she has friends who can show her around," Gavin mused cluelessly.

"Don't be a child, Gavin. We want the two of you established as a pair well before the wedding this summer. It won't be the event of the season if the two of you don't make a good showing this spring," Edward explained.

Gavin felt like the walls were closing in on him. "Me and Hillary Lauder?" There was a good chance he was going to be sick. He had *heard* the Lauders mentioned regularly as a child and remembered meeting Hillary before he was packed off to live with Uncle Henry. But he didn't *know* her and there was the small, yet crucial fact that Gavin was gay.

It was small in that Gavin was nineteen and cared very little about his sexuality at the time. His closest friends were gay and were exploring and experimenting, but Gavin was too focused on his grades and too busy with practices and rehearsals. And he was too scared to dip his toes in the college dating scene. Everything was too fast and too much.

"I'm sorry, but I...can't. I'm..." Gavin's voice had cracked and his nose had begun to run, making him feel and look even more like a child. He *never* imagined having this conversation with either of his parents. "I'm...not attracted to women," he mumbled, his gaze dropping to the rug.

"You keep that to yourself," Edward growled, jabbing Gavin in the chest. "I know all about you and your friends. Including that Marshall boy. I've kept a closer eye on you than Henry has and I don't want you associating with him or the rest of that group anymore. People will suspect that you're like them but you'll put an end to that with Hillary," Edward concluded.

Gavin saw the trap looming ahead and every cell in his body instinctively screamed for him to *run*. "I'm sorry, but I won't do it." His voice had wavered and his knees were knocking against each other, yet Gavin raised his chin and shook his head.

Edward gave Gavin's shoulder a hard shove. "You don't have a choice. This was decided when the two of you were infants and we've signed contracts. The Lauders have given you their place in Water Mill for your starter home."

"No. I'm sorry. But I won't—" Gavin was dizzy and his skin began to prickle. "I won't do it." He had to put his foot down if it was the last thing he did before he cast up his accounts or his dignity by fainting at his father's feet. "I won't marry her and I'm not giving up my friends," he stated with as much bravado as he could muster. Gavin saw flickering, floating shapes as his father snarled at him.

"You'll do what I tell you and you'll keep your mouth shut," he said, his palm clapping hard against Gavin's cheek, nearly knocking him off his feet.

Gavin clutched his jaw and shook his head. "No. I won't do it."

Edward thumped Gavin's chest, making him stumble back. "You'll do what I say or I'll destroy you," his father explained simply. "I'll close all of your accounts and I'll stop paying for your school. You'll be a nobody and you'll be worthless because I'll make it very clear that you are no longer a Selby."

But my life won't be worth anything without Reid. I'm no one without my friends.

"Very well," Gavin said with a stiff bow, then turned and promptly left.

There was no car to drive him back to the city that day so

Gavin took a bus and then the train to Lenox Hill. He was indeed penniless by the time he returned, but Uncle Henry had promised that everything would work out and it had. Henry had paid for the rest of Gavin's education and left him Briarwood Terrace and a comfortable inheritance when he was twenty-four.

It had been close to two decades since Henry had passed, but Gavin thanked him every single morning when he awoke in his beloved Briarwood Terrace and when he prepared to play his clarinet. It had never been Gavin's dream to perform with an orchestra or to tour the world as a musician. All he had ever wanted was for his parents to be proud and to love him.

That never happened. When Gavin was twenty-six, he received a letter from his father's attorneys informing him that his mother had died during a cosmetic procedure and had been laid to rest at Heathcote a week earlier. His request for permission to view her resting place had been denied, but Gavin took comfort in the knowledge that he had found a much better replacement for his parents' affections.

He and Reid had created a big, beautiful life and Gavin could hear it filling Briarwood Terrace as he played his clarinet. Gavin's heart sang when he heard Fin call a good morning from the kitchen and the low rumbles of Penn's and Walker Cameron's voices as they teased each other. There were cheers when Riley arrived and it was so easy for Gavin to forget that he was a Selby.

Now, he played for himself and did his best to express his feelings for Reid and their friends through his music. Gavin wished they understood how much they meant to him as they gathered in the kitchen while he put away his clarinet and finished dressing. They were Gavin's world, but he was—to his own disappointment—still too much of a Selby to ever tell them with words. Instead, he serenaded them on Saturdays and wore more festive ensembles to cheer them up and send them out into the world feeling as loved and supported as they made him feel.

Gavin was feeling particularly pleased and content as he wound the ends of a red paisley tie around and over and under, giving the knot at his throat a slight tug at the end. He went to the dresser mirror to make sure it was straight, smiling at the pattern. The paisleys were actually poinsettia petals and there were tiny green holly leaves and berries hidden within the pattern as well. Gavin gave the tie and his reflection one last check, then reached for his coat on the valet stand by the door. He'd been in a flashier mood earlier and had selected a brown tweed instead of black or gray.

"Is it too much?" He asked himself as he returned to the mirror. His head tilted as he considered the green pocket square. He'd almost chosen a red one. Now, *that* would have been too much. Gavin snorted as he smoothed back his hair to make sure it was neat.

Pleased with his appropriately festive appearance, Gavin opened his door and hummed contentedly when he was greeted by the smell of coffee and the sound of chatter in the kitchen. Everyone was still milling around and catching up on the week's gossip as Gavin sidestepped around Penn. He was holding a bagel out of Riley's reach and Fin and Walker were seated and flirting over their coffees. Penny and her wife, Agnes, were on the window seat, whispering conspiratorially as they watched their brothers, hatching God only knew what manner of mischief.

"Morning," Reid said cheerfully. He was watching the group's newest newlyweds and chuckling as he handed Gavin his tea.

"Morning. Glad to see you made it back from the trenches in one piece," Gavin murmured over the rim, sipping as he turned and headed for his seat in the living room.

"'Love is like war; easy to start but hard to end and you never know where it might take you,'" Reid quoted back, making Gavin snicker.

Fin and the gathered rabble would be scandalized if they knew what Reid had been up to while they were enjoying their blissfully domestic Friday nights. They assumed their competent, responsible leader spent his evening at home in urbane dignity and that he would one day find a decent and respectable man. Neither Gavin nor Reid had any intentions of doing so, but happily encouraged Fin and their friends to believe they were healthy, functioning adults.

Gavin silently applauded Reid's ability to present himself bright and early every Saturday morning without fail for brunch. Anyone could drop by as early as 9:00 and there was often a crowd by the time Gavin was finished practicing his clarinet. Reid had a warm smile, a cup of coffee, and pastries from the shop around the corner ready and no one was ever the wiser.

The back door opened and Gavin braced himself as a rich, rising laugh filled the kitchen. The sound warmed Gavin like playing his clarinet in a beam of sunlight at the window but he remained outwardly calm, sipping his tea and awaiting his turn.

"Check it out, Gavin!"

There he was: Mr. Sunshine. Mr. *Everything*.

Dash giggled as he hurried into the living room with his hands outstretched, cupping a large ball of snow. Gavin shut his eyes, savoring the tickle in his belly and the way the hairs on the back of his neck stood.

"Hmm?" He looked up from his tea, raising his brows politely, but not too much. It wouldn't do to encourage Dash. In addition to being a full decade younger, Dash was incredibly wholesome and a touch naive so Gavin did his best to avoid misleading him. And Dash was far too beautiful and energetic for a bland, faded fuddy-duddy like Gavin.

"Penny bet me I couldn't gather enough snow to make a snowball but look! If we had a hoop, I could dunk this," Dash said as he carefully raised it like he was going to, causing Gavin to lean away. "I wouldn't!" Dash insisted and went to the front door to dispose of it.

A soft sigh escaped Gavin and he craned his neck slightly so he could watch as Dash's sweatshirt tightened around his broad, muscular shoulders and biceps. The waist of his jeans slid down as he rolled the ball out the door at invisible pins, revealing a hint of bright blue elastic, making Gavin's heart race. Dash really did have the most spectacular ass.

"Yes!" Dash cheered as if he'd scored a strike and Gavin's gaze dropped into his teacup before he was caught staring.

"Bravo. Now, close the door before I get a chill," he muttered and pulled in his shoulders.

"Sorry! I'll go get you a muffin while they're still warm," Dash said, zipping past the sofa before Gavin could tell him it wouldn't be necessary. Dash reappeared a moment later with a plate bearing a perfect muffin. "It's orange and cranberry. I made them this morning because I know they're your favorite," he confided with a wink.

Gavin flinched, his jaw and body locking as he resisted the urge to smile and squirm. He stared while his ears popped and his shirt stuck to his body beneath his wool vest and coat. There was a warm tingling in Gavin's trousers and he prayed his face wasn't turning red.

For the love of God, why did I think I'd need a vest? I'm suffocating.

"I did skip dinner last night," Gavin said in a low mumble once he could trust his voice. "Thank you," he added awkwardly and nodded as he accepted the plate and set it on the table next to him.

"Enjoy!" Dash stunned him with another wink before spinning and racing back to the kitchen, leaving cheerful charm and warmth in his wake.

Gavin savored that as well, quietly pulling in the smell of Dash's shampoo and fabric softener and the gentle glow of kindness still lingering in the room. He was the human equivalent of a breath of fresh air and filled every room he entered with light. And Dash was happy to play the empty-headed himbo because *he* was happiest when everyone around him was smiling. Nothing that pure and good had ever existed in Gavin's world and he'd already been blessed with beautiful, loving friends before Dash became a regular at Briarwood Terrace.

The addition of Penny's best friend to Gavin's social orbit had been one of the many beautiful consequences of Reid's agency. Of course, they had known of Dash before and he had visited Briarwood Terrace with Penny on a few occasions. But Dash became a permanent fixture and Reid's shadow after Penny recruited him.

Young and full of curiosity and passion, Dash put his heart into everything he did and flourished everywhere he went. And *everyone* mattered to Dash. He made time to remember people's names, where they were from, and what made them smile.

Gavin had noticed all of this because he noticed everything Dash did and paid very close attention to every word he said. There wasn't a cruel bone or jealous hair on Dash's spectacular body and that was why Gavin was hopelessly in love with him. But there wasn't a damn thing Gavin could do about it and it was only a matter of time before someone better came along and swept Dash off his feet.

The two of them had been a source of speculation within their little group for a while, but Gavin thought the entire notion was rather obvious and absurd and couldn't understand the fixation with them lately.

It was obvious because how could Gavin *not* want Dash with the burning intensity of a thousand suns? Dash had a pure and gentle soul, a mind that was far sharper than most people gave him credit for, the face of an adonis, and a body...

Gavin groaned into his cup and cursed himself for wearing a vest *and* tweed when he had no plans to leave the house. He was dressed for the blustery day outside and slowly cooking in four layers, counting his undershirt. One of the many reasons why he and Dash were absurdly incompatible. Gavin swaddled himself in tweed and wool like a geriatric toddler while Dash looked like Superman or a star quarterback in jeans and a hoodie.

Literally anyone would be attracted to Dash, you'd have to be dead or have an actual heart of stone. No one was impervious to Dash's brilliant smiles and magnetic charm, certainly not Gavin. He went absolutely haywire, silently imploding because Gavin had no idea what to do with a man like Dash.

In most cases, a forty-two-year-old dating a thirty-two-year-old wouldn't be all that brow-raising, but Gavin was a dinosaur compared to someone as vibrant and outgoing as Dash. Their friends were all too kind to admit it, but Gavin was barely out of the closet. He was woefully—but willfully—inexperienced when it came to men. He had preferred to live quietly and it was safer to act as if he was hard-hearted and sexless whenever Dash was around because Gavin could never have him.

Aside from the fact that Dash was far too good and too beautiful inside and out for Gavin, there were the awful consequences that were bound to follow. Because if there was one thing Edward Selby would not stand for, it would be Gavin finding real love and living happily ever after. Any sign of that would be like waving a red flag at a wrathful bull. In fact, he was so sure his father would strike hard and fast if there was so much as a *hint* of a rumor that Gavin was romantically connected to anyone, anything more than basic kindness towards Dash was strongly prohibited. Especially outside of Briarwood Terrace.

Unlike Gavin, Dash had his family's love and unconditional support. Edward was too smart to risk upsetting the Mooneys by publicly attacking Dash himself. Instead, he would find underhanded ways to smear Dash's wholesome, heart-of-gold reputation on the internet and social media. Gavin had lost hours of sleep worrying about all the possibilities. But in reality, all it would take was a few compromising photos and a handful of ugly accusations to do real harm to Dash's standing in the community and his prospects outside of the agency.

Which left Gavin no choice but to watch from his armchair in the living room, quietly collecting winks and smiles until Dash grew tired or found a more worthy man or woman to bestow them upon.

"I have a muffin," Gavin reminded himself, plucking a cranberry from the top. They were his favorite, but only because Dash added a drizzle of orange frosting to his. No one else did that, as far as Gavin was aware, and every muffin tasted as bright and sweet as one of Dash's laughs and his heart-stopping smiles. "I can have that, at least."

Bright & Spicy Cranberry Muffins

- 2 cups all-purpose flour
- ¾ cup brown sugar, packed
- 2 teaspoons baking powder
- 1 teaspoon ground cinnamon
- ½ teaspoon salt
- ¼ teaspoon baking soda
- ½ teaspoon ground ginger
- ¼ teaspoon ground cloves
- ¼ teaspoon ground nutmeg
- 1 cup unsweetened pumpkin puree
- 1 Orange, for juice and zest
- ½ cup unsalted butter, melted
- ¼ cup buttermilk
- 2 eggs
- 2 teaspoons vanilla extract
- 1 cup fresh or dried, sweetened cranberries
- 1 cup confectioners' sugar

- Preheat the oven to 400 degrees F (200 degrees C). Line a 12-cup muffin tin with paper liners.

- Mix flour, brown sugar, baking powder, cinnamon, salt, baking soda, ginger, cloves, and nutmeg together in a mixing bowl.

- Beat pumpkin puree, 1/2 teaspoon orange zest, melted butter, buttermilk, eggs, and vanilla in another large mixing bowl until well combined. Gradually beat in flour mixture, then stir in dried cranberries until incorporated. Fill prepared muffin cups about 3/4 full with batter.

- Bake in the preheated oven until a toothpick inserted in the middle of a muffin comes out clean, 20 to 25 minutes. Remove from the oven and let rest for a few minutes before turning muffins out onto a wire rack.

- For glaze: add orange juice and 1/2 teaspoon of zest to confectioners' sugar to make a glaze and drizzle over muffins. Serve warm or at room temperature.

Chapter Two

There was absolutely *nothing* better than winter in New York City as far as Dash Griffin was concerned. The decorations, the *extra* twinkling lights, the holiday music, the window displays, and the parades. Dash loved the parades! But the possibilities were endless if you were looking for a magical holiday experience. There was the tree in Rockefeller Plaza, Santaland at Macy's, the world's largest Menorah at Grand Army Plaza, the Lantern Festival in the Snug Harbor Botanical Garden, the Winter Village at Bryant Park... New York City was a winter wonderland!

The cloudy, blustery weather never failed to put Dash in the mood for romantic, snowy walks in Central Park, cups of hot cocoa, and soup dumplings. And there was only one person Dash was interested in taking romantic walks or sharing cocoa and soup dumplings with.

The object of Dash's intense and unwavering affections had settled into a wingback by the fire and was contently sipping Earl Gray and humming Rachmaninoff's Symphony

No. 2. Dash had stayed behind after brunch to help with the dishes and was pretending to read a cookbook in the kitchen.

After more than a decade of hopping from career to career and living a charmed, but somewhat aimless life, so many of Dash's biggest questions were about to be answered. It was a crisp, snowy day outside and Dash could *feel* the holiday magic twinkling around them as he waited to make his move. He hadn't solved all of Gavin's riddles yet, but the answers were finally within Dash's reach.

The plan to secure a good job *and* save Gavin from his scary secret had turned out to be Dash's destiny and it was wrapped in a big red bow and waiting for him in the living room. What started as a crush had bloomed into love and an intense attraction once Dash had noticed that Gavin was actually rather handsome behind his glasses and his grumbles. After that, it was hard to stop noticing that he had really nice eyes, lips, and hands or that he always smelled like a clean shave and a cup of tea. His low, rumbling voice made Dash's stomach flip and God help him when Gavin smiled. It rarely happened, but when it did, Dash wanted to lick it right off his face. And then lick just about every other inch of Gavin's tall, lanky body.

Then, Dash noticed that Gavin was full of secrets and most of them were lovely. He pretended to be annoyed when number 4 was full and bursting with noise and activity, but Dash saw Gavin hiding little smiles behind his teacup. There were even occasional chuckles from the wingback chair by the fire and Dash had even caught Gavin wiping a tear from his eye once while Morris was singing a sweet but silly song to Penn. He did his best to hide it, but Gavin quietly lived for his friends and was devoted to Reid and their agency. And that's what Dash loved most of all about him.

Dash had come to share Gavin's devotion, although being a

floating or substitute nanny wasn't exactly his passion. But there wasn't really a title for the position Dash currently held within the Marshall Agency or a demand for it outside of Briarwood Terrace. Whatever it was called, Dash finally felt like he'd found his calling as an ambiguous childcare professional and felt happiest and most useful when he was at Reid's side, solving puzzles for fellow nannies and clients. And Dash was putting his social media prowess to good use, focusing on the agency's branding around its mission to provide inclusive, family-focused, and highly-skilled childcare.

Dash had his days at the library on East 79th Street as well. Volunteering at his favorite library was the perfect outlet for Dash's enthusiasm for books and learning and his love of service. The librarians there were always overworked and underappreciated and there were a million ways to be useful. It was easy to find someone who needed help finding something and there were always things to put away. Plus, the elevator was often out of service so it was a great way for Dash to burn up extra energy. Which he always had an abundance of.

The library had also provided Dash with the key to solving his most vexing riddle after spotting Gavin reclining in an armchair in the corner of the periodicals area. Dash was about to swing by and say hello when Ashley, one of said overworked librarians, whispered in his ear that she'd nicknamed Gavin "Tall, Stark, and Stuffy" because he *did not* like to be disturbed. Ashley continued to tell Dash about how Tall, Stark, and Stuffy had been arriving early and occupying that same chair in the corner until lunchtime nearly every weekday *for months*.

Because the elevator was cursed and eternally broken, Dash's main area of responsibility was running up and down the steps for the aforementioned librarians and maintaining order in the busier kids' section upstairs. Dash rarely visited the quieter corner of the library's first floor, but upon conferring with Penny, they agreed that the best course of action was to gather as much intel as they could before alerting anyone else. They spent weeks covertly observing Gavin at the library, tailing him to the Olympia, The Killian House, and Penn and Morris's place.

Penny had also "interrogated" Agnes and they had pieced together a rather concerning picture: Gavin no longer had a job at the prestigious accounting firm, Ernst & Waterhouse. He pretended to leave Briarwood Terrace every morning to go to the office and was hiding at the library, instead. Reid believed that Gavin spent his days at the office and made house calls on his free afternoons to do basic low-level accounting work for their friends and to practice with the Cameron and Ashby children for the annual Christmas Eve eve party.

But for some reason, Gavin was hiding the truth from Reid and the rest of their friends. Walker and Giles knew about Gavin's unemployment and had given him work out of pity, but even they didn't know the full details and had been sworn to secrecy. After weeks of spying, Dash and Penny had yet to uncover the reason or why Gavin was hiding and had agreed that it was finally time for an intervention.

They didn't know why Gavin was lying to everyone, but they assumed he had a good reason. It was agreed that a subtle approach was needed and Dash had volunteered to quietly confront Gavin with their suspicions. He was just waiting for the right opportunity and the perfect solution had presented itself Friday morning in the guise of a Santa mishap and Dash had sprung into action.

Ashley's husband, James, had dressed up and read to children during the library's Stories With Santa evening for the last six years and had committed to doing it again this year. But James had thrown his back out *again* and was having emergency surgery the day before the library's most popular holiday event.

Dash would have been an obvious choice if he wasn't so well-known to the library's younger patrons. Plus, Dash had his heart set on being Santa's helper and wearing his "Buddy the Elf" costume again. Dash had promised he'd come through and find a substitute Santa. But with less than two weeks to the library's big holiday party, every decent Santa in the city was booked. Dash had called several talent agencies but the Friday night before Christmas was one of their busiest nights so a safe and reliable amateur Santa would have to be found.

Luckily for Dash, he had a bunch of friends who were great with kids and would be happy to do it. Gavin was not one of them, but Dash was going to make him a holiday offer he couldn't refuse.

"It's for his own good," Dash whispered, his eyes twinkling with anticipation. He was biding his time until they were alone and then he'd stage his one-man holiday intervention.

Thankfully, it didn't take long for Briarwood Terrace to clear out after brunch. Everyone except Dash, Gavin, and Reid had spouses and children to return to and there was much to do with the holiday season in full swing and their big Christmas Eve eve party just around the corner.

"I'm heading out," Reid announced as he returned from his room, pulling on his coat and scarf and heading for the door. "Meeting Mom for Christmas shopping so don't wait up for me. You know we'll end up having dinner and then martinis at Bemelmans."

"That sounds like an amazing day," Dash said, hurrying around the counter and into the living room.

Reid's head tipped from side to side as he knotted his scarf. "Let's see how hungover I am tomorrow and how my feet feel after a day with my mother. She's like a terminator in heels and won't stop until she's maxed out all her spending limits."

"That can be quite a feat these days," Gavin observed from his seat by the fire.

Reid humphed and rolled his eyes. "Dad usually has the good sense to check their accounts around sunset. He'll beg Mom to put down her debit cards and pick up a cocktail."

"Smart," Gavin said, shaking his head as he sipped his tea. "Stay safe and tell her not to buy me anything," he grumbled over the rim of his cup.

"Have fun and don't listen to him!" Dash said as he waved Reid off at the door. He closed it and cleared his throat softly, taking a large step toward the sofa. Dash flashed a wide, sheepish smile as he skipped his fingers across the leather cushions while Gavin raised a brow warily from his seat on the other side.

"Is there something I can do for you?" Gavin asked in his low, flat rumble.

Which was exactly the question Dash was hoping for. "Yes, actually!" He made a giddy sound as he raced around the sofa and sat on the coffee table, startling Gavin.

"I meant that figuratively. Did everyone...?" He leaned and looked around the side of his chair.

"It's just us and don't be silly," Dash said as he gave Gavin's knee a playful swat, making him jump.

"Silly? I'm never silly."

"Sure you are," Dash said dismissively, then hesitated. "The thing is... I need help and I'm a tiny bit desperate."

Gavin's neck craned and he looked concerned. "Desperate?"

That was a good sign so Dash went with it. "My coworker's husband usually dresses up as Santa for our library's Stories With Santa event in two weeks, but James hurt his back and he has to have surgery the day before. You have no idea how hard it is to book a decent Santa on such short notice."

"I'm afraid I don't know any Santas." Gavin attempted to get up and flee and swore when Dash grabbed his elbow.

"It's for the kids!"

"Whose kids? Not mine," Gavin said, shaking his head. "I don't even like children."

"That's weird," Dash replied as he rubbed his chin. "Because you help run a *childcare* agency."

"I 'run' the accounts," Gavin corrected. "No one would leave me alone with a child."

"Why not? You're...quiet, but you'd never hurt a child."

"No." Gavin shook his head, frowning. "For my own protection. Children are terrifying."

That made Dash laugh. "They are not! But they can be overwhelming for some people and that's okay. You could do it...*for me.*" He widened his eyes and made his lower lip wobble, doing his best puppy impersonation. "I'll owe you," he added suggestively, causing Gavin to flinch and draw back.

"Owe me? What could you possibly...?"

Dash shushed and waved wildly. "Fine. Do it so you'll be on the nice list," he said, earning a dubious frown.

"It would take a lot more than a costume and a story to get me on the nice list."

"What are you talking about?" Dash protested. "You're nice."

Gavin snorted into his teacup. "I don't know who gave you that impression, but I most certainly am not on anyone's nice list."

"You're one of the nicest people I know," Dash informed him, defiantly crossing his arms over his chest. "And I'm going to prove it."

"How?" Gavin asked warily.

"Did you know that kids come from *all over* Manhattan for Stories With Santa? It's the library's most popular event of the year and it's a tradition for a lot of families. It's one of the reasons why I *had to* get a job there. I'm not smart enough to get a master's degree in library science, but I can volunteer and every year I get to be one of Santa's elves and give out cookies and cocoa and free books!" He pumped his fists and squealed excitedly.

"I don't understand how..." Gavin blinked at Dash, mystified.

Dash gave Gavin's knee a poke, making him jump again. "Think. A. Bout. It," he said, punctuating each syllable with a jab. "You're not gonna let *all those kids down.* Are you?" He asked dramatically and batted his eyes even harder.

"Me?" Gavin's face fell. "Why do I...? What about Penn or Morris? I have to be the least Santa-like person you know," he mused as he shook his head.

"And me!" Dash added quickly. "I know you'd never let me down."

"I let you down almost daily when you ask me to have dinner or coffee with you."

That was true and stung a little because Dash wanted to go on a date with Gavin so badly. But Gavin was never cruel when he said no and Dash sensed that something else was holding him back. "Not when it really matters. You never let your friends down. It's one of the reasons you're one of the nicest people I know," Dash said brightly.

It didn't have to be anything fancy or exciting. Even though, a walk in the park and two cups of hot chocolate could change the trajectory of their lives if Gavin would just give them a chance. But they rarely ever saw each other outside of Briarwood Terrace. Except at the library.

"I'm only returning the favor. Everyone puts up with me,"

Gavin said dismissively and shifted in his seat, looking very uncomfortable.

Dash shook his head. "That's not true at all. You pretend to be Gavin the Grouch but I can see that you *love* us."

There was a bored chuckle as Gavin stared Dash down over the rim of his cup. "You've discovered my dark secret and this is the price for your silence?" He added with a sarcastic snort.

"Sort of..." Dash chewed on his lip anxiously, deciding it was time to reveal that this was also an intervention. "Speaking of secrets, why haven't you told Reid that you're not working anymore?" Dash asked and Gavin fumbled his teacup and it clattered onto the saucer.

"What...? What are you talking about?" He shook his head, but the color drained from his face.

"You know I volunteer at the library three days a week and you're always there. And Ashley told me you come in just about every morning and stay until around lunchtime. She said you've been a regular for months," Dash explained gently.

Gavin swallowed loudly and he blinked at the rug between them. "Of course, I knew. I..." He stared silently for a moment, then shook his head. "You spend most of your time on the second floor and I thought you wouldn't notice me. It's a very large library."

"You thought you could hide from me?" Dash asked in confusion. "There?"

"Yes." The cup and saucer rattled as Gavin set it down. "I manage to blend in rather well everywhere else and go unnoticed. I don't know why *anyone* would notice another boring businessman reading a paper."

"But you're not a boring businessman to me," Dash argued. "Why don't you go to work anymore?"

There was another long pause and Gavin had to clear his

throat several times before his voice would work. "They didn't want to do it and my boss, Mark, tried to protect me for as long as he could. But my father put so much pressure on him and the firm, they had to let me go."

"Your father? Why would he want you to lose your job?" Dash had always paid extra attention whenever the subject of Gavin's parents came up because one, *he* had parents who loved and supported him unconditionally so it didn't make sense, that Gavin's parents could be so cruel and abandon him like that. And, two, Dash couldn't imagine what Gavin could have done to deserve any of it. If anything, Dash wondered how Gavin's father hadn't seen the man he had become and had a change of heart.

Gavin snorted. "He'll take whatever he can away from me."

"Wait." Dash's head tipped to the side as he considered everything he had learned about Gavin and his family. "Your father's *still* punishing you for being gay? Because you wouldn't marry some girl when you were in college?" He verified.

"And other reasons," Gavin said vaguely.

"Why go after you now, though? What could you have possibly done?" Dash asked, then gasped because there was only one thing that had changed in Gavin's very quiet and very routine-oriented existence. "The Marshall Agency. He's punishing you because you're helping Reid with the agency," he realized.

"It was the agency," Gavin confirmed, scrubbing his face and groaning. "And Wolford. The old asshole and my father are close friends, believe it or not," he added facetiously. "My father wrote a letter ordering me to intercede on Wolford's behalf when Giles retaliated against the old bigot for firing Fin and costing Riley his job. I replied saying I would do nothing. My father wrote back and said it was his final warning, that he'd destroy me if I didn't help Wolford, turn Reid out, and end the Marshall Agency at once. I refused, of course. A week later, I lost my job. None of that matters, though. The agency and Reid are practically untouchable now thanks to Walker and Giles," Gavin said, but the muscle in his jaw twitched and his nostrils flared.

"How can you say that? You *loved* your job! Being an accountant is...your thing!" Dash protested and gasped again when he remembered the tantrum he had observed in the kitchen. "That's why you were so angry that day. I saw you slam the refrigerator door because you couldn't find your teacup. But I knew something else was going on."

Gavin reeled for a moment, then shook his head. "It doesn't matter. The agency keeps me busy enough."

"But it doesn't!" Dash said and Gavin held up a hand, shushing him.

"Please! I'll be your Santa if you'll let this go. You *cannot* say anything to Reid about this."

"But—!" Dash began and stopped when Gavin gave him a pointed look.

"I'm perfectly fine. My uncle Henry was very generous and I've invested wisely. I don't need the income, but our friends have sent what work they can my way to keep me busy and I'm looking after Morris's finances."

"So Giles and Walker do know that you're hiding this from Reid," Dash confirmed and covered his mouth to hold back a nervous laugh as he imagined Reid's reaction. "Reid doesn't know that you lost your job, but Walker and Giles know..." He widened his eyes, hoping Gavin appreciated how *mad* Reid would be if he found out.

"Please." Gavin pressed his hands together. "Reid will blame himself and who knows what he'll do to get back at my father."

Dash threw his hands up, flabbergasted. "Who cares?

Whatever Reid decides, I'm in. *Someone* needs to teach him a lesson."

"*No.*" Gavin grabbed Dash's wrists and softly pleaded for him to listen. "You can't teach Edward Selby anything. He's one of the most feared and revered men on Wall Street. Banks turn to *him* when they're in trouble and the chairman of the Federal Reserve doesn't make a move without my father's blessing. He might as well be the Pope. All it would do is make things worse."

"But...what about you?" Dash's eyes blurred as they filled with tears. "You've been dressing for work and going to the library every day to protect Reid. That has to be killing you because I know how much you loved your job and working at Ernst & Waterhouse."

Gavin shook his head. "It doesn't matter. Reid can never know. You have to promise me, Dash."

"You've been doing this for a long time, haven't you?" Dash was so sad as he imagined how lonely it would be to keep this kind of secret and was struck by how easy a burden it was for Gavin to bear. As if he'd been doing it his whole life.

"My father has been trying to put an end to this 'Marshall business' since we were children," Gavin admitted. "He's never approved of Reid and Fin and he blames them for my homosexuality."

"You have to stand up to him," Dash whispered, earning a wry snort from Gavin.

"Why? He can't live forever."

"But he could live for several more years!"

Gavin shrugged. "I find comfort in the concept of karma and knowing my father will never see Heaven."

"Probably not," Dash agreed, crossing his arms over his chest and squaring up to Gavin again. "You're not going to like this, but your days of suffering alone are over and you're going on the nice list," he informed Gavin, earning a confused frown.

"I don't mind suffering alone. I prefer it, actually, and I don't think I want to be on the nice list. It probably requires me doing something tedious and a great deal of discomfort," he predicted.

A calculating grin spread across Dash's face. "Only if you consider a Santa costume uncomfortable."

Gavin nodded quickly. "Extremely."

"Maybe just a little," Dash made a mental note to have it dry-cleaned before Gavin wore it for Stories With Santa. Ashley's husband did say that it could get a little hot and itchy. "But it'll be so worth it," he promised. "You're my new Santa and you've got yourself an elf for the rest of the season, buddy."

"The rest of the season?" Gavin's voice rose warily. "Why would I want to be on the nice list and what do I need an elf for? I don't really celebrate after Christmas Eve eve. Reid goes to Park Slope to spend Christmas with his family so I...keep to myself."

Dash stifled an excited gasp at the sparkly, snowflake-filled explosion of possibilities. There were so many ways that Dash could give Gavin the warmest, happiest, and most loving holiday season of his life. And some of those possibilities were very kinky... "I was worried about how I was going to get through the holidays without Penny but this is going to be so *awesome!*" He pumped his fists as he let out a squeal. Dash was so happy, he felt like doing cartwheels. "You'll see!" He grabbed Gavin's face and kissed him loudly on the lips, startling him. Dash enjoyed the flutter of joy in his tummy and Gavin's shock. "I'm going to prove just how *nice* you are and we're going to have so much fun."

"But I don't like...fun," Gavin whispered, his neck craning

conspiratorially. "And I prefer to suffer alone. Why would I agree to—?"

Dash held up a hand, halting Gavin. "I'll keep your secret *until* you tell Reid yourself, but you're our new Santa and you're mine for the rest of the season," he stipulated with an imperious tilt of his chin. He had made up his mind.

"I think I can endure the rest of it but why can't you ask Penn or Morris to be Santa?" Gavin asked, slouching as he pouted. "They'd be much better at it."

"Nope." Dash beamed back at Gavin, laughing when he jumped and leaned away. "This is for your own good, Gavin. You're going on the nice list and you're gonna like it."

"This is a terrible idea," Gavin warned and they both looked when the front door opened and Reid rushed in.

"I left my wallet! What are you two up to?" He asked as he ran past the sofa.

"Hey, Reid! Need help finding it?" Dash asked cheerfully and swung around, raising his arms to jump up and join him but Gavin snatched his sleeve.

"Wait!" He whispered while Reid shouted from his room that he'd found it. "I'll be your Santa and do as you ask. Just don't tell him," Gavin begged under his breath.

"Yes! I got my Santa!" Dash's fist shot into the air triumphantly. "And you've got yourself an elf for the rest of the season."

Chapter Three

Gavin had spent much of his Sunday evening fretting over the deal he'd made with Dash and praying that having an elf wouldn't be as bad as he was expecting. Stories With Santa already sounded like holiday hell on Earth. But apparently, Gavin was at Dash's mercy for the entirety of the season with no real indication as to what that might entail.

He had received one cryptic hint as Dash was preparing to leave after dinner. Dash had shared a glass of wine with Reid as they went over a prospective nanny's resumé and there was a mischievous tilt to the younger man's lips as he wound his scarf around his neck. "I hope you like hot cocoa."

"And getting caught in the snow?" Reid had guessed over his shoulder, chuckling and humming the tune to "The Piña Colada Song" while he did the dishes.

That had amused Reid for the rest of the evening, but the statement turned into an ominous warning that became an ache in Gavin's gut.

Who didn't like hot cocoa? Unless they were up to their

armpits in it and fighting giant marshmallows. Which was where Gavin found himself a few hours later, during a particularly vivid nightmare. Dash was steering a gondola and laughing when he threw Gavin overboard and pushed him downstream with the oar. Gavin was fighting off his pillow and drowning in his comforter when he woke up an hour before his alarm.

He told himself over and over again that Dash would never throw anyone overboard and that it had all been a nightmare as he showered, shaved, and dressed. If anything, Dash would be the first person to dive in and save someone if they were drowning in cocoa—or any substance, probably. Which caused Gavin to imagine Dash emerging from a river of hot chocolate like a messy Mr. Darcy as he was eating his breakfast.

Gavin had choked and dribbled his tea, requiring a quick tie change before he headed out. "Message me if you need me to pick anything up on the way home," he told Reid as he gathered his trench coat and briefcase by the door.

"I can't think of anything, unless you'd like something special for dinner this week," Reid mused from his seat at the kitchen table. "Have a good day at work, dear," he said sweetly as he turned his attention back to a paper he was reading on the long-term effects of early, extensive daycare.

"I'm sure I will," Gavin replied as he let himself out.

Once outside the building and safely around the corner, Gavin's strides slowed and his shoulders dropped as he made his way to the library on East 79th Street. If he was being honest, Dash was what had initially drawn Gavin to that particular location. There were larger and grander libraries Gavin could have chosen to hide in during the day. But knowing it was Dash's favorite library somehow made it safer. And Gavin thought it might feel more like home knowing that Dash spent so much time there.

It was comforting to sneak up to the second floor for a little peek while Dash was helping children find books and use the computers. Gavin believed he had been undetected, arriving an hour before Dash and staying in the periodicals until the library was busier. And why would Dash notice another drab businessman?

But Gavin had made the same mistake most people made by underestimating Dash and forgetting how intuitive he was when it came to those he cared about. He didn't have an odd sixth sense like Penn and Penny had. Dash's intuition came from watching and caring so much that he could anticipate a friend's thoughts and desires before they could.

The terrible "tea tantrum" had been the beginning of Gavin's nightmare. His father was furious about the agency and had demanded Gavin put an end to it or Edward would. Gavin had ignored him and Reid was turned down for a loan the following week despite having immaculate credit. His father had obviously interfered—hence the tantrum—so Gavin had lied and said he'd found Reid a better loan. It had been from Gavin's savings and he wouldn't have been able to support the agency for more than a few months if Walker Cameron hadn't stepped in. He'd done it out of guilt for "stealing" Fin from Reid's new agency, but that infusion of advertising and PR revenue and the influx of wealthy clients had saved them.

Then, Giles went after Wolford and Gavin lost his job. He'd managed to hide the fact from everyone except Walker and Giles, but all of Gavin's secrets began to unravel the moment Dash caught him in the library. Gavin had no idea when that had occurred, but it was over as soon as Dash found out because he would have no problem putting the rest of the pieces together. Which begged the question: did Gavin *want* Dash to find him?

The rational parts of Gavin's brain denied it, but the

weaker, lonelier parts and his heart whispered that he craved the comfort of Dash's smiles and his laughter. And because even though Gavin would never admit that he'd been completely devastated when he'd lost his job, it helped *tremendously* having Dash close by when it hurt the worst. He couldn't run upstairs and tell Dash or ask for a hug, but Gavin could stand a few aisles away and hear Dash calmly encouraging a young reader or laughing with one of the librarians.

The library had been his sanctuary within the city. And perhaps it was Pavlovian, but Dash had become as soothing as a cup of tea and a seat by the fireplace for Gavin. Now, Gavin was drifting as he trudged to his destination. Whether intentional or not, Dash knew most of Gavin's secrets and it was only a matter of time until he knew *everything*.

If there was one thing that was truly annoying about Dash, it was his ability to see right through Gavin and read him like a book. *That* was why Gavin couldn't risk accepting any of Dash's invitations. A cup of tea at the shop around the corner would have been an unmitigated disaster because it would take Dash all of two minutes to figure out that Gavin was a lovesick idiot. He couldn't pretend he was ignoring Dash and reading the paper when he was too nervous to speak, could he? He couldn't 'ignore' Dash on a date or offer distracted shrugs and impatient scowls when he was afraid of saying something silly or sappy.

Gavin was out in the cold—literally and metaphorically—as he stared at the library's turn-of-the-century limestone facade and classic arches. Sanctorum was no longer sanctum and he was having nightmares about Dash.

"Good morning!" Dash called from behind Gavin, making him jump.

"No!" He shouted as he turned and found Dash's bright blue eyes and megawatt smile beaming back at him. "I mean, good morning," Gavin corrected, then frowned at the two coffee cups in Dash's hands. "I've already had my tea and I only—"

"I know!" Dash informed Gavin with a toss of his chin at the library's steps. "One of these is for Carolyn. She's a little crabbier on Mondays so I like to bring her a peppermint latte. It never fails to put a smile on her face," he whispered out of the side of his mouth.

"I don't enjoy peppermint lattes," Gavin said. "They taste like they have toothpaste in them."

Dash laughed as Gavin got the door for him. "I'm an unapologetic pumpkin spice guy myself."

"I've never had the pleasure," Gavin said. "I'm not sure if I want my coffee to taste like a dessert. And I prefer tea."

"You're kidding!" Dash said as he searched the tables and

the area behind the desk. "I'm definitely adding PSLs to our nice list."

"There's an actual list now?"

Dash winked at Gavin before making a beeline for the desk. "It's a mashup of reasons why you're nice and deserve the best holiday season ever *and* nice things for us to do between now and New Year's."

Gavin's steps faltered. "But New Year's is...almost three weeks away."

"I know!" Dash whispered at him, his eyes twinkling. "We've got a lot of ground to cover so keep up!"

They were greeted by a surly-looking older woman when they reached the desk. She had limped from the back office, only cracking a smile when Dash stretched over the counter to kiss her cheek.

"Good morning, Carolyn! You're looking even lovelier than yesterday."

"Morning, handsome," she grumbled. "The elevator's still out and all this wet weather is making my knee act up."

"That's what you've got me for!" Dash told her, then set his hands on his hips and did a few fast squats. "I'll be your knees and your gopher," he declared.

"Do that again but turn around so I can see your ass while you're doing it," she said, twirling her finger and making Gavin laugh. He coughed to cover it and waved awkwardly when she raised a suspicious brow at him. "Did I give you permission to check out his ass?"

"It's okay, he's with me," Dash said. "And I'm always trying to get him to notice my ass." He threw an arm around Gavin and gave him an affectionate squeeze. "You're looking at our new Santa!"

"This is the guy you're always going on and on about?" Her nose wrinkled as she eyed Gavin up and down, shaking her head dubiously. "More like the North Beanpole or jolly old Saint Stick."

Dash made a dismissive sound. "Look at his *hands*, Carolyn. Look. At. His. Hands." He wiggled his brows at her, scaring Gavin.

"My hands?" He raised the left and searched it. All Gavin saw was a normal hand, but Carolyn grunted in a sexually suggestive way while sipping her coffee.

"That's some Grade A hand porn," she conceded.

Gavin shook his head as he stuffed his left hand into his trench coat pocket while the hand with his briefcase swung behind his back. "What is that? That's not a thing," he said to Dash, making Carolyn smother a wheezing giggle.

"Now I get it," she said, waving at them. "You two go on. Take your adorable asses upstairs and find Ashley."

"Message me if you need *anything*," Dash told her, then steered them around and toward the stairs. "Let's go! I don't want Ashley to put the returns away!"

Gavin followed, jogging up the steps next to Dash. "I knew I should have worn gloves."

"I have bad news if you think your leather gloves would look less pornographic," Dash said, wincing apologetically, then took a right when they reached the second floor. "You could try mittens. Mittens might work."

"I can't wear mittens. I'm not...cute like Riley."

"Stop it! You're cute," Dash said, stunning Gavin with another wink and making him trip.

"No. I'm not, but thank you." His face was hot and Gavin missed his newspaper dearly.

Dash stopped, pointing at Gavin. "Ah ha! Caught you being adorable *and* nice! That's another one for the list."

"What are the chances that we could stop with the list? I'm sure you have enough for us to do and I have a feeling you'll find more things that are boring and disappointing, the longer we're together." He grimaced in the direction of the children's section. "What if I waited in periodicals?" He suggested hopefully.

"Not a chance. There's Ashley," Dash said when he spotted a tall, *very* pregnant woman in brightly-colored patchwork overalls pushing a cart loaded with books. "Keep up!" He waved over his shoulder, sipping his latte and leaving Gavin in his dust. "Let me take that!" Dash said once he'd caught up to her. "Say hello to Gavin and then go and put your feet up somewhere," he told her, then flashed her a huge grin as he stepped aside and waved at Gavin. "Ashley, this is *the* Gavin and he's agreed to be our Santa next week. Gavin, this is Ashley."

Her eyes lit up and she covered her mouth, muffling a shriek. "Oh, my God! You are real!" She giggled and rolled her eyes. "I mean, I could see that you were real when we were spying on you downstairs. But I kind of thought Dash was making it up when he said he knew you. Kind of like I keep saying the incredibly hot FedEx guy is this one's father," she whispered as she cradled her belly, making Dash snort.

"Don't listen to her. I told you, she's happily married to a lovely man named James who is currently at home with their twin boys and nursing a bad back."

She shrugged and braced her lower spine. "He's the one with twins in the family and I could tell him a thing or two about back pain. Only difference is, he'll be on the good drugs week after next and I'll still be pregnant with his fourth behemoth. And the FedEx guy is..." She kissed her fingers, groaning appreciatively.

"He really is," Dash said before flailing a hand. "Anyways! I finally got this hottie to speak to me in public." He tossed his chin at Gavin, making him recoil.

"Don't say things like that."

"That you're a hottie?" Dash asked and Gavin shushed him.

"Yes. And you know I do my best to speak to as few people as possible."

"Hmmm..." Ashley tapped her chin thoughtfully while giving Gavin a thorough once over. "Tall guys who dress like Victorian prime ministers usually don't do it for me, but I have to agree with Dash on this one. I'd let you pull my hair and bend me over that broken copier if I were him," she said, hitching a thumb at the copy machine in the conference room behind her.

Dash coughed and rested a hand on Ashley's shoulder. "I'm a little concerned with how specific that was. Is it normal for women to be this horny in their third trimester?"

She smirked at Dash. "Yes. And I've got a husband with a bad back so you do the math."

"Mmmm..." He hummed and canted toward Gavin. "Ask her how he threw out his back this time," he whispered behind his hand.

"Ha! I dare you," she challenged Gavin, but he shook his head.

"I wanted to stay in periodicals."

Ashley and Dash burst into laughter. "You're right!" She gasped as she held onto him. "He's a riot!"

"Are you two always this loud?" Gavin asked, looking around but there was no one else on the second floor as far as he could tell. "Shouldn't you be quieter?"

"Nah. It's still early," Ashley said with a weary groan. "I need to pee. You got these?"

Dash gave her a jaunty salute. "Go put your feet up." He shooed her off, laughing at Gavin. "Oh! I need that Santa costume so I can get it dry-cleaned for Gavin," he called after her and she held up a thumb.

"That's probably a good call. Jimmy was wearing it when he threw out his back."

"You're an animal, Ashley," Dash said, widening his eyes at Gavin. "That's how you have four kids in four years."

"Not me," Gavin replied with a shudder. "I'm in charge of music for Christmas Eve eve this year because Morris has his hands full with Cadence's preschool holiday pageant. I can barely manage June, Milo, and the triplets, but Morris volunteered to help an entire class of three and four-year-olds learn a holiday routine."

"But that sounds like fun," Dash argued and Gavin let out a disgruntled grunt.

"I enjoy Amelia, Bea, and Charlotte tremendously in small doses and individually, but all together... And then you add Fin and Riley and their diva-like demands. Why does a holiday medley require dry ice and where the hell am I supposed to find that?" He asked, rubbing the back of his hand across his forehead in distress. "I'm not built for that much noise and chaos."

"I'm sure you've got it all under control and it's going to be an amazing showcase," Dash said encouragingly.

"Probably," Gavin concurred. "But will it be worth the psychic damage? I told Morris he's not allowed to volunteer next year unless Fin or Riley want to handle the entertainment for the party. Or, you and Penny."

By Gavin's estimation, he was the least festive person in their friend group and was a terrible choice to coordinate the holiday talent show and group singalong. With Henry's passing, the holidays stopped after Christmas Eve eve for Gavin. Once the party was finished and everyone else went off to spend Christmas with their spouses, children, and loving parents, Gavin settled in for a solitary respite. He thought of Henry and their quiet Christmases as he opened a fresh box of tea and a tin of butter cookies, then enjoyed his papers and his chair in peace until Reid and their friends returned from their joyful family holidays.

"Maybe you and I could do it together next year," Dash suggested brightly, but Gavin shook his head and scowled at the thought of *more* practices with the triplets and Fin's and Riley's bizarre demands.

"Let's see if I survive *this* Christmas, Dash. I'm already stressed out just thinking about it. I need to read my paper," he said as he held up his briefcase, then left before Dash could put him to work.

Chapter Four

Once again, Dash's favorite library had magically revealed another one of Gavin Selby's closely guarded secrets. He was *wonderful* with children.

There had been only one question in Dash's mind as far as Gavin's suitability as a future life partner. And prior to falling head over heels for Gavin, Dash had been extremely bisexual and his primary requirement for a partner had been: must like kids.

His approach wasn't consistent with *any* of Reid's methods and he'd probably pull his hair out if he were observing Gavin at the library. But to Dash, the morning had been a revelation and refreshing. Once all the returns were put away and kids began to arrive, Dash parked Gavin next to the computers since he was internet savvy and would be a great homework helper.

Children rarely visited Briarwood Terrace so Dash had yet to see Gavin interact with one beyond a few patient smiles at June Cameron and Milo Ashby. Gavin tended to have an errand or an appointment when Fin and Walker brought the triplets around. That was understandable. They were a delight, but holy hand grenades, the triplets were *a lot*.

Dash looked up to Fin because parenting three chaotic, headstrong girls was not for the weak. And if Dash was being honest, he loved kids with all his heart, but he didn't want to live with them. His idea of a perfect life was finding someone he felt complete and right with, celebrating *that* and putting 100% of his focus on making them happy. Part of the reason why Dash hadn't found his passion in life was because he was waiting to find the other half of himself first.

Some people were driven to be doctors or actors or politicians because something in their soul guided them in those directions. Not Dash. He could see himself doing too many things and being happy as long as he was making other people's lives better while he was doing it. For Dash, his soul had a different kind of compass and it had always guided him toward *love*.

It began when he was a child and felt the first stirrings of affection and then arousal. He had his first crush at the very early age of six on a little boy with bright orange hair and freckles. From that moment on, Dash didn't dream of becoming a firefighter or the president, he dreamt of being someone's *husband* and wondered who his future spouse would be.

How and when he would find his soulmate seemed far more crucial to Dash than his profession. Dash understood that he lived an extremely privileged existence and that his priorities would probably be different if he didn't have wealthy parents who were still willing to support him while he "found himself."

But it did hurt Dash's feelings whenever he was asked why he had squandered the opportunity to be a football god like his father. How could a *Mooney* not love football? Or, when people asked Dash why he hadn't "done something" with his life yet. Dash was aware that to some, he'd failed to launch despite having doting parents and unimaginable privilege. But Dash had seen too many kids from backgrounds like his fall victim to the lure of fame and social media popularity. And Dash had learned that he wasn't built for the pressures and scrutiny that came with being a celebrity.

His family's legacy had been both a blessing and a curse for much of Dash's life. On and off the field, everyone adored Dash and treated him like he was Swift Griffin's clone and destined for football greatness. Those expectations got to be too much for Dash when he was in high school. He was "supposed to" play football for Michigan like his father had, but Dash had his first major panic attack his senior year.

It had been a storm that had been building for a while because even though Dash was really good at football and wanted to be like his father and make him proud, the game itself was intensely stressful for him. And it only grew more so for Dash as the players around him grew larger and faster.

He'd been hurt a few times in his push to get into Michigan and follow in his famous father's footsteps. Then, a serious head injury had left Dash with post-concussion syndrome, resulting in memory loss, terrible fatigue but trouble sleeping, increased anxiety, and depression—on and off the field. Dash's grades suffered and he was psychically *unwell*. He did his best to hide how sick and scared he was when he played until a catastrophic panic attack took Dash down in the middle of a game with scouts from Michigan in the stands.

To Dash's great relief, his parents didn't care if he ever stepped foot on the field again after that if his heart was no longer in the game. That had been life-changing for Dash and he was able to bounce back thanks to his amazing friends and his parents' love and support. And *a lot* of therapy once he "came clean" with everyone about his fear of—of all things

—*football*. Ironically, it had been easier for Dash to come out as bisexual than admit that he didn't really enjoy the sport.

For Dash, football had been a way to bond with his father. Dash idolized Swift and wanted to be exactly like the goofy, lovable teddy bear the world universally adored. He'd inherited his father's *dashing* good looks, corny charm, easygoing personality, and natural athletic ability. He just hadn't inherited his father's ambition, passion for the game, or fearlessness on the field.

For his mental health, Dash's parents encouraged him to get off society's radar. He followed Penny to Sarah Lawrence College instead of going to Michigan and entered the pre-health program. It turned out that nursing wasn't the right call for Dash either because he also suffered from vasovagal syncope. He fainted twice at the sight of blood during his first clinic visit.

After that, Dash went into early childhood education but his introduction into the world of elementary school teaching was rocky as well. He was willing to put up with the low pay and long hours because he had the energy and a passion for educating children. It was the other many emotionally draining aspects of teaching that had Dash rethinking his career yet again when Penny steered him toward the newly-formed Marshall Agency.

But having a famous athlete as a father and being heir to a famous football dynasty paled —for Dash, at least—to being the product of an iconic celebrity love story. In the late '80s and early '90s, football fans and much of the American media had been obsessed with Swift's fairytale courtship of Hannah Mooney shortly after his first year in the NFL. Hannah, a socialite and philanthropist, was heiress to the Mooney football empire. Her grandparents on both sides owned football teams, but she was famously down-to-earth and a devoted fan of the sport herself.

Their courtship and marriage had been widely covered and celebrated and the Griffins moved to Manhattan after Swift retired and began calling games on the major networks and doing sneaker commercials. Both of Dash's parents became beloved television fixtures with Hannah often making appearances on the morning news and talk shows, occasionally filling in as a guest host on the *Today* show. As a result, their famous love story was just as much a part of the legacy Swift had passed on to Dash as football. And that came with responsibilities and expectations as well.

That was why finding the person he'd *live with* for the rest of his life and then seeing what profession made the most sense for them was the logical route for Dash. And now that Dash had found Gavin, working at the Marshall Agency as Reid's assistant, being a "floating" nanny, and volunteering at the library felt like a positive and harmonious answer to the question of what he was going to "do" with his life.

Introducing Ashley and Carolyn to *his* Santa and finally seeing Gavin interact with children felt like the beginning of Dash's very own holiday miracle. Gavin didn't have to adore kids like Dash did or even want to be a parent. But it was important that the love of the *rest of Dash's life* at least respect children and treat them with kindness. And rather shockingly, Gavin was phenomenal with children. He may have claimed to dread and misunderstand them, but to Dash's now well-trained eye, Gavin was a natural.

Dash hovered whenever he wasn't helping hunt for books and was charmed as Gavin answered their littlest patrons' many questions. Unlike most adults, Gavin had infinite patience and gave their questions honest consideration instead of trying to entertain them or "get on their level." He talked to the library's younger visitors like they were people and he was *honest.* Not in an inappropriate or harmful way, thank goodness.

A girl whom Dash estimated to be around six-years-old gasped up at Gavin in wonder as he got her chair for her. "You're really tall!" She noted. "Are you all done growing yet?"

Gavin looked rather serious as he shook his head. "I thought I was done growing, but then I found out about feelings and now I will never know rest."

One boy stood on a chair, attempting to get eye-to-eye with Gavin. "Am I gonna be as tall as you one day?" He asked and Gavin's brow furrowed as he studied the child.

"I don't think so. You appear to have a personality and you can either be tall and that is your personality, or you can have a personality and use it to overcompensate for the fact that you are not tall."

Dash's favorite moment of the day occurred when a boy of around seven yanked on Gavin's sleeve. "Can I sit next to you?" He was hugging an encyclopedia of great composers and Dash had sent him over because Gavin was practically a walking encyclopedia himself when it came to classical and jazz music.

"This is a public space so there is little I can do to stop you," Gavin had replied dryly as he read his paper. But Gavin's neck craned curiously as the boy climbed up onto the seat and opened the large book. The newspaper was set aside and Gavin humphed in approval when he read over the boy's shoulder. "Bartók," Gavin said, scooting his chair closer and the boy nodded.

"I have to do a report about a composer because I got in trouble during music class," he confessed, receiving another serious hum from Gavin.

"I'm sure you've learned your lesson," he said, his tone dismissive as he slid the encyclopedia closer so it was between them. "Bartók was a very important composer and would be a good choice," he murmured. "He left Europe because of the Nazis and was a fellow at Columbia so you might get extra points for the New York connection. And he was a pioneer of ethnomusicology, the study of music and the people who make it," he explained in his calm, quiet tone, enthralling his new pupil. "Because of Bartók we know what folk music sounded like from faraway parts of the world most of us will never get to visit. A lot of the music he recorded would have disappeared before we could hear it," he explained.

"Can I hear it?" The boy asked in wonder, earning an enthusiastic nod from Gavin.

"You should. We'll go to the media room and I'll see if I can find some of Bartók's recordings and headphones for you," he said as he stood and helped the boy gather his book and Gavin collected his paper and briefcase. "His own works were a fascinating mix of modern and folk elements and I am particularly fond of his piano compositions, although I don't play it myself. I'm a clarinetist but I do enjoy playing a bit of Bartók when I'm in the mood for something light and...folksy," he added, making Dash clutch his back and bite a knuckle as he hid behind a bookshelf and eavesdropped.

He had never been more turned on by another human being in his life and Dash was certain that even Ashley would be scandalized if she knew what he was envisioning. Dash was unabashedly wholesome and enjoyed being a bit corny because happiness was his drug of choice. He was pretty much the exact same person in the bedroom, but Dash was into just about everything as long as it wasn't mean or caused serious pain.

Sometimes, Dash liked it really wild and really rough and that's what he had in mind as he leaned around the end of the row, reconsidering the photocopier in the conference room. It was a silly place to keep it but after the last remodel, that was the only place it fit on the second floor. Dash could see the potential now and wanted to ride Gavin until they were both jammed and out of toner like the copier. His back was already aching because like James—who had played football in college —Dash was now paying the price for his youthful athletic ambitions at the "advanced" age of thirty-two. Dash had to keep in shape because he had the spine of an octogenarian and it was fussy when the weather was really cold and wet or he got a little too wild in bed.

He knew it would be worth it as he glanced at the media room where Gavin carefully placed a set of headphones over the boy's head. Dash let out a swooning sigh, his hormones receding as he heard violins. "I want the filthy stuff but I just want to smother him in *love!*" He whispered, hugging himself as tight as he could, the way he'd squeeze Gavin once he was allowed to.

Dash was still sad and angry whenever he thought about all the awful things that Gavin had quietly endured over the years. He couldn't imagine how lonely it must have been for Gavin, even with amazing friends, hiding the pain of his parents' rejection and his father's cruelty. Everyone assumed the falling out had been over Gavin's homosexuality and his refusal to marry the girl his parents had chosen, but it was so much more than that from what Dash gathered.

Gavin had used himself as a shield around Briarwood Terrace, Reid, and the agency for over twenty years. Everything in Dash's heart told him it was time to release Gavin from his father's awful spell so he was finally free. But Dash had to accept that those were Gavin's secrets and it was *his* life. Only he could decide when the truth came out.

In the meantime, Dash was going to bring as much joy and magic to Gavin's world as possible. Without overwhelming

Gavin, of course. Dash chuckled as he watched Gavin sitting next to the boy, both wearing matching headphones and nodding in sync. Gavin would probably be shocked to his toes if he knew what Dash wanted to do with him.

"It's what he deserves," Dash decided with a smile, then went to check the midday returns and put them away before it was time for him to walk Gavin to the Olympia for the first of the afternoon's accounting appointments. "I'll have to come up with something *nice* for us to do along the way."

A walk through Central Park was the obvious answer since the Olympia was right there. They could take a practice stroll for when they went back to enjoy all the lights and see the tree at the plaza. Dash had a feeling ice skating was out of the question, but that was okay. He didn't want a sprained ankle or wrist putting a damper on the rest of their romantic holiday adventure. And there was always next year or the year after that.

Awkward and silly made for better anniversaries than first dates, Dash decided, and he wanted to prove that falling in love didn't have to be as disruptive and stressful as Gavin was expecting. He was going to curl Gavin's toes without stepping on his feet or pushing him too far outside of his comfort zone. Because there were lots of ways to sweep your lover off their feet and sometimes, slow and gentle was the way to go.

Especially if you were hoping to get your back blown out over the photocopier in the future.

Chapter Five

Monday was far more pleasant than Gavin had expected. Tuesday, on the other hand, had been dreadful. Dash wasn't at the library and hadn't been available to walk with Gavin because he was caring for a family who was staying at the Waldorf. He'd been away all day and the only bright spot had been the two hours Gavin spent at Penn and Morris's.

He'd known both men for decades, but Gavin had met Morris first at Saint Ann's and the two of them shared a unique bond. Morris played the trumpet—among *many* other instruments—and the two had gravitated to the back of the class as shy seven and eight-year-olds. Like Gavin, Morris was quiet and intensely focused on his studies. They clicked instantly and Morris invited Gavin to tag along and hang out at his mother's bakery after school. Morris's best friend, Reid, was part of the package and the two became Gavin's first and closest friends.

Morris also had his twin sister, Michelle, and their at times bizarre, but beautiful connection. Then, Morris's music career took off during their sophomore year, leaving Reid and Gavin to stumble along awkwardly through the rest of high school together. Reid became the pillar of Gavin's existence and was the closest thing he'd ever have to a brother. Instead of attending Juilliard, Gavin had defied his parents and chose Columbia so he could follow Reid.

Morris's recording career came to a sudden halt with the tragic loss of Michelle to a stroke. Thankfully, Reid had the good sense to send Penn to take care of Morris and Michelle's newborn daughter, Cadence. Morris had helped Penn heal as well and they surprised everyone by falling in love and getting married.

Hanging out with Penn was a surefire way to brighten any day, but Gavin was glad he had taken Cadence to Hoboken to visit his father. Morris had called Gavin down to the studio in the basement instead of working at the kitchen table or in the garden. It was soothing and Gavin was enjoying a bit of nostalgia as they listened to old jazz records and went over Morris's accounts.

"How are you doing?" Morris asked. He was sitting backward and hugging the back of his chair.

Gavin looked up from the contributions page of Morris's solo 401k. "Me?"

"Yes, you. Reid's been worried and we both think you're extra quiet and cranky lately."

"Could it be that you and Reid are more irritating lately?" Gavin held up the page and squinted at the columns, hoping Morris would take a hint and hush. "I think Reid's on the verge of burning out and could use a vacation, and I think you might be watching too much *Paw Patrol* with Cadence. You're obsessed with solving everyone else's problems and I think you've said the word *teamwork* a dozen times in the last hour."

"When was the last time *you* went on vacation?" Morris

countered, widening his eyes at Gavin. "Have you ever gone on a vacation?"

When was the last time I went to work?

"I went up to that godforsaken cabin with Penn three years ago," Gavin said, shivering as he recalled that awful weekend.

"Right! You lost some silly bet and then he bet you you couldn't last a weekend with him up there."

"I still don't understand how Penn knew that TPL was going to take off. He barely touches the internet and he'd rather barter like a medieval peasant than keep a bank account, but he knew that Texas Pacific Land would be one the year's top performing stocks."

Morris nodded as he laughed. "Knowing Penn, he probably thought the TP had something to do with toilet paper. He said you handled the cabin like a champ, though."

"I drank tea and refused to do anything but sit in a folding chair on the porch for two days like an invalid."

"But you survived!" Morris said, reaching and giving Gavin's shoulder an encouraging punch. "How about you and Dash?"

"What about me and Dash?" No one was supposed to know about their arrangement.

"Come on! You can't tell me there's *nothing* there."

"Why?" Gavin asked, raising a brow and challenging Morris. "Why does everyone keep assuming something's there? We've barely seen each other outside of Briarwood Terrace."

Morris's eyes narrowed as he rolled his chair closer until their knees bumped. "Liar!" He whispered.

"Do you mind?" Gavin used his foot to slide the chair back to a reasonable distance. "Nothing is happening between me and Dash."

"Sometimes, I think you forget that I've known you longer than the rest of them."

"True, but is it possible that I've known you for too long?" Gavin mused, making Morris laugh.

"Nah." He waved dismissively. Unlike the rest of them, Morris gave as good as he got and rarely let Gavin's crankiness be a deterrent. "You *watch* him!" He whispered.

"So? I watch everyone."

A loud snort answered. "No. You don't," Morris stated, shaking his head. "You will tune out everything except your tea, especially when things get *too loud* and too busy, but you watch Dash. You watch him like you're trying to learn or memorize the way he does things."

"That's ridiculous." Gavin set the page on the opened file on his lap because his hand was shaking. "If I watch him it's because he's always in motion and one never knows what wild thing Dash will do next."

"I know. Isn't it *great?*" Morris said sincerely, rolling closer again. "You need someone who will keep you on your toes and give you something better than tea to keep you warm."

Gavin had insisted he was seeing things and wasting his time, but Morris's astute assessment had been unnerving. It followed Gavin as he did his rounds and returned home to a quiet apartment. Reid was still out and had yet to return with dinner, so Gavin had a few solitary hours to fret over who else might notice his distraction as he spent more time with Dash outside of Briarwood Terrace.

Even with that worrisome warning, Gavin woke up Wednesday morning feeling hopeful and impatient as he dressed and calmly chatted with Reid in the kitchen before leaving. Dash didn't have a family to care for and was usually at the library on Wednesdays.

He was waiting when Gavin came around the corner on 79th Street. Gavin was stunned by Dash's big smile and perfect two-day beard. He had on a gray peacoat and his pink scarf had adorable candy cane hearts that brought out the red highlights in his brown hair. He was almost too handsome for a Wednesday morning and Gavin's steps faltered as he crossed the street and stepped onto the curb to join him.

"Good morning," he said, avoiding the dazzling sparkling of Dash's eyes. "Is that Carolyn's?" he asked and nodded at the coffee cup in Dash's left hand.

"It's your pumpkin spice latte!" Dash bounced excitedly as he passed it to Gavin.

"I don't know..." Gavin raised it and sniffed warily, then grunted in surprise at the pleasant aroma.

"Ha! I bet you you're going to love it!" Dash said, leaning forward as he waited for Gavin to take a sip. "Go on."

"It's just that I don't like a lot of different flavors, unless it's whatever flavor my Earl Gray is." He humored Dash with a sportsmanlike salute, then took a drink. Gavin's eyes widened at the warm creaminess and subtle cinnamon pumpkin flavor. He also detected a hint of nutmeg. "That's...acceptable." Gavin nodded, taking another drink and gesturing for Dash to lead the way.

"I think I won that bet!" Dash declared, humming happily as he drank from his cup. "They don't need me at the library today. Ashley's training a new librarian so I thought we could cut through the park and hit the Columbus Circle Holiday Market. I'm in the mood for cider donuts and I'm willing to bet you haven't started your Christmas shopping yet."

"I have made a list," Gavin said defensively. He was glad for the cozy spiciness of his latte, dreading the thought of being outdoors and around so many people instead of the library. Dash didn't need to know that Gavin's list was merely all the names of people he needed to buy gift cards for. He always did that because how in the world would he know what to buy everyone? And children were never disappointed by gift cards.

Some adults claimed they were, but Gavin found that difficult to believe. "What if someone sees us? Reid might see us."

"He's supposed to be in Park Slope helping his parents decorate the tree since they're both free today," Dash reminded Gavin. "And we have the perfect cover: we're sneaking away to do some Christmas shopping!" He whispered, hooking his arm around Gavin's and towing him down the sidewalk.

"What about my briefcase?" He wouldn't take that if he was sneaking away to do some shopping. "And I would never sneak away and go Christmas shopping."

"That's literally what we're doing and that's the beauty of this: we don't have to lie if anyone catches us! We can leave it at the library."

"Alright," Gavin conceded. "But I'm waiting outside. It's too early for that much bawdy banter." He shuddered and hugged his cup.

"Deal!" Dash said, then sped up the library's steps with Gavin's briefcase. He reappeared a few minutes later, his cheeks pink and chuckling about Carolyn being on the naughty list because of her language. "Shall we?" He asked, turning toward Park Avenue and heading for the park. "What's wrong?" Dash asked when he caught Gavin frowning at his cup.

"We have a problem," Gavin said, sighing heavily at Dash. "I enjoyed that," he said quietly and leaned closer so no one would hear. "And I'm sad that it's almost gone."

A huge smile spread across Dash's face. "I knew it! I have a theory," he said as he pulled Gavin along. "There are two types of people in this world: pumpkin spice people and peppermint mocha people. I could tell that you were a pumpkin spice guy like me, you just didn't know it yet."

"I can't imagine who wouldn't like them or why they're scorned the way they are." Gavin gave his head a shake and decided to enjoy the decadent velvetiness of the whipped cream and mild espresso flavor as he took in the early morning park. It was far less crowded than the last time he visited, although he couldn't remember when that had been. Gavin decided he liked all the decorations and the way the snow was still white and clean in most places. "It's like having a sip of coffee after a bit of pumpkin pie," he observed. "Is Penny a pumpkin spice or a peppermint mocha girl?" He asked as they walked.

Dash's nose wrinkled. "Neither! She gets a chai tea latte with oat milk. Which I think you'd love!"

"A chai tea latte with oat milk?" Gavin parroted. "That's a lot to remember, but I'd like to try it."

"Hold on!" Dash pointed when they came around the corner and saw three pairs of snow angels. "How sweet are those?" He took out his phone and swiped and tapped quickly. "Gavin!" He gasped and spun around. "Let's add another pair!"

"What?" Gavin spluttered and looked around. "Out here?" People would see him. Not many and no one would probably care...

"You can't make snow angels inside, silly!" Dash laughed and pushed his lip out. "Come on, Gavin. You owe me a dare and a pumpkin spice guy would definitely make the snow angel."

"What are you talking about?" Gavin wrinkled his nose as he considered the sets of angels. The odd thing was, he had always wanted to make one but had never dared. He was always too worried someone might see him and think he was intoxicated or searching for his missing childhood. "Just because I *might* be a pumpkin pie spice guy doesn't mean I would make a snow angel."

Dash's neck craned and he squinted at Gavin. "A pumpkin

spice guy jumps in a pile of leaves, surprises his friends with baked goods, and lives for scarves and festive accessories," he said with a dramatic wave of his hand at Gavin's red plaid tie. "Don't think I haven't noticed and appreciated your efforts!" He said from behind a hand and winked. "And a pumpkin spice guy would definitely stop and make a snow angel if he spotted a parade of snow angels in a patch of snow in Central Park," he stated with absolute certainty. "I dare you." He widened his eyes excitedly, then hopped off the trail and tiptoed around the other angels. Gavin looked around nervously while Dash carefully laid down next to the angel at the end, setting his cup on the ground above his head where it was safe. "Get a picture and then come and join me!" He called and began waving his arms through the thin layer of snow. There was just enough and Dash giggled as the sun peaked through the clouds.

"Just a moment," Gavin said as he juggled his coffee and his phone. "I don't do this a lot..."

"Take pictures?" Dash asked, raising his head.

"No. I'm not very good at it and everyone sends me plenty as it is," Gavin murmured but he thought he was doing a pretty decent job as he swiveled and made sure he got all the angels in a row with Dash.

"That's good. Get your adorable backside over here!" Dash said, pointing sternly at the ground next to him.

"Fine," Gavin said as he stepped over and made his way around, avoiding the other angels. "No pictures," he stipulated, tucking his phone back into his pocket. He turned and awkwardly lowered and eased back with his cup and mimicked Dash. Gavin felt oddly light and like laughing but he bit down on his lips and humphed instead, using his arms to sweep away the snow. "Am I doing this right?"

"Of course, you are! Let's get a look!" Dash got up then turned without disturbing his angel and offered Gavin a hand.

"Thank you." Gavin reached up and wasn't prepared for the heat of Dash's palm as it closed around his or how easily he was pulled up. "Thank you," he repeated breathlessly.

"No problem." Dash blinked at Gavin's lips and swallowed loudly. "Any time," he said as he swayed closer and Gavin was mesmerized as Dash's tongue slid along his lips.

If Gavin wasn't a colossal chicken he would have kissed Dash. He desperately wanted to know if Dash's lips and tongue still tasted like pumpkin spice. They looked sweet and Gavin could smell cinnamon and spices as their breaths huffed between them. "Nice," he whispered.

"What?" Dash's eyelashes spread across his cheeks as his chin brushed Gavin's.

"This is..." Gavin shut his eyes, praying he'd get away with this.

"Jeffrey! Come back!" A woman shouted as a golden retriever in an argyle vest galloped toward them.

"No, no, no, Jeffrey!" Gavin pleaded in terror when the dog veered in his direction.

"I've got him!" Dash intercepted the dog before he could trample Gavin and their angels or make a run for the lake.

"I am so sorry!" The woman was breathless when she caught up with them. "He thinks every man in a trench coat is my husband. I was fixing my glove and lost hold of the leash when he saw the two of you." She babbled apologies at them and offered to take a picture, but they insisted she was forgiven and sent her on her way.

They laughed about it and gathered their cups, took a few photos, and returned to the trail. The moment had clearly passed and it was probably for the best, Gavin decided. There was no telling who else might have seen them and he couldn't explain their outing as two friends doing a little covert Christmas shopping if someone saw them kissing.

At the market, Gavin was easily tempted to buy a gorgeous glass lamp for Penny and Agnes. He wasn't sure what the style was called but it looked like it was made of blue mosaic tiles. Gavin found a daring pair of handmade shoes he was sure Reid would have no trouble pairing a suit with, being the flashier dressed of the two of them. The perfect tacky Christmas sweaters for Fin and Riley practically jumped into Gavin's shopping bags, they were so loud and chaotic.

The morning passed all too quickly and Gavin was sad to have to part with Dash when they reached the library. "I have practice with the triplets this afternoon," he said with a heavy sigh after Dash ran in for his briefcase. "How a thing can be both a joy and horrendous I will never understand."

"How about this?" Dash said, taking Gavin's bags. "I'll drop these off at your place and leave you some soup for dinner. Reid's probably going to be late and I have to cover a family from Toronto tonight. The dad's a famous hockey player so Reid thought I'd be the obvious fit," he added quickly. "But this was definitely nice. We should do this again the next time I'm off. You only got through half of your list," Dash noted with a hopeful smile.

"I wouldn't mind that," Gavin admitted. "I'll see you later, then," he said with a bow.

"Wait!" Dash grabbed the front of Gavin's overcoat and pressed a quick kiss to his cheek. "You were really nice and today was perfect."

What was perfect?

Gavin's brain had been completely erased and all that was left was the feel of Dash's lips brushing his cheek. "It was. Thank you," he managed before they parted ways.

For some odd reason, Gavin's hand kept brushing his cheek

where Dash had kissed him. He could still feel a slight pressure and a tingle there and had lost control of his own lips. He hadn't meant—or wanted—to, but Gavin had even *smiled at a child*. He couldn't help himself. She was precious in her puffy pink coat and her red hat had big pink pom poms.

"I like your hat," he informed her while waiting for the lights to change so they could cross the intersection.

"I like your..." Her lips twisted as she studied Gavin and he raised a brow at her, wondering what a small girl of four or five would find likable in him. "You have neat glasses!"

"Thank you for noticing," he said, pleased that she could appreciate his new frames. "Goodbye and have a very good day," he told the girl when they reached the other side and went in different directions.

Unfortunately, the rest of Gavin's afternoon wasn't very good for him, personally. The triplets asked him a dozen questions about Dash apiece. Apparently, they had heard from Fin that "something" might be happening and attempted to interrogate Gavin instead of practicing "The Twelve Days of Christmas."

Common sense warned that if the news had already made it back to the triplets, it was likely that his father was hearing whispers as well. But Gavin knew there was no going back and it wasn't going to stop him from meeting Dash again and finishing his Christmas shopping.

Now that Gavin was on the nice list with Dash, he didn't want off of it.

Chapter Six

Unlike Fin and Riley, Dash and Penny didn't need weeks to prepare their performance for the Christmas Eve eve talent showcase. All they needed was a few drinks and for Dash to pull out one of his guitars. They weren't the strongest singers in the group *by far*, but what they lacked in natural talent, Penny and Dash made up for with enthusiasm and chemistry. No one was more fun to sing and dance with than Penny Lane and she hyped Dash up like he was Johnny Cash.

But some planning was necessary so they met for a little bit of thrifting, hitting two stores before heading over to Penny and Agnes's new place on East 63rd. They were greeted by a doorman, but had the townhouse to themselves because Agnes was out Christmas shopping while June was at school.

"It's just over a week away," Dash said as he hung his coat. "Are you two ready?"

"Yes and I can't wait! We get to host it here this year!" Penny spun in the foyer like Mary Tyler Moore and tossed her hat in the air.

Dash skidded across the marble on his knees so he could catch it. "It's going to be epic!" He hopped up, then winced when his right knee twinged. "I keep forgetting that I am not a kid anymore," he said under his breath and shrugged as he went to hang Penny's hat. "I'm going to dedicate something to Gavin, but have you decided what we're performing?"

"Yes!" Penny's eyes lit up. "I think we'd kill with 'Run Run Rudolph' if you bring your electric guitar too."

"Yes!" He agreed as he envisioned himself rocking out in his elf costume.

"June has been practicing with Bea twice a week. She's playing 'Have Yourself A Merry Little Christmas' and I'm pretty sure Reid will play the piano again."

Dash hummed in agreement. "June's going to do *amazing* and Reid always makes me cry," he said, making Penny chuckle.

"Birthday cards make you cry like a baby," she said as she patted his arm.

"Some people put a lot of thought into picking those, though." He got a little emotional just thinking about someone pausing in front of a wall of cards and looking for one that would put a smile on his face or make him laugh. "Sometimes, that's just as good as the gift!" He whispered, hugging Penny's hat.

"Come on!" She tugged on his sleeve to get him moving. "Reid is going to do something sentimental and classy so I thought we should rock out."

"Agreed. Gavin, Morris, Milo, and the triplets are doing 'The Twelve Days of Christmas' for the singalong. I can't wait for that!" Dash said while jogging up the stairs at Penny's side. "I wish I could eavesdrop on Gavin's practice sessions with the triplets. He says it's like a rollercoaster ride."

"Fin told Aggie that Gavin's great with them and that he

would have made a brilliant music teacher," Penny relayed as they headed for her "office."

She skipped ahead and threw the double doors open and Dash was right beside her when she crashed onto the giant beanbag. It was one of Penn's creations and covered in a patchwork of bright florals. There was also a standing desk with two monitors because Penny actually did a lot of work while June was at school. But the rest of the space was overrun by potted and hanging plants. Dash loved it because it was like their own miniature jungle in Manhattan.

"He says he doesn't like kids, but I think we've all rubbed off on him," Dash said, brushing the end of one of Penny's braids against his lips thoughtfully. "And he acts like he's so stuffy and cranky when he's actually really, really nice."

"How are things going with Gavin, by the way?" Penny asked, rolling toward Dash.

He sighed happily. "We're finally making progress and it's so...nice being able to spend time with him away from Briarwood Terrace. Although, it has been kind of icky, keeping it a secret from Reid. I want to tell him about how sweet Gavin is at the library or about how he charmed an old woman in the market the other day, but I can't because he's supposed to be at work. I can't tell anyone but you about all the awesome things we did this week and that stinks. And I'm really worried about how Reid's going to take it when he finds out."

"Ew..." Penny grimaced. "I would not want to be there for that. Are you going to be okay? You don't handle confrontation well and secrets stress you out."

He nodded, concerned too. "I've been worried, but I'm a lot stronger than I was in high school." He knocked his forehead against hers.

"I know!" She smacked his stomach, making him gasp.

"You're one of the strongest, bravest people I know. But even dragons have tender bellies. Or, they're ticklish!" She dug her fingers into his ribs.

"No!" Dash gasped and laughed as he twisted. "Uncle!"

She grabbed his hand and they flopped onto their backs. "This is kind of like when you're scared your parents might get a divorce. And you're doing your best to keep everything normal for your other siblings because they don't know."

Dash's lips twisted. "Kind of. Except I want to sleep with one of the dads. Like, *a lot*."

"It's a poly situation for sure," Penny said to the ceiling. "You'll be the husband Gavin sleeps with and Reid is the one who nags him."

"Would that make me your step dad? This is a really weird metaphor," he said out of the side of his mouth.

Penny shook her head, suddenly serious as she looked at Dash. "It isn't, though. Reid and Gavin are life partners, in just about every sense *except* romantic and sexual. That would scare a lot of men off."

"True, but they're different." Dash understood exactly what he was getting into with Gavin and Reid. Their bond was beautiful and Gavin's loyalty to Reid only made him even more appealing. "They're kind of like us, they're just more dependent on each other because they're not as outgoing and high strung," he said, smiling as he hugged her hand. "They're like *Frog and Toad*, except the tall one is the uptight one. I love that about them and it's one of the reasons why I spend so much time at Briarwood Terrace. Who would want to break that up?"

"They are!" Penny rolled toward Dash. "Which iconic literary duo are we?"

He didn't even need to think about that one. "Merry and Pippin, obviously."

She laughed and kissed him. "We would find the best short-cuts to the mushrooms."

"And go on the best side quest," he agreed. "I think I can help them work this out. Or work through it if Reid is really, really upset with Gavin. I won't let this break them up. That would mean that Gavin's dad won."

"Not on our watch," Penny growled, narrowing her eyes. "Reid trusts you and he'll listen to you."

"If he isn't mad at me for keeping secrets," Dash worried out loud.

"He'll understand. Reid has a little bit of a temper and he can be stubborn, but he knows you have to keep your word. And he'll expect you to have Gavin's back like that."

"I hope so. But I also want what's best for Gavin and getting it all out in the open would take so much weight off his shoulders. He wouldn't have to pretend to go to work every day and I could tell Reid that Gavin made a snow angel."

"No, he did not!" Penny laughed and searched his face to see if he was serious. "There's no way!"

Dash made a dreamy sound and his eyes watered as he marveled at how something as silly as snow angels could turn a mundane Wednesday stroll through a park into a magical adventure. "We saw a chain of them and I dared Gavin. Did you know, he's a pumpkin spice guy?"

"Really? I'd peg him for a peppermint mocha drinker," she replied, but Dash shook his head.

"No way! Deep down, Gavin's a romantic and a little corny like me. I can tell!"

"I guess I can see that. What else?" She gave him a poke. "I know there's more. You keep making little swoony sounds."

"We would have kissed if it weren't for an adorable golden retriever named Jeffrey. He thought Gavin was his dad and came charging at us. Gavin almost had a heart attack but I rescued him and stopped Jeffrey's argyle rampage. I had to work last night until late and I'm working again tonight and tomorrow morning, until the family flies back to Canada. So I won't see Gavin until tomorrow evening or Saturday morning at brunch."

Penny made a sympathetic pouting sound. "If it makes it any better, I bet he's wondering when he'll get to see you again and misses you when you're apart."

"I don't know… Do you think he's there yet? It's still a little soon," Dash wondered out loud and a snorting laugh fluttered from Penny.

"Hello! You got him to drink a pumpkin spice latte and make a snow angel. You've never seen the way he stares at you, but I think the snow angels are proof enough that Gavin is deeply in love. I still can't believe it happened and there's only one logical explanation."

"No!" Dash said, tossing a hand at Penny. "Do you think…?" He felt a rush of hope as he thought about how close they'd come to kissing in Central Park. "Do you think we might be boyfriends by Christmas Eve eve? Everyone keeps adding more and more mistletoe traps every year and it would be nice to have someone to kiss this time."

"We are a cheesy bunch and we do get a little heavy-handed with the mistletoe," she confirmed, shrugging a shoulder. "You and Gavin and Reid are the only single grownups left, the rest of us are newlyweds or still act like it so it's fun embarrassing each other."

"Oh, no." Dash shook his head. He thought the traps were fun before, but now they had the potential to be harmful.

It started after Fin and Walker were married and Penn came up with the idea for everyone to bring some mistletoe to hang around The Killian House since they were hosting that year. Agnes had been up at her cottage in Sagaponack with her elderly, retired nanny, but it was Dash's first Christmas Eve eve with the Briarwood crew and he'd had a blast making mistletoe traps with Penny beforehand. But Gavin didn't enjoy them and tended to skirt the room to avoid crossing paths with anyone and having to endure a kiss.

"I don't want our first mistletoe kiss to feel forced or be embarrassing. I need to find some and keep it in a jar of water so I'll be ready when the perfect opportunity presents itself," Dash said distantly as he plotted.

"I'll get you some by the end of the day!" Penny said as she held out her fist so he could bump it. "Any idea when this perfect opportunity might occur?"

"Not yet, but I hope it's soon. Preferably before Christmas Eve eve and we find ourselves in a mistletoe minefield," he said and Penny chuckled deviously.

"I have a feeling you'll be way past kissing by then. Which reminds me, have you given any thought to how the rest of us will be loosening our inhibitions? You're in charge of the punch as usual."

"It's going to be a giant cranberry Moscow mule!" He clapped and pumped his fist. "Ginger beer, cranberry vodka, fresh lime juice, and some cranberry juice cocktail. I'm going to make sugared cranberries to float on top but I'm adding super finely diced fresh mint to the sugar."

"Oh! That sounds delicious. I'll make sure we have every-thing you need to keep the punch flowing," Penny promised.

"Good. Because that's half of our plan," Dash said, making Penny giggle.

"We always sound better after three or four glasses of punch. Come on!" She sat up and tugged on Dash's hand, pulling him upright. "Let's work on our choreography!"

"Just remember that I'll be wearing my elf boots and they

don't have as much traction," he said as they got up and she found the song on her phone.

"Got it. What about overhead lifts? Do we want to try that again?"

Dash shook his head. "If last year taught us anything, we're not better at *that* after four glasses of punch."

Chapter Seven

I t hadn't seemed possible at the outset of the week, but things were actually looking up. Gavin had braced himself for a series of grueling trials and tedious tribulations. Instead, he had experienced and *enjoyed* pumpkin lattes, was dazzled by window displays, finished half of his Christmas shopping, and had even been convinced to make a snow angel in the park. Gavin had never visited any of the many holiday markets around Manhattan and had done his best to avoid all the popular holiday attractions so he had been treated to a whole new, and at times, dazzling city thanks to Dash.

The best part was Dash knew the perfect times to visit and it often felt like he had turned down the volume on the sidewalks and parks, making them surprisingly bearable. Dash had promised that the holiday city was even more magical at night and Gavin was secretly excited to see it all through his eyes.

Gavin was even anticipating the weekend and whatever Dash had in store for them as he made his way home to Briarwood Terrace. He had a stop to make, first, and regretted that he couldn't join Reid when he waved from their stoop.

"Where are you headed?" Reid asked, holding the door.

"I'm meeting Kyle Vanderlake for coffee," Gavin explained and waved his paper at the shop at the end of the block.

Reid squinted as he nodded. "Right. I remember Kyle. He's from...upper...what's it—?"

"Yes, that Kyle," Gavin said dryly. "He's from upper what's it. Or, as I like to call him, a senior partner. He sent me a rather vague text about coffee and catching up this morning."

"Maybe it's a promotion." Reid held out a hand so Gavin could slap it.

That was highly unlikely, but Gavin slapped it back and smiled. "Possibly. Shouldn't be long," he guessed as he checked his watch and grimaced at the time. "Why he'd want to meet this late on a Friday evening is beyond me."

Reid humphed as he narrowed his eyes at the shop. "Maybe they're finally getting around to making you a partner." His lips tightened. "Want some backup?"

"No," Gavin said quickly. "I don't know what Kyle wants to meet about but I don't need you badgering him about promotions."

"You gotta stand up for yourself and tell them you want it or it'll never happen," Reid advised with an encouraging pat on Gavin's back.

"I'll keep that in mind." He checked his watch again, clearing his throat loudly. "It wouldn't do to be late."

"Right! See you later," Reid said, tapping his brow before heading inside.

The coffee shop was just as busy as Gavin feared and he had to sidestep around the crowd at the door to get in. He scanned until he spotted Kyle at one of the tall tables by the window and went to join him.

"Selby! It's been a while," the older man said as he offered his hand. He was in his mid-sixties, but his black hair had been

perfectly trimmed and colored to hide any gray and was styl-
ishly messy.

"It has," Gavin agreed, hugging his briefcase and stepping
closer to the table so a couple could squeeze behind him to get
to the bar.

"Don't just stand there! Take off your coat and stay a
while," Kyle laughed as he stood and came around to help
Gavin with his overcoat. "I picked this place because it was
right around the corner from you. I didn't count on it being this
busy."

"I'd rather not—" Gavin started, but Kyle laughed and gave
his shoulders a quick knead, unlocking a buried memory. Gavin
recalled the bourbon fumes and Kyle's hands gripping and
assessing in the men's room, just after Ernst & Waterhouse's
holiday party.

*"There's something I've wanted to discuss with you, Selby.
Why don't we step in here?"*

Gavin had joined Kyle in the larger handicapped stall
because...it would have been rude to decline and Gavin didn't
necessarily object, per se. Kyle was an attractive man and
Gavin generally preferred his partners on the older and quieter
side when he did engage in sexual intercourse. They were more
"his speed" and less intimidating.

The entire encounter had been rather brief and pleasantly
impersonal. Kyle had unzipped Gavin's trousers and
murmured husky compliments as he petted and tugged until
they were both erect. And it was not unpleasant when Kyle
dropped onto the toilet's seat so he could perform fellatio upon
Gavin. It only took a few moments for Gavin to climax and for
Kyle to spill on the tile between their feet.

They had exchanged a few bland pleasantries as they
fixed their suits and washed their hands but neither had felt
the need to mention the encounter once they'd left the

restroom. It had been... Gavin frowned as he tried to remember the year.

"Nice of you to dress up," Kyle said with a chuckle while draping Gavin's overcoat on the back of the empty chair.

"I...just left a meeting," Gavin lied, looking down at his suit. It was a perfectly acceptable charcoal wool single-breasted suit and what he would normally wear "to work."

"Good! I'm glad you're staying busy. We've missed you," Kyle said as he pulled out Gavin's chair but he shook his head.

"I'd rather not. I'll stand," he said, resting an elbow on the table. He didn't like sitting on the tall stools. He was already 6' 4" and they made him feel like he was perching and he didn't like seeing over everyone's heads. And Gavin felt like everyone was staring while he sat there like a great, gangling dunce.

"So, tell me. What have you been up to?" Kyle asked as he returned to his stool. He waved down a server, gesturing impatiently before flashing Gavin a wide grin. "I lost track of you after you left the firm. Where have you been hiding yourself?"

"Mostly private work. I handle some of Walker Cameron's accounts. I make a lot of house calls these days," Gavin replied with a bland smile. "Why? Is there interest in me 'returning'?" He asked, but grew confused when Kyle winced and hissed sheepishly.

"Not until your old man..." He raised his brows suggestively.

Gavin understood that he was still in exile and that no one was willing to touch him until his father was dead. He eased aside when a young woman hustled to their table to take their order. "Earl Gray," he mumbled to her. "Then, why did you want to meet?" Gavin asked Kyle after she went to fight her way to the bar to get his tea.

Gavin watched her go, grimacing in irritation. It was so unnecessary because he had the exact same tea at his place and it was quieter there. And all things considered, it would have been so much faster and more pleasant to go home and prepare it for himself.

"You can't be serious, Selby."

Gavin's head whipped around. "I generally am," he replied warily, earning a boisterous laugh from Kyle as he put an arm around Gavin.

"I might be able to help with that." Kyle gave his shoulders another squeeze before Gavin's ass was patted.

Gavin jerked away and took a large step to the right, sliding around the table so it was between them. "How?"

"Easy!" Kyle reached and set his hand on Gavin's. "I heard a little rumor through the grapevine that your father had taken a turn and that it was just a matter of time."

That was news to Gavin. "Oh?"

"You haven't heard?" Kyle laughed when Gavin shook his head. "They've moved him to the city because he needs round-the-clock care. All that's left is for you to pull the plug and you're a free man, from what I'm hearing."

"I believe that's considered murder," Gavin mused to himself, then thanked their server when she arrived with his tea. It had been prepared in a paper cup, thank goodness. "Wait," he said, pulling his wallet from inside his coat and finding a $20 so he could escape.

"I'm kidding!" Kyle slapped the table, his eyes twinkling as he grinned at Gavin. "But I was thinking about the possibilities *for you*," he explained, increasing Gavin's confusion.

"You just said the firm wasn't interested in hiring me—"

"Hiring you?" Kyle reared back as if Gavin wasn't making sense, then sneered. "Why would you give a single fuck about Ernst & Waterhouse? And we'll all be working *for you*, I hope. You wouldn't forget your friends there, would you?"

"No." Gavin shook his head quickly. "I wasn't aware that

my father's...passing was imminent, but I have no reason to believe that I'll be inheriting a dime or get so much as a memento from the estate."

"That's not what I'm hearing at all," Kyle replied, resting a forearm on the table so he could smirk and stare into Gavin's eyes. "And I was thinking that we might—"

"Hold on!" Gavin gasped and finally noted Kyle's sleek black suit. He didn't look like he'd come from the office or a meeting. The collar of his powder blue shirt was unbuttoned and he wasn't wearing a tie. A cautious sniff revealed that he was wearing a very expensive and intoxicating cologne as well. "I'm afraid I misunderstood," Gavin said, just as the door opened and the sound of the street and a blast of cold air filled the shop. He spotted Dash, laughing over his shoulder at Penny as they pushed their way inside.

"No way!" He heard Penny shout, gesturing at the bodies between them and the counter.

"I just have to grab his tea for tomorrow," Dash replied, making Gavin feel like the biggest coward as he looked for someone he could hide behind. He knew exactly who Dash was buying tea for. "Gavin?" Dash called in surprise when their eyes met.

"Ugh. I'll wait outside," Penny decided and turned back as Dash waved wildly over people's heads to get Gavin's attention.

"Hey, Gavin!" Dash was hopping and waving excitedly, scooting his way through the crowd. "What are you doing here?" He asked when they were finally face-to-face. He offered Kyle a sunny wave, then raised his brows at Gavin expectantly. "You know I always stop by on Friday nights to make sure you have enough tea for the weekend."

"I...um..." Gavin croaked. He cleared his throat as he stalled while Kyle watched them over his demitasse cup, his pinkie pointed out as he sipped.

Dash's gaze slid back to Kyle and then to the table and Gavin's coat on the chair. "Oh!"

Kyle raised a brow at Gavin. "You prefer tea in the morning. Good to know," he said and there was a sharp squeak from Dash.

"Oh, God. I'm sorry. You're on a... You're on..." His voice had cracked and his eyes were huge and glittered when they swung back to Gavin's. "You're on a date."

"No!" Gavin shook his head quickly.

Kyle snorted into his tiny cup. "What are we, teenagers?" His sneer slid down the front of Dash's jean jacket, scarf, and hoodie. He let out a groan at Dash's distressed jeans and black sneakers. "A date?" Kyle rolled his eyes. "Why don't you run along, kiddo? Selby and I have some catching up to do."

"Right!" Dash turned bright red, nodding quickly as he backed away. "I didn't mean to—" He spun when he bumped into a pair of young women. "I'm so sorry!"

"Dash, wait!" Gavin called, but Dash shook his head.

"It's fine! I keep an extra box at my place in case you ever —" He choked out, then shielded his face as he ducked into the crowd.

"Wait!" Gavin begged and swore when he lost sight of Dash. "Do you have any idea what you've done?" Gavin demanded as he turned back to Kyle, furious as he snatched his coat off the chair.

"I honestly thought you'd have better taste than that," Kyle said with a bored sigh.

"Go to hell, Vanderlake. You're not fit to kiss his Converse." Gavin didn't look back as he fought his way through to the front door, but there was no sign of Dash or Penny once he made it out and searched the sidewalk and the street. "Briarwood Terrace!"

He took off, his overcoat flapping behind him as he raced

like a madman. Gavin shouted apologies as he checked shoulders and kicked bags, skidding around the corner and dodging a couple walking their dog. The stoop in front of his building was empty, but he hurried and was digging in his pocket for his keys as he ran up the steps.

Gavin let himself in and gasped when he found the front desk unoccupied, then recalled that Norman had called in because he had a cold. Gavin rushed through the lobby, scaring 2B's cat as he came around the corner and tripped toward his door.

"Is Dash here?" He demanded as soon as he threw it open and fell inside.

"What? Why?" Reid asked, leaning around the refrigerator.

Gavin let out a strangled roar, swinging his coat and briefcase onto the sofa. "It was a date!" He said loudly, then braced his hands on the back of the sofa so he could hang his head in shame. "I was blind and didn't see that it was a date until Dash walked in and he saw me with Vanderlake."

The fridge door swung shut. "Oh, no!" Reid was panicky as he came around the counter. "Poor Dash! Why would a *senior partner* even think you'd be interested in going on a date with him? Isn't he like...?"

Gavin threw up a hand, warning Reid before he jumped to conclusions. "We may have...once. But it was years ago. And I forgot," he added in a quiet mumble.

"You forgot?" Reid laughed in disbelief and Gavin nodded.

"You know that I don't have intercourse very often. And when I do, it's usually in a bathroom, or an office, or a conference room, and it's rarely anything worth remembering," he said, making Reid's face twist.

"I want so much more for you than that and have you ever thought of saying no? Especially to a creep like Vanderlake. You've never had anything nice to say about that guy."

Gavin shook his head. "No, because I had a chance to get off with another man—quickly and easily—without having to engage in any witty banter or social posturing. And afterward, we both went back to our lives as if it had never happened. It was utterly unremarkable and *ideal* because I didn't want more than that."

"Looks like Vanderlake does," Reid said suggestively. "Doesn't sound like it was unremarkable to him."

"He heard that my father is dying and wanted to 'catch up.'" Gavin curled his fingers sarcastically.

"Ew. Do you want to talk about that or...your fath—" Reid started carefully, stopping when Gavin cut him a hard look.

"Not at all."

"Good," Reid said, swiping Gavin's overcoat off the sofa and pushing it at him. "Because you have to get over to Dash's and fix this. He's probably devastated. You know how long he's been waiting for you."

"He is, but—" Gavin attempted, gasping as he was spun and shoved at the door.

"Go!"

"Wait!" Gavin braced a hand on a panel before Reid could pull it open. "I don't know what to say to Dash!"

"How about the truth?"

Gavin's lips pursed and his eyes narrowed. "You want me to tell Dash that Vanderlake and I had intercourse several years ago?"

"No. Don't do that." Reid shook his head quickly. "I meant the other truth."

"About my father?"

"Gavin!" Reid reached for his throat but smiled as he straightened Gavin's tie and tightened it. A touch too tight. He held onto the knot, grinning threateningly at Gavin. "I meant the part about you loving him—and only him—to complete and utter distraction."

"No. I—" Gavin coughed as his windpipe was squeezed.

"Do you really want to lie to *me*? And when time is of the essence? Dash is probably at his place crying his eyes out and double-fisting emergency margaritas as we speak. I'm not having it, Gavin. Not when he's done literally everything humanly possible to prove that you're it, you're *everything* to him."

"Yes, I know. But I can't give him false hope," Gavin argued and gasped when Reid backed him into the door.

"False hope?" Reid barked angrily. "You love him! I don't know what you're so afraid of or why you can't accept it, but you can't hurt Dash while you're working that out."

"You don't understand! It's...complicated," Gavin attempted. But there was no way he could explain it to Reid.

"I don't care! Not right now. Not when Dash is hurting." Reid turned Gavin and yanked the door open. "We can have our come to Jesus chat after he's feeling better," he said, but Gavin had his own epiphany as he stumbled into the hall and the door slammed shut behind him.

He could trust Dash, Gavin realized. Dash would understand once he learned the truth and he wouldn't tell Reid because he loved Gavin too much to betray him.

Chapter Eight

O f all the times to be out of tequila and limeade concentrate. But in Dash's defense, there hadn't been as much need to keep ingredients on hand for emergency margaritas after Penny moved to East 63rd with Agnes and June.

Life had been pretty close to perfect and Dash believed that happily ever after with Gavin was just around the corner. Why would he possibly need to lock himself in his apartment and get hammered in the shower?

"It was never gonna happen, kiddo," he muttered as he lifted a bottle of spiced rum to his lips and took a long pull. He gagged and let out a whimpering "Yar!"

Dash didn't like rum, but it was leftover from the pirate punch he'd made for the last Halloween bash at Briarwood Terrace and the only alcohol he had in the apartment.

"I thought I'd stop tasting it after..." He held up the bottle and pointed to where the rum had been when he carried it into the shower and where the line was now. "That's like a quarter of the bottle," he noted.

But he was still *so sad* and thanks to the rum, he couldn't stop picturing Gavin in his pirate costume. The theme had been "Pie, Rats, and Pirates" and Reid had browbeaten Gavin into dressing up and had conveniently supplied him with a costume so he had no excuses.

The long black hair, eye patch, and faux five o'clock shadow had worked so well on Gavin, Dash hadn't been able to keep his eyes off of him.

"That's right..." Dash said as he scowled at the bottle, recalling why he didn't like rum and what had happened after he'd drunk several glasses of pirate punch. "Sexiest pirate in the seven boroughs, indeed" he muttered, putting his thumb over the mouth of the bottle and reaching up to turn on the water when he started to cry in earnest again.

That was why everyone thought he was nothing but an empty-headed himbo. Dash *knew* there were only five boroughs, but there were seven seas and he was standing on the coffee table and pointing a foam sword at Gavin. Dash had attempted to leap over the sofa so he could ask Gavin to dance. But several critical factors were not in Dash's favor—mainly that it was a very large leap up and over the back of the sofa and he had greatly overestimated his coordination at the time. The result had been a dramatic backflop onto the cushions that had caused everyone to erupt into wild cheers while Reid, Morris, Penn, and Walker announced their scores for the maneuver.

"Pathetic. And for what?" Dash turned off the water and took another drink.

When he was a child and afraid to cry in front of others, Dash would run home to the nearest shower so A. no one would see him, and B. he had an excuse for being a walking puddle afterward. His therapist helped him understand that crying was actually healthy years ago, but Dash still preferred to do his hardest crying alone in the shower and this was the hardest he had ever cried.

All this time, Dash believed with all of his heart that *they* were inevitable and worth waiting for. He could feel it every time Gavin walked into the room. His whole body jittered with excitement and Dash was pretty sure that if he was lucky enough to have a tail it would wag like crazy. No one, not even Penny, made him *that* happy just by walking into a room. And Dash knew without a doubt that he could make Gavin happier than the jerk with the perfect hair in the coffee shop.

"How could Gavin take him to *our* coffee shop?"

Everything hurt worse and Dash let out a sob as he turned the water back on. They had never actually stepped foot into the shop together. Dash had just fantasized about it every time he asked if they could get coffee sometime and whenever he popped in every Friday evening for Gavin's Earl Grey. The baristas had even begun to tease Dash about buying it for his boyfriend and he had looked forward to finally confirming their suspicions.

"How could I be so stupid?" He asked the ceiling, squinting through the water. "And for so long?"

The doorbell rang loudly, mocking Dash, but he shook his head. It was probably Penny coming back to make sure he wasn't drinking in the shower. Or, she had told Penn to come over and make sure he wasn't in the shower. He turned off the water and slid back the curtain so he could use the towel hanging from the bar to dry his hand and grabbed his phone off the toilet seat.

It only took a few swipes to call Penny and her face filled the screen. "Hey! How are you holding up? Are you sure you don't want me to come over?" She asked tenderly.

They had parted ways outside the coffee shop after he shrieked that Gavin was *on a date* and took off running. Dash then screamed a "No!" when she asked if she was supposed to run after him or stop for tequila and meet him at his place. She had clearly listened and had gone home to East 63rd.

"I didn't want you to see me like this," he said, waving the bottle at the phone before taking a drink. His head swung toward the hall when the doorbell rang again. "Call Penn and tell him I appreciate his concern, but I'm not answering that."

"Penn? I didn't call Penn. He's having dinner in Park Slope with the Mosbys," she reminded him.

"Right..." Dash nodded, jumping when there was a loud knock at the front door. "Who...?"

"Maybe you should check?" Penny suggested helpfully.

"Fine. If I'm lucky it's the Seven Boroughs Strangler coming to put me out of my misery."

Penny giggled. "Sweetheart! I'm so, so sorry and I'm sure this is all a big misunderstanding."

"There was nothing to misunderstand, Penny," he said as he pulled on the fluffy pink robe she had left him when she moved. They had laughed over it in a thrift shop and bought it as a lark. But it quickly became their "snuggle robe" and they would pull it on to signal that they were having a rough day or had received bad news and needed to be handled with a little extra care. He mopped at his face with the sleeve on the way to the door. "It was very clear that they had hooked up before and were heading back to Briarwood Terrace."

"That doesn't sound at all like Gavin, though," Penny argued.

"I don't know what to tell you except that maybe Gavin's into older guys who get too much Botox and wear expensive suits. He called me kiddo and laughed at me."

"Who?" Penny demanded angrily.

"I don't know what his name was," Dash said as he went to the door and peeked through the hole.

Penny let out a determined grunt. "I'll find out and when I do, I'll make him eat that *kiddo*," she vowed.

"Gavin?" Dash asked, squinting through the hole harder to be sure he was seeing right.

"No. The other guy. The one who called you kiddo."

"Oh, no. You should leave that guy alone. I don't think he's hooking up with Gavin again."

"Why? Is he at your door?" She asked in alarm.

"What?" Dash checked to see if anyone else was with Gavin but shook his head. As far as he could tell, Gavin was alone and pacing on the stoop. Gavin scrubbed his face in frustration, then banged on the door again.

"Ah!" Dash and Penny yelled.

"Who is it?" Penny asked.

"Would you please answer the door?" Gavin begged.

"It's Gavin!" Dash whispered at his phone, making Penny giggle.

"Answer it!" She shouted, then hung up.

"Right!" Dash dropped his phone into the robe's pocket and unlatched the deadbolt. He eased the door open, leaving the chain on. "Yes?" He asked, doing his best to sound and look completely composed as he angled his head to see through the crack.

"May I come in, please?" Gavin asked gently.

"I'm afraid that now is not a good time," Dash said, shrinking away when Gavin moved into view and offered him a pleading look.

"I am so sorry and I promise it wasn't what it looked like. I'll explain if you'll let me in."

Dash sniffled and dabbed at the end of his nose with an oversized sleeve, then looked down at himself. He looked like a kid in his mother's robe. "The thing is, I've had a lot to drink while I was in the shower and I look like..."

"I don't care, Dash. I hurt you and I can't leave until I know you're feeling better."

"Oh. See? That's...*nice*."

"Thank you, but you don't understand. Reid won't *let* me go home until I make this right. But I want to explain. Everything."

"Okay," Dash said hesitantly, unable to resist Gavin's cryptic "everything" or the thought of Reid worrying about him. He gathered his courage, tightening the robe around him as he unlocked the door and eased it open so Gavin could pass. "It's fine. You're allowed to date anyone you want and you don't owe me an explanation," he said in a rush as he shut the door, his sleeve catching on the knob. Dash yanked it free. "It's not like you gave me any reason to believe something would happen between us."

"I didn't know it was a date," Gavin said clearly, gripping Dash's arms and shaking him just enough so he'd focus and listen. "We used to work together and I misunderstood the purpose of our appointment when I accepted his invitation."

"Oh! I thought you two—" Dash started, but stopped when Gavin nodded.

He turned bright red and his gaze dropped to their feet. "We did. But it was a long time ago and it meant absolutely nothing. I completely forgot."

"You forgot?"

Gavin nodded. "I do my best to ensure that every encounter is as brief and unremarkable as possible and then promptly pretend it never happened," he stated simply.

A shocked laugh burst from Dash. "I am so relieved and I'm done crying in the shower, but who *wants* to have bad sex?"

"Someone who already has everything he needs," Gavin said, holding up his hands. "I like my life—our life—just the way it is and I don't want anything to change. So, I say yes whenever an opportunity arises so I can know what it's like to be touched and touch someone else again. It...isn't ideal, but I can't imagine many men would understand that Reid and our weird little family will always come first or find that acceptable. Nor would I expect anyone to."

"But I do!" Dash insisted. "I know that you and Reid are platonic soulmates, like me and Penny, and I *love* that! I think it's beautiful and I understand why you're more protective of each other. Well, why he's more protective of you and why you need Reid more than I need Penny."

"You do?" Gavin looked dubious and wary as he rested his shoulder against the door.

Dash nodded, smoothing Gavin's tie and his lapels. He must have been in a hurry to get across town, his suit and hair were a mess. "I was born into a wonderful family who loved me no matter what. You had to build yourself one from scratch. Of course, you wouldn't let 'some guy' come in and turn everything upside down."

"No," Gavin said, chuckling as he caught the end of Dash's sleeve and rubbed it between his fingers. "Soft," he noted, letting out a heavy sigh. "You're not just some guy, Dash. But there are other reasons why I can't date you."

"Other reasons?" Dash parroted. "You can't tell me you don't feel *something*," he said, his voice rising with frustration. "You wouldn't be here if you didn't care."

"I do." Gavin nodded seriously. "I've done my best to discourage you, but only because I do, in fact, care rather deeply."

Dash's eyes widened in shock. From anyone else, it would have been rather tepid and possibly disappointing, as far as romantic declarations went. But from Gavin, it was *a lot*.

"Just not enough to have coffee or brief and unremarkable

sex with me?" Dash teased, earning another heavy sigh from Gavin.

His eyes were sad as they touched Dash's. "Something tells me it would be the opposite of brief and unremarkable and there are times when I would give *anything* for just one..." Gavin rasped and his hand shook as he cradled Dash's cheek. "Just one hour with you. But I'm afraid..." He grimaced and gave his head a shake, breaking the spell and setting Dash away from him. "I'm afraid that wouldn't be enough and that I can't protect you."

Dash snatched Gavin's hand back and pulled it against his chest. "Protect me?"

"You don't understand what my father is capable of. There's no telling what he'd do if he found out about you."

"Oh, my God!" Dash released Gavin's hand so he could give him a hard swat on the chest. "You've been blowing me off because you're protecting me!" Dash accused and Gavin nodded like it made perfect sense.

"Yes. My father is a vindictive monster. He'd try to destroy you and I'm certain I'd be a terrible disappointment as a lover. I can be dreadfully boring. Given *all* of that and my many, many other personality flaws, I thought it best to spare you."

Dash threw his hands up, completely flabbergasted. "And everyone thinks *I'm* clueless." He grabbed Gavin's face and kissed him. *Hard.* Gavin was startled and his hands hovered around Dash's face, but their tongues swirled and thrust hungrily and they both groaned as their bodies slid together.

"Dash!" Gavin scolded but his fingers twisted in Dash's hair and the other hand locked around his ass. They fell back against the door and Gavin angled his head, taking the kiss deeper. Dash moaned encouragingly and fought to get his arms free of the robe and wound them around Gavin's neck, letting the fluffy pink garment slide to the floor. Gavin's hand snaked between them and Dash whimpered in approval as his hard-on was cupped through his wet boxers. "Wait!" Gavin pulled his lips free and his chest heaved as he stared at Dash. "I'm sorry. I got carried away."

"But I want you to!" Dash reached for him, but Gavin shushed loudly and held him off.

"The thing is—! I'd rather not. I don't like it when I'm not in control of myself, especially when there could be serious ramifications."

"Serious ramifications? What could your father do to me? I'm a nanny and a part-time elf," he joked.

"I don't know!" Gavin said and wagged a finger at Dash scoldingly. "You have no idea how many times he's tried to punish Reid or take him from me. Reid has no idea because he's never needed to look for a place to live and has no desire to own a car, but he wouldn't be able to rent a movie in this town without my father shutting it down. The Marshall Agency wouldn't exist if Fin and Walker hadn't fallen in love. Reid's loan applications were getting turned down despite his excellent credit. I was covering all of the agency's initial expenses, but I couldn't have carried us for more than a few months. I never had to tell Reid how dicey things were in the beginning because Walker played the knight and paid for advertising, hired a PR agency, and brought a dozen high-paying clients."

"But what if Reid finds out!" Dash covered his mouth and his stomach when it ached. Reid would be livid and that much confrontation and conflict made Dash queasy when he wasn't drunk. "Your father really is a monster!"

"I know. That's why I can't risk him finding out about you. He lashes out every time I do something overtly homosexual and my parents have always blamed Reid."

"Fine. I'll wait him out. He can't live forever," Dash said with an easy shrug.

"No. He's expected to die any time now."

"*What?*" Dash shook his head, certain he'd misunderstood. "Did you just say...?"

"Apparently, my father is dying," Gavin clarified. "If I'm to believe Kyle. *That's* why he invited me for coffee."

"Oh, no! I'm so sorry," Dash said, but Gavin's brows knitted together and his lips pursed.

"Why? I just explained that he'd destroy your life if he knew what you meant to me." He made an exploding gesture with his hands that mimicked the explosion of glitter and snowflakes bursting in Dash's heart.

"Wow!" He whispered as he canted forward and pressed his lips to Gavin's, giggling when he felt another happy burst. "I'm sorry your father is a miserable man and that he'll probably die before he can make things right with you," he mumbled faintly. "I don't care how long it takes. I'll never give up on us."

"Dash." Gavin breathed his name like it was a miracle and it felt miraculous, the way their lips clung and their noses brushed. "How can you be so sure when I can't imagine why?"

Dash laughed softly as he leaned back and searched Gavin's face. "Why?"

There was still a confused furrow to his brow as he nodded. "Why would you settle for me and why are you so sure we'll work?"

"Come on!" Dash protested and tried to swat Gavin's chest but he caught his hand.

"I'm being serious, Dash. I see the way you look at me and it feels like a moment in the sun. But everyone looks at you like that. Everyone loves you and you could have damn near any man or woman you please. Why in the world would you choose me?"

Dash rolled his eyes as he looped an arm around Gavin's and pulled him to the mirror. He kept their arms linked and gestured at their reflection. "What do you see? Aside from the fact that one of us is drunk and wearing soaked boxers."

"Is there anything else?" Gavin asked distantly, his eyes lingering over the semi pressing against the nearly transparent fabric.

"Kind of making my point, though," Dash noted as he got harder and the bulge became more obvious. "*We* make me really happy."

That earned a chuckle and Gavin was blushing when their eyes touched in the mirror. "Is that all?" He asked flippantly, but Dash gasped.

"That's *everything*! You know my dad, right?"

"Not personally, but I know of him."

"Obviously," Dash said, waving dismissively because his dad was on TV just about every Sunday calling a football game. And he was now a spokesperson for a line of sneakers with memory foam soles that aired on most news channels during prime time. "But when I was a kid, I told my dad that I was worried because boys made my tummy tickle the way girls did and I had heard mean things about people like that."

"Oh my God," Gavin said woodenly.

Dash could tell by the tone and the way Gavin's eyes watered that a terrible memory had been triggered. "I will *never* take for granted how lucky I was that that was a safe space for me to admit that. Or that it was my dad who planted a little seed in my heart that day, and that he's responsible for the man I grew into. He said that it didn't matter who I loved as long as they made me happy. And not just happy when I'm with them, but happy with who I am when we're together," he said, his voice trembling as he realized how close he was to making that dream come true.

"That's...*wonderful*, Dash," Gavin stated, a tear sliding down his cheek as they watched each other through the mirror.

"It was. But it was more than that!" He explained as he hugged Gavin's arm and bounced excitedly next to him. "I saw how much my dad loved my mom and how happy *loving* her made him. Not just being in love with mom, but he found so much happiness in all the little ways he expressed his love for her. He showed the whole world every day and in every way he could that there was nothing better than making mom happy. And then, when I blurted that boys made me feel funny too, he told me it didn't matter *who* made my heart light up as long as the happiness was there. My parents are about to celebrate their thirty-fifth anniversary and I know the secret to their happiness is...happiness."

"Happiness," Gavin echoed as if it was a new concept.

"Exactly," Dash replied without a hint of doubt. "It might be a little thing, but nothing feels better than preparing your tea just the way you like it and seeing how content and *happy* you are while you're drinking it."

"You have to be joking."

"Nope," Dash stated with a firm nod. "And I know that if I'm this happy *now* over a cup of tea, I'll feel like the luckiest man in the world if I'm still the one who gets to make it thirty-five years from now."

This time, Gavin threw his hands up and captured Dash's face for a desperate, breathless kiss. "You are the most...ridiculously beautiful person I have ever met," he whispered shakily. "I keep waiting for you to slip through my fingers but—"

"I'm stuck and there's nothing you can do about it now." Dash made a giddy sound, ecstatic at the turn his evening had taken. He couldn't wait to tell Penny that their first kiss had finally happened and they were making *real* progress. "Unless you want to go back to my room and stick your fingers—"

"Not yet!" Gavin shushed loudly and squeezed his eyes shut as if he was afraid someone had heard Dash. "I'm not willing to risk it while there's still a chance my father could find out and make serious trouble for you."

Dash made an appropriately serious sound despite not giving a solitary damn about that sad, sick man. But Dash understood that Gavin cared and that he had suffered years of fear and trauma and that was what mattered most at the moment. "We've got time," he agreed, turning Gavin toward the door. There was no point standing around in wet boxers and catching a cold if neither of them were getting blown. "What's a few more months or a year?"

"I doubt it'll be that much longer, but, Dash?" Gavin paused at the door.

"Hmm?"

"How are you so sure that happiness is enough? How do you know I won't disappoint you when we do...?" His voice trailed off suggestively as a bright pink rash spread up his neck and across his cheeks, making Dash blush as well.

"You try to hide it, but I can see that there's a healthy imagination in there," he said, pointing between Gavin's soft gray eyes and causing them to cross. "And I've seen how passionate you can get over a teacup."

"A teacup?" Gavin asked cluelessly, then groaned and held on when Dash leaned in and stole another kiss.

"You can get really worked up over a teacup," Dash panted against his lips. He was getting turned on again, remembering how hot Gavin was when he lost his temper over his misplaced cup. "And I can *really* work with that." In fact, Dash was going to as soon as he was alone. "Goodnight, Gavin."

"Goodnight," he said as he opened the door and leaned back when the wind howled.

"It's not too late to change your mind," Dash teased, but raised his brows and bit into his lip hopefully.

Gavin opened his mouth, and for a moment, Dash thought

he'd say yes. But he shook his head and stepped over the threshold. Gavin slowly eased the door closed until they were back to peeking at each other through the crack. "This is probably safer for the time being. Do you think you'll be able to make it to brunch tomorrow? Reid will be worried until he knows you're alright."

"I'll be there," Dash stated with a firm nod. He was going to prove how happy they could be and they were going to check something special off their list tomorrow. "I wouldn't want you to run out of tea."

Chapter Nine

Dash had made a full recovery by the time he turned up for brunch with Penny, smiling as if he didn't have a care in the world. Fin and Riley were already seated and had badgered Gavin about his date with the "senior dickhead from upper whatever." Neither could believe the man's audacity and were concerned about Gavin's father's failing health. But Gavin promptly shut down the conversation, simply stating that the situation with Kyle had been a terrible misunderstanding and that Edward Selby could go to hell for all he cared. And that he wasn't wasting another moment of his weekend worrying about either of them.

"*Well done,*" Reid said sincerely, toasting Gavin with his coffee when Dash arrived with Penny, laughing as he hung his coat on a hook by the door.

Gavin humphed into his teacup from his spot on the bench. "Everything's fine now and we're putting it behind us," he said, silently wishing that were true. He'd cleared things up with Dash and his secret was still safe from Reid, but Gavin had never felt like he was less in control.

At the moment, he was entirely at Dash's mercy and Gavin had no way of knowing what the effervescent younger man had in store for them. It wasn't an entirely unpleasant turn of events, though, because there was no doubt that Gavin was in the safest hands possible. Gavin just wished Dash had provided him with an actual list so *he* could analyze and mitigate any risks.

Penny skipped into the kitchen with Dash on her heels. "Hello, all!" She waved over her head, summoning everyone's attention. "I can't stay long because I'm meeting Aggie and June at the movies in an hour. But I wanted to remind you that we're having an ugly stocking contest on Christmas Eve eve so get to glittering and gluing, people."

There were nods and murmurs as Reid, Dash, Fin, Riley, and Gavin all agreed to comply. A lively conversation followed as Reid questioned Penny about what he should bring. Gavin offered a sedate nod when Dash edged around the group and dropped onto the bench next to him.

"Hey! I have something to show you but we have to go outside," Dash said, tugging Gavin's charcoal tweed sleeve. He'd picked a more conservative three-piece suit and had paired it with a sensibly festive red and white-striped tie, hoping to feel more grounded and like himself.

But Gavin was questioning Dash's judgment as he frowned at the kitchen window. "Outside? It looks like the weather's about to turn," he noted and wrinkled his nose.

"Come on, we won't even notice," Dash said, sliding toward the door and gesturing for Gavin to follow.

"Alright..." He said as he rose and was towed around the table. No one seemed concerned as Dash opened the door and gave Gavin a gentle push out onto the terrace. Gavin checked the sky and it was overcast, the sun hidden. "I won't feel over-dressed, for once," he noted as he considered the small, paved courtyard and the simple bistro table at the other end. Penn and Reid had built raised gardens along the walls, but they were covered for the winter.

"Look what I've got!" Dash pulled a sprig of foliage from his front pocket and waved it at Gavin.

"What is—?"

Dash beat Gavin to it. "It's mistletoe!"

"Oh," Gavin said and his face pinched as he shook his head and reached for the doorknob.

"No, you don't!" Dash hurried around Gavin and pressed his shoulder against the door, trapping him. "I know better now and I know you *want* to kiss me," he boasted, raising the mistletoe over his head and making Gavin snort.

"Of course, I want to kiss you, Dash. I'm conscious and incapable of thinking of anything else whenever you're around. But the ramifications could be—"

A finger pressed on Gavin's lips, halting his warning. "Shhh!" Dash held the sprig over them as he backed Gavin into the wall next to the window and out of view. "I've been waiting a long time for someone special to kiss under some mistletoe. And after our little 'date' mix-up last night, I thought it would be really *nice* if you kissed me."

Gavin hummed thoughtfully, doing his best to appear serious despite the flutter of anticipation and his twitching lips. The thought of kissing Dash—*him* kissing Dash—had unleashed a rush of adrenaline and had him ready to flee, but Gavin's mouth wanted to spread into the goofiest grin as well. "I still feel terrible, knowing I hurt you, and I deserve to be punished," he agreed, letting out a low groan as Dash's tongue slid across his lips, taunting Gavin.

"It was a misunderstanding and it all worked out," Dash murmured, his eyelids sinking as he stared at Gavin's lips, making them itch.

They wanted to stretch into a laugh and Gavin wanted to mash them against Dash's. It was maddening. "Just a kiss?" Gavin confirmed.

Dash hummed drowsily, craning his neck. "Just a kiss. I'll even stick this other hand in my pocket so you know you're totally safe." The hand that wasn't holding the mistletoe promptly went into the back pocket of Dash's jeans.

"I know I'm safe," Gavin whispered, taking hold of the front of Dash's hoodie with shaking hands. "It's you I worry about."

"Stop," Dash said firmly, his tone no longer playful and light. There was a faint shudder as he pulled in a deep breath. "It hurts more when you don't kiss me."

Gavin angled his head so he could search Dash's eyes, suddenly concerned. "What do you mean?"

"You love me and you *want* to kiss me but you're holding out on us. You know I can be patient. Tell me you're not ready and I'll set aside our list until next year or the year after that," Dash said with an easy shrug, but his eyes filled with tears and his lip wobbled. "That's not what this is about, though, and *that* hurts, Gavin."

"Damn it!" Gavin pulled Dash into him and pressed their lips together, thrilling at the instant burst of heat and joy. A contented sound swelled from Dash, vibrating against Gavin's chest and lips and spreading through him.

"That's better," Dash said, his breath a sweet, minty huff.

Gavin opened his mouth, sucking it in as his tongue flicked cautiously at Dash's. "Yes," he agreed, then moaned as Dash's tongue swirled around his.

So warm.

Heat spilled through Gavin, heady and filling the cold, aching hollows in his chest. Dash was right, they could have been standing in the midst of a blizzard and Gavin wouldn't have stopped kissing him. He gathered Dash in his arms, licking, pulling, groaning, desperate for more magical warmth. There was an encouraging chuckle from Dash, but it was ragged as they fell against the wall.

Dash's erection dug into Gavin's thigh, shocking him and demanding his attention. It took just a slight adjustment and they both gasped in relief when Gavin bucked his hips, grinding his hard-on against Dash's. Gavin mumbled an apology as his hand locked around the hand in Dash's back pocket, pressing them together. He guided their hips in a jerky, urgent dance, enthralled by the pressure and heat building in his core.

"Dash!" Gavin gasped as he yanked his lips free so he could fill his lungs. "Don't stop," he said in a pleading whisper, clutching at the back of Dash's head and writhing against him. Dash's lips and tongue dragged over Gavin's jaw and up his neck, the scalding wetness creating a wave of goosebumps down his back and chest. "Oh! Yes!" He nodded frantically, his eyes crossing as Dash hummed and sucked. The scrape of teeth against Gavin's skin made his cock throb harder and heat and pressure surged in his core when Dash rolled his hips. Gavin's toes came off the ground as every nerve in his body flared, then burst into bright light.

Dash swallowed Gavin's yell as he came, wet heat soaking the front of his boxers. But, ever true to his word, Dash's left hand remained deep in his jeans pocket. It was still being crushed by Gavin's as Dash's right hand kept the mistletoe dangling over their heads.

"That's why I waited for you. I knew it would be heaven when it finally happened." Dash rubbed their noses together, smiling as his lips clung to Gavin's. "Go as slow as *you* need to, but don't hold back out of fear. Whatever happens, it can't be worse than keeping us apart. Not when we could be happier and stronger together."

"You don't know that. You don't know what my fath—"

Dash cut Gavin off with a slow but intense kiss that left them both breathless and shaking. "I know it's the season of giving and good cheer, but what if you gave spite a chance?" Dash suggested, waving the mistletoe before tucking it into the pocket on Gavin's chest. "You've quietly rolled with the punches so he'd stay out of our lives and look at where that's gotten us. What if you stopped doing his work for him and gave happiness a shot instead, just to stick it to your old man? Wouldn't that be the best revenge?"

"Stick it...?" Gavin echoed as he stared over Dash's shoulder. He'd never considered spite or how disappointed his father would be if he knew Gavin was deliriously happy. His eyes widened as they slid to Dash's. "I do like that."

"There you go!" Dash pressed an encouraging kiss to Gavin's lips, then stepped back. "Oop!" Dash laughed and caught Gavin when he pitched to the left. His legs weren't ready to work yet, apparently.

"I beg your pardon," Gavin murmured, shaking his head and righting himself. "You make a very good point, but I need to think. It's taken almost everything I have to protect us from him. I'm scared I won't be able to shield you if he decides to lash out at me one last time," he explained.

Dash pushed out a hard breath and nodded. "That's understandable, considering how much he's taken from you. But I'm not helpless and you have friends—some really powerful friends—who will always have your back."

A wave of gratitude filled Gavin and his eyes watered as he was momentarily overcome. "Can't you understand why I would do anything to keep him from poisoning those relationships? And, for the love of God, I do not want to be pitied! Not when I have so much."

"So much? You lost a job you were passionate about and he's kept us apart," Dash argued gently, but Gavin shook his head.

"Most people don't have a golden safety net when their parents abandon them or friends like mine. I *could* lose my job and break my own heart because I already have more good fortune and love than I deserve," he said, then jumped when Dash's hands clamped around his shoulders.

"Gavin!" He whispered loudly, giving them a firm knead. "I have never wanted to shake someone so badly in my life and I am *this close* to begging you to mount me right now."

"No!" Gavin jumped and shook his head, appalled and baffled. "Out here? I wouldn't even know how to... No."

"We'll work our way up to that," Dash said as he turned Gavin.

"I hope you're joking." He frowned at Dash as he opened the door.

"Am I?" Dash wiggled his brows, then winced at Gavin as they overheard what must have been a punchline from Fin and a burst of laughter. "You do look a little..." He cleared his throat, causing Gavin to duck and block his face as it became hot. There was no telling what his hair or his collar looked like and Gavin could see that his tie was pulled askew.

"I have to go," he said, rushing past everyone around the table, receiving stunned looks and nearly crashing into Reid.

"Whoa! Did you two—?" Reid asked as he spun back to Dash.

"A gentleman never tells," he replied, earning boos and appreciative whistles.

Gavin swore under his breath and kept his head down until he was safely in his room and on the other side of his door. He banged his head against it as he held onto the knob, waiting for his heart to stop racing and his face to stop burning. Once it did, Gavin took a deep breath and smiled at the mistletoe in his pocket.

He was a disheveled mess. One look at his reflection in the mirror confirmed what everyone in the kitchen had already observed. Gavin's hair, collar, and tie were all in disarray and his lips were red and swollen. Bright pink blotches stained his cheeks, further proof that something salacious had occurred on the back terrace. But Gavin found that he didn't regret a single bit of it. *Yet.*

Chapter Ten

D ash was still celebrating and feeling extra pleased as he rode the M15 back uptown from the East Village the following Tuesday morning. He wasn't needed at the library and Gavin was off doing super sexy accountant work for Giles and Walker. Dash had popped over to 9th Street to pick up a surprise for Gavin from a friend's antique shop.

"It's a teacup!" Dash whispered to the elderly woman next to him. She had been eyeing the pink box on his lap since 14th Street and he figured it was safe to let her in on the secret. He made an excited sound as he opened the lid and pushed back the tissue paper.

"Look at that!" She gave him a few jabs with her elbow, signaling that she was impressed.

Dash was beaming as he admired a perfect replica of Gavin's precious teacup. "It's *just like* my boyfriend's!" He said, enjoying the way the word boyfriend sounded as it came out and feeling rebellious. Dash knew it was way too soon and would give Gavin palpitations if he were there. But it was lovely, finally being able to say the word out loud without wondering if it was all wishful thinking.

"I was hoping you were single and straight. I have a niece," the old woman said with a weary eye roll. "She should look for a boy who drinks tea, instead of these weirdos with the rings and tattoos on their faces." She gestured at her face and sneered in disgust. "That's a nice teacup, though. He's a lucky man."

"He is, but he knows." Dash sighed happily, tracing the cup's handle. It was mostly brown and painted to look like a branch but it turned green near the bowl and he loved the delicate little leaves and flowers painted along the outside of the cup. "I asked my friend Clarence if he could find one Royal Copenhagen Flora Danica cup and saucer so *my boyfriend* would have a backup. It took four months, but Clarence came through. These are still only made to order, but Clarence thinks this set was made right around the same time as my boyfriend's. I had to do a little digging because he inherited it with the house and all he has left is one teacup set and a few of the larger serving pieces," Dash explained. "I smuggled this weird bowl called a monteith to Clarence's shop so he could match the pattern and I guess it was worth like $8,000!"

"You better not have lost it," she said heavily and Dash shook his head.

"No way! I carried it back like a baby!"

"Good."

"*This baby* set me back a few hundred dollars, but it's going to be priceless when Gavin sees it. I'm hoping he'll let me use it during brunch so we can be tea twins," he confided, feeling a burst of delight at the thought. "This is me," he told her when the train came to a stop and quickly repacked his treasure and gathered the rest of his things.

He hadn't stopped beaming when he greeted Norman and let himself into unit number 4 with the key Reid had given him.

Reid was reclining on the sofa and waved a stack of papers at Dash. "I was *just* wondering if you'd be dropping by," he said as he sat up and hopped to his feet. "You were right about adding a testimonials page to our website and including all of our nannies' languages for international clients."

"Awesome! I'll get right on it!" Dash said, leaving his backpack by the door and heading to the kitchen with his pink box.

"What's that?" Reid asked, trailing behind Dash.

"I found Gavin another teacup so he has a matching set!"

Reid groaned adoringly and pressed a hand against his chest. "You couldn't be more perfect if I had designed you myself," he said and sniffed as he dabbed at the corner of his eye. "You have no idea how long I've waited for this."

"Me too," Dash said, chuckling as he set the box on the table and backed away. "That will be a nice surprise when he gets home later," he predicted as he crossed his arms over his chest and turned back to Reid. He was still staring at Dash like he'd rescued Gavin from a burning building. "It's just a teacup," he said, laughing when Reid tackled him.

"It's so much *better* than that, though!" He hugged Dash tight, lifting him off his feet. "You're the perfect man *and* you're perfect for Gavin because you think he's perfect."

"Well...your expectations might be a touch high, but I think we're perfect for each other," Dash said and gave Reid a good squeeze because it had been a while since their last hug. He tried to disengage so he could get his laptop, but Reid held on, resting his head on Dash's shoulder.

"I started worrying about him when we were in college. He said he was fine when his parents cut him off and disowned him, but Gavin...shrank."

"He shrank?" Dash's brow hitched. "He's 6'4."

Reid laughed softly. "Not like that. He was always quiet, but he was in clubs and had more friends and he was getting up the nerve to ask guys out. All of that stopped after he came back from Heathcote. I did everything I could to get the old Gavin back, but it's like they snuffed out his light and his world just got smaller and smaller. Even with this agency and our family getting bigger, Gavin keeps shrinking and getting dimmer. I can't figure out why except it started that night at Heathcote when we were nineteen." He paused his ramble, raising his head and scowling. "Fuck, I hate that place and I hope Gavin burns it to the ground if he gets it. And I hope he lets me help," he added, his voice trembling with hatred.

"I get that," Dash said, patting Reid's back soothingly. Hate wasn't an emotion Dash was well acquainted with, thankfully, but he'd show up with a bag of marshmallows. He knew why Gavin had shrunk and regretted that he couldn't tell Reid the truth. Gavin had retreated to the safety of their friendship and Briarwood Terrace, building his defenses around the people who mattered the most out of fear. He'd kept his circle tight because he could only do so much to protect Reid and their little family from his father's wrath. Dash couldn't tell Reid the truth so he told him something that would make him feel better. "But I have a plan and we've already made a lot of progress."

"That's so great!" Reid smiled at Dash like he was an angel and gave his cheek a tender pat. "I have complete faith in you and I won't let Gavin sit this one out. It's his turn and I've been waiting for someone. Just. Like. You." He slapped Dash's cheek softly before giving his face an affectionate squish.

"Thanks! What about your Mr. Perfect?" He asked, then yelped when Reid pinched Dash's nose between two knuckles and slapped them in the classic "Stooge" maneuver.

"No! Bad, Dash!" He scolded and pointed across the room. "Go sit in the corner."

"What did I say?" Dash cupped his nose and held up a hand cluelessly.

"We are so close to having it all!" Reid raised his arms and gestured around them. "We've created the perfect home base and everyone's got a great job, except you but I'm not gonna push my luck there because you do seem happy," he said out of the side of his mouth, winking at Dash. "Penn, Morris, and both of my little brothers and honorary little sister are all settled. All that's left now is for you and Gavin to..." He pressed the pads of his index fingers together and made a kissing sound. "And we *all* lived happily ever after."

"But what about—?" Dash started but stopped when Reid stomped a foot.

"We're nearly there, Dash. Focus! I don't need some...guy messing this up. And you don't need me tonight. You should have the place to yourself when you give Gavin his teacup," he decided, nodding as he went to the door to get his coat and scarf. "I think I'll drop in at The Killian House and spend the evening with my nieces. Don't wait up for me and don't even think about those website updates until tomorrow."

"You don't have to leave for the whole evening," Dash said, but Reid waved him off.

"I already told Fin I'd stop by. It's pizza night. Order some takeout. You know what Gavin likes," he suggested with a soft laugh. "I can't tell you how happy it makes me, knowing he's in good hands."

"Of course, I'll take good care of him," Dash promised as he got out his phone. "He's probably in the mood for something warm and cozy like pasta and garlic bread," he predicted, hunting for Gavin's favorite Italian place as a plan came together.

"Open a bottle of red wine. He'll drink a glass if there's

pasta and garlic bread," Reid said with a suggestive wiggle of his brows.

"Maybe..." Dash was already making little adjustments around the living room in his head in preparation for their evening. "I'll have the kettle ready and let Gavin decide what he's in the mood for."

"I will leave it in your capable hands," Reid said, bowing before he opened the door and left Dash with roughly two hours to prepare before Gavin typically returned to Briarwood Terrace.

"I can do a lot in two hours!" He ran to the kitchen to see how much tape Reid had and if there was any ribbon in the apartment.

Chapter Eleven

Just when Gavin thought he had everything under control and there was some hope of his life returning to its quiet routine after New Year's, the other shoe dropped. It was probably in poor taste for Gavin to think of his own discomfort as word spread of his father's impending demise. But everywhere he went, the residents of Manhattan seemed to have conspired to make it his business—along with everyone else's—despite Gavin's insistence that it was of no great importance and would have very little impact on his life.

Even Giles had been compelled to inquire as to how Gavin was doing during their appointment. Giles was a client of Ernst & Waterhouse and had heard that Gavin had been let go. Thankfully, Giles had honored Gavin's wishes and hadn't told Riley. That pact had come with a price as well, and Gavin had accepted Giles's pity and found himself balancing basic household accounts for the reclusive millionaire.

"Listen," Giles began with a hard wince. "You know I prefer to never discuss our personal affairs and wouldn't ask if

Riley wasn't making me, but I do understand what it's like to have a terrible father. And I imagine if I were in your shoes I would feel..." His brows fell as he studied the rug between them. "I would feel nothing and probably more conflicted about *that*," he admitted, then shook his head. "But I'd probably want to take that up with my therapist, not an uptight agoraphobe."

Gavin nodded slowly. "You're right, I don't feel anything and I'd rather not talk about it."

"Great," Giles replied. "Just tell Riley I asked and that we had a good chat when he asks because he will."

"Thank you for the warning."

Riley had taken their daughter, Luna, to have a tea party with Cadence at Morris and Penn's, thankfully. But Gavin's reprieve only lasted until he reached the Olympia's lobby.

"I've been waiting for you, Selby," Muriel Hormsby announced to Gavin, the doormen and several tenants. The wealthy, elderly widow and renowned busybody rolled toward Gavin like a turbaned burgundy hurricane. The feathers of her shawl swirling around her as she preened and aimed a garnet-encrusted lorgnette at him. "You certainly turned out better than I was expecting. Shame on you for keeping yourself hidden away."

"Ma'am?" Gavin asked, looking around in confusion. "I can make some recommendations if you're in need of an accountant, but I—"

"Jonathon!" She shouted, snapping her fingers and cutting Gavin off.

"Yes?" A bored younger man with long blond braids presented himself. He was wearing a bright blue overcoat with a frilly white blouse and a red neckerchief.

"Yes?" Gavin echoed, wondering if Jonathon had meant to look like the Swiss Miss on purpose.

Muriel let out an impatient grunt, giving Jonathon a shove and propelling him toward Gavin. "He's single, Selby," she said to Gavin.

"I'm sorry?" He attempted with a questioning look at the Swiss Mister but the other man was just as disoriented as he looked around them. "Have you considered a dating app? I've heard that younger people prefer those..." He bowed his head and made to leave but Muriel sidestepped, blocking his path.

"Don't be absurd. My nephew isn't looking for a man on an app. He's attended the finest boarding schools and has *millions* of followers on social media."

"Perhaps he should look there," Gavin suggested.

Muriel spluttered. "Quit playing stupid, Selby! Do you want to date Jonathon or not?"

"*Not.* Not even a little bit," he replied, his neck stretching cautiously. "Why would you imagine...?"

Muriel narrowed her eyes at Gavin as she stepped up to him. "I'll bet that Reid Marshall's been keeping you on a leash for years, just waiting for this."

"Reid?" Gavin straightened, all caution and good grace immediately draining from his demeanor. "I don't know what twisted scheme is rattling around that dusty brain of yours this time, madam, but you'll keep my friend's name out of your mouth."

She reared back, stunned and horrified. "How dare you? Do you have any idea what your father would say if he—?"

"I have no idea whatsoever, nor do I care," Gavin interrupted, enunciating loudly and clearly over Muriel's tantrum. "And I cannot imagine what he has to do with me or what bearing he has on the situation," he added, then raised a brow expectantly.

Muriel blinked up at him, looking utterly bewildered as Jonathon stepped into the open elevator and pressed a button, leaving his aunt to fend for herself. She gave her head a quick shake, regrouping. "Don't you try to play me for a fool. I've checked and Briarwood Terrace is worth a fortune and you'll be one of the wealthiest men in Manhattan when you inherit. You're about to have a very merry Christmas, from what I hear, and you'll need someone to share it with. Why not someone with a good name and good breeding?" She widened her eyes suggestively at Gavin.

He was completely dumbfounded as he stared down at her, not sure of where to begin. She was laboring under so many astounding misconceptions. "I think that turban might be too tight."

Muriel reached up, scowling and patting around her ear. "What are you talking about, boy?"

"My personal affairs and finances are no concern of yours, but I will not be inheriting anything from my father when he passes aside from his name. Even if I were and that somehow required me to marry, nothing—and I mean absolutely *nothing* —could ever compel me to date your nephew," he explained carefully and Muriel's face twisted as she clutched at her collar and her shawl.

"Well! There's no need to be uncivil about it. And I'll have you know that I've had it on good authority that you're still Selby's heir."

Gavin squinted at Muriel for a moment, baffled and a touch disgusted that she would know and care more about his own family and personal affairs than he did. "I'm certain you own a television, madam. Perhaps you should turn it on from time to time as you're in such desperate need of entertainment."

With that, he bowed his head and left before Muriel could load another nonsense cannon and fire another shot across his bow. It might have been his imagination, but Gavin felt like more people were watching him as he made his way from the Olympia and around the corner to The Killian House. He was so used to being invisible, to seeing passersby look through him, but Gavin noticed people whispering and pointing as he left the Olympia's lobby and had caught someone staring while at the newsstand.

"*Mr. Selby.*" Even The Killian House's über proper butler, Pierce, was acting differently. He had announced Gavin to the empty foyer as if he were attending a ball, as opposed to Walker Cameron's household accounts. "This way, sir," Pierce said, gesturing at the hall on the left of the grand staircase.

"I...know where it is, thank you."

Gavin rushed past Pierce and around the corner, striding quickly down the hall. The soles of his Oxfords *clack, clack, clacked* on the marble floors, the sound soothing his frayed nerves as it echoed in the empty hallway. He found Walker at his desk, quietly jotting down notes in his planner.

"Afternoon," Walker murmured without looking up.

"Afternoon," Gavin replied, crossing the room to retrieve his folder from the tray on Walker's desk. He was relieved to find that everything was normal between them, at least. "I'll take this to the library," he said as he turned to leave.

"Just a moment, Gavin," Walker said and closed his planner, disappointing Gavin.

He sighed as his head fell. "Not you as well."

"I thought it might help to talk to someone who understands what you've walked away from and what you're about to get sucked back into," Walker explained, sitting back and propping his cheek on a fist.

Gavin shook his head, frowning at the carpet. "This is both precipitous and preposterous. I know nothing about my father's condition except that he is still alive. And while I do not wish that he were dead, I do not particularly care one way or another. The one thing I do know is that my father made it very clear that *I* was dead to him and has wished nothing but misery for me. So I can only assume that whatever is circulating about me inheriting is either gossip made from whole cloth or my father's idea of one last cruel joke."

"Perhaps…" Walker conceded with a wince. "I'm hearing similar things from very reliable sources."

"You can't seriously believe this. It's gossip, Walker," Gavin groaned as he rubbed his temple.

"Your father and I have several lawyers in common at Davis & Ellis. And from what I hear, you've got the whole firm shaking and sweating. They can't court you yet because your father still despises you, but they're terrified of losing their relationship with the Selbys when he dies. They're in a particularly sticky situation at the moment, caught between your father and you. There's a lot of handwringing about whether you'll be keeping your legal business there or you'll be taking the family accounts elsewhere. But I think we can safely deduce that you'll be inheriting." Walker flashed Gavin an apologetic smile. "And Agnes. She hears everything and she says your father's about to kick the bucket and it's all going to you."

"Why is this happening?" Gavin pinched the bridge of his nose under his glasses, hoping to alleviate the throb behind his eyes.

Walker chuckled as he stood and came around his desk. "Most people would be pleased." He gestured at the sideboard, inviting Gavin to join him for a drink. It was a bit early in the afternoon and he *rarely* drank, but Gavin decided the day had warranted it. "I can understand why you're not thrilled about the estate and all the responsibilities that come with it—"

That made Gavin laugh wryly. "I can assure you I don't give a single damn about the estate or my father's money and I don't anticipate that changing. Ever." He thanked Walker when a tumbler of amber liquor was handed to him and took a cautious sip. It burned and tasted like hot sewage so Gavin assumed it was good scotch or whiskey and hummed appropriately.

"I see," Walker replied, looking concerned as he took a drink. "I'm sure you won't do anything rash and you'll give the matter more thought when the time comes. But you'll finally be able to live your life without your father interfering. You won't have to hide anymore," he added, but Gavin shook his head.

"I haven't been hiding and I'm perfectly happy with my life, with a few...exceptions."

Walker gave him a severe look. "My God, Gavin. You've lost your job and who knows what else you've sacrificed to protect Reid from the truth."

"What else—?" Gavin started to deny that he'd sacrificed anything else, then thought of Dash. Walker would probably have something to say about that as well, if he knew how afraid Gavin was of his father hurting Dash. He set down the drink and held up the file. "If it's alright with you, I'll skip the lecture and take care of this."

"Of course," Walker said, waving at the door. "But I wish you'd talk to Reid," Walker said, but Gavin shook his head.

"I've told you and Ashby, Reid *cannot* find out. He'll blame himself and the agency and I won't have that. He's worked too hard and he's helped too many people."

"I understand," Walker said, his voice softening as he studied Gavin. "You're protecting him, but you do your friend a disservice by denying him the opportunity to help you in return. You don't have to face this alone. Tell Reid and let us help you," he urged gently.

"Not right now." Gavin waved dismissively. "This season has been hectic already for the agency and it's going to get worse as we get closer to Christmas," he predicted. "And we're uncles, now," he reminded Walker with a warm grin, sincerely delighted at the prospect of Christmas Eve eve with the Camerons and the Ashbys. They had Penn, Morris, and Cadence to celebrate with as well. "I won't have my awful family putting a damper on *our* holidays. We have too much to be grateful for and we don't want any trouble from him."

"We?" Walker chuckled and shook his head. "I dare him to come after me and *we* can protect you."

"Please." Gavin clutched his stomach as it soured and clenched. His heart raced and he panicked at the thought of how cruel and petty his father could be. There was no telling how much more vindictive he had gotten and how bitter he was as he drew closer to the end. Edward Selby could still make trouble for them. Even on his deathbed, he carried a lot of weight and was still feared around Manhattan because he didn't let go of grudges or forget when debts were owed. "I don't want to give him another reason to go after Reid."

"You forget that this is *my family* you're talking about as well," Walker said, sounding severe as he rose. "Reid is my brother-in-law and you're not just my household accountant, Gavin, you're my friend."

Gavin held up a hand, grimacing. "The sentiment is deeply appreciated and reciprocated," he said in a quick rush and prayed Walker wasn't expecting them to hug. "But if it's all the same, I'd like to do these in peace," he said as he waved the files. "You've already done enough for us and I owe you too much. My father wouldn't have let the agency get off the ground if you and Agnes hadn't put your weight behind it. And I'm safe working for you and Giles even though neither of you actually needs me. You both hired me out of pity and Morris thinks I started handling his finances and making house calls out of sympathy. It's already cost me a great deal of pride to accept your help and I'd like to salvage what I have left if that's alright," he said and Walker's head pulled back and his brows pinched.

"Pride? You've done nothing wrong and it doesn't make you weak to ask for help," he said, his tone becoming frustrated and urgent. "You're stronger than you think and we can help you get your life back."

Gavin cleared his throat loudly. "I appreciate your counsel and I know you mean well, but I'd rather...*not.* What you're suggesting sounds like a spectacle and would only be inviting more attention and gossip. And for what? It sounds like my father doesn't have much time left and it's clear that I'm never getting my job back. I'll never be able to be a simple accountant again. So I'd rather wait it out, if that's okay, because everything else was shaping up rather nicely and there was the promise of normalcy before all of Manhattan became fixated on my father's death."

"I understand. Just remember that you have friends who care very deeply," Walker said with a warm smile, then finally excused Gavin so he could take the household accounts to the library.

Alone, Gavin *didn't* reflect on his father's impending death or his many wonderful friends. He'd made his decision all those years ago at Heathcote and Gavin hadn't regretted it once. He knew he was blessed, that was why he had sacrificed so much to hold onto Reid and the beautiful family they had built together. He did wish that he had been a little braver when he was with Dash, but Gavin was working on that.

Chapter Twelve

Briarwood Terrace had been transformed into Heaven. Not that it wasn't a lovely place before, but Dash was tickled as he stepped back and admired his handiwork.

A large basket containing six rolls of wrapping paper and supplies was waiting by the sofa for later and the coffee table was set for dinner. Dash had also assembled fabric scraps and sewing odds and ends so they could get a start on their stockings for the contest. The smell of garlic and oregano wafted from the takeout containers and Dash's favorite Christmas movie was cued up on his laptop because Reid and Gavin didn't own a television. Dash looked down at his "Buddy the Elf" costume and smiled. He bought the fun plastic ears and costume "for the library" a few years earlier and jumped at any opportunity to wear them.

He heard the key in the lock and hurried around the sofa, snatching his pointy green hat off the armrest and pulling it on. "Surprise!" He cheered when Gavin opened the door.

"Oh!" Gavin jumped, then checked his watch. "Were we doing Stories With Santa tonight?"

"No, that's still on Friday night." Dash went to help Gavin with his briefcase and overcoat.

"I see," Gavin said, even though his expression suggested otherwise. "Reid said he was having dinner at The Killian House so I wasn't expecting anyone."

"Reid left me in charge!" Dash boasted while he eased Gavin out of his tweed coat.

"Did he?" Gavin's head swung around warily, but his lips tipped up at the corner when his eyes met Dash's. "That was probably a good call. Is that garlic bread? Something smells amazing." He sniffed at the air and Dash cheered again.

"Yes! I ran out for a few supplies and takeout from your favorite Italian place. Wait until you see all the *nice* things I have planned for us." Dash wound his arm around Gavin's, turning them toward the kitchen. "Now, how was your afternoon? Was it a tolerable, run-of-the-mill, a-cup-of-tea-will-do sort of day? Or, do you need me to pour you a glass of wine?"

"After the day I've had? I could use a glass of wine. Or a gallon," Gavin added with a weary groan. "Everyone—even Giles—asked about my father. And while I appreciate their concern, I just wanted to go about my day in peace. But no one seemed to understand."

Dash was glad he hadn't planned to bring up Edward Selby. If anything, his intentions for the evening were to keep Gavin's thoughts as far away from his father and the past as possible.

"Well, I'm ordering you to leave all of that at the door. We've got better things to do tonight," he said while gathering the bottle and opener he had ready on the counter.

"Thank you," Gavin said sincerely and his head tilted

when he spotted the pink box on the table. "What's that? Is it from a bakery?" He guessed as he went to inspect it.

"Take a look! It's for you," Dash said, feeling sneaky as he filled two glasses.

"For me?" Gavin asked as he opened the lid and lifted the tissue and there was a soft gasp. "It's my—!" He looked at Dash with huge watery eyes. "How did you find this?"

Dash shrugged, not wanting to make it too big of a deal after Gavin's terrible day. "I asked my friend Clarence to see if he could find one so you'd have a backup."

"It's exactly like my Uncle Henry's," Gavin said as he took it out and carefully turned the cup, examining the design. "Henry said he'd bought the set in an antique shop in Paris in the '80s. By the time he left it to me, all that was left was the tea set and a few pieces I'll never use. But all I cared about was that I still had *his* teacup. I've kept it and used it all these years because I miss him terribly and wish he was still here to have a cup of tea with me."

Now, Dash was crying. "I had no idea!" He sniffed hard and wished he wasn't holding two glasses of wine as tears rolled down his cheeks and his lip wobbled like a toddler. "I know it's not as good as Henry's teacup, but now you have two!" Dash attempted cheerfully, but Gavin shook his head as he set the cup and saucer on the counter.

"No. It's the same. Or, maybe it's a little better because it will hold all the same memories as Henry's teacup and remind me of him, too, but this one is from you."

"I didn't realize it was your Uncle Henry's. I thought you were just a little picky about your favorite teacup. My friend Clarence was the one who found it," Dash said dismissively. He'd hoped that Gavin would love it, but he didn't realize he was co-opting something *that* sentimental. "Here!" He held out a glass. "I need my hand."

"Sorry." Gavin took both of them and set them on the counter. He allowed Dash a moment to swipe at his cheeks and drag the back of his hand under his nose. "Thank you," Gavin said softly, stepping closer and tipping Dash's chin back. He was trembling as he cradled Dash's jaw. "I am picky and I am cranky and I am...difficult. But you see past all of that and you see me and I *thank you*." Gavin's head lowered and his neck craned tentatively. "Thank you," he whispered so reverently as he set his lips on Dash's. It was the faintest shiver of a touch, but it set off an explosion of glittery confetti in the center of Dash's chest.

A watery laugh burst from him. "I love you!" He grabbed Gavin's tie, leaning into him and mashing their lips together.

He felt Gavin's lips spread into a smile and he laughed softly, the sound warming Dash. "I know and...I do too, even if I'm too afraid to show you."

Dash's hand slid around Gavin's neck and into his hair. "I regret to inform you that we will be adding a naughty list to our holiday itinerary."

"Will we?" Gavin asked, his voice cracking as he stumbled forward, backing Dash into the counter. As a taller guy, Dash appreciated Gavin's height. Being 6'2" meant that Dash usually had to duck to kiss his partner, but Gavin's lips were within easy reach and their hard-ons fit perfectly into each other's hips.

"Yup. Unless you've already been blown by an elf," Dash panted, his other hand slipping between them.

Gavin's eyes widened as Dash pulled his belt through the buckle, and then a loud laugh rolled from him. "No!" He held onto Dash's shoulder, shaking his head as he wiped his eyes and giggled. "I can't say that I have."

"Well, you're in for a treat, mister," Dash said, turning them and pushing Gavin against the cabinets.

But neither of them were laughing when Dash yanked Gavin's trousers open and pushed them down his thighs. He cupped the bulge tenting Gavin's boxers and they both groaned against each other's tongues as Dash stroked.

"Fuck!" It was a strangled huff as Dash freed Gavin's erection.

"In every possible way *you* can imagine," Dash whispered, giving Gavin's lip a playful nip before sliding to his knees. "Let's start with this." He trailed his lips up Gavin's length, breathing him in. The smell of starch and soap and the taste of warm, aroused skin thrilling Dash and setting his own nerves alight. He was *finally* touching and tasting Gavin. "Giving you a slow, dirty blowjob has been at the top of my list for a while."

"Dirty? Dash!" Gavin held onto the counter and Dash's head. "I had no idea you could be so..."

"Dirty?" Dash hummed euphorically as he dragged his tongue up Gavin's cock and swirled it around the head, earning a strained yelp and a taste of pre-cum. "Mmm... Dash can be so dirty. Let's see if we can do this without knocking my ears off."

"I'm rather worried about my own," Gavin babbled, his jaw gaping as he watched Dash's lips stretch and slide down his length. "Dear Lord." His hips began to buck slightly in time with the rise and fall of Dash's head and it was incredible, listening to Gavin's frantic swears and awkward, adoring compliments. "Oh, fuck, that's very lovely! You're so, so *good*, Dash!" His body jerked and twitched as he fought to maintain his control and it had to be the sexiest moment of Dash's life.

He could feel Gavin's orgasm building with every slick glide of his lips and it was beautiful seeing and hearing him come apart as he gave into the pleasure. "Go ahead," Dash purred when he raised his head and found Gavin's dazed gaze. "Get rough and let go," he said, angling his head so he could lap at Gavin's sac.

"I couldn't!" Gavin shook his head wildly, whimpering when Dash sucked at his tender flesh.

"Sure you can." Dash crooned as his lips trailed back up Gavin's cock. "I'll show you." He gave the head a saucy flick before he opened wide and slowly swallowed him to the hilt.

"Jesus!" Gavin squeaked, his hand cradling Dash's head and alternating between gingerly pats and desperately gripping. "How can you—?" He said in scandalized awe as Dash quietly gagged and moaned around his shaft.

Dash was too busy to explain that he'd dated some pretty dominant guys and girls and liked to practice with his toys. The pressure in his throat as it strained around Gavin made the pressure in Dash's tights nearly unbearable. He'd much rather show Gavin that there were all kinds of ways for them to get off together. There was no need to rush because this was more than enough and Dash was into *anything* Gavin was into. Dash made a grateful, greedy sound when Gavin began to buck against his face and beg his name.

"Dash! I'm getting close!"

"Mmm*hmmm!*" Dash shoved the front of his tights down, releasing his aching length and giving it a few tugs.

"Oh, yes! Fuck, fuck, fuck, yes!" Gavin cried as he watched Dash and became more frantic. "Fuck, you're so good, so beautiful! *Dash!*" He covered his mouth to hold back a sob and a hoarse yelp. His body jumped and his sac tightened before Gavin's frame went limp and he swayed with every hot pulse of his cock, deep in Dash's throat. Dash could taste Gavin, crisp yet softly salty, just before he shattered into bright, glittering bits and came all over the tile between his knees. "Come here!"

Dash was pulled up by an armpit and they were both breathless as they slid and fell against the refrigerator, leaning against it for support. "We can definitely cross that one off the list," Dash said, making Gavin grin and blush as he nodded.

"I had no idea that you could be so...naughty. Or that I would like it, if I'm being honest."

Dash's eyes lit up as he lowered and pulled up his tights with a mischievous shimmy. "I hope you're ready, Santa, baby. Because I'm gonna ride you like a sleigh and let you come down my chimney," he said with a wink.

"Dear God, Dash!" Gavin hissed and looked around like someone might overhear them.

"It's cool! I'm on PreP and I get tested every other month and I know you go with Reid whenever he gets tested," Dash said, even though he knew why Gavin had scolded him. "I'm wholesome and corny, but I'm also vers and super horny."

"So I see," Gavin said, then thanked Dash when he helped fix his trousers. "This has been truly nice, though," Gavin murmured as he raised Dash's hand and kissed his knuckle tenderly. "Today was terrible and I was looking forward to its end, but you made this evening magical. I don't know how you do it, but you always make everything better."

"The night isn't over yet! I have penne alla vodka, lots of garlic bread, and those clams you like. After that, we're making my special, decadent hot cocoa, starting our stockings, wrapping all those gifts you bought, and watching 'Elf!'" He informed Gavin as he steered him into the living room.

Gavin paused and held up a finger. "All of that sounds wonderful, but I can't watch that movie now."

"'Elf'?" Dash asked, his head tipping in confusion. "What's wrong with 'Elf'? It's my favorite Christmas movie."

"What's your second favorite Christmas movie? Because there's no way I can watch 'Elf' without getting turned on and being utterly mortified," Gavin said in his dry, flat rumble.

"'Home Alone' it is!" Dash declared and didn't stop giggling for the rest of the night.

Chapter Thirteen

I t turned out that Dash was far more than the most perfect man in the world. He was also Gavin's breaking point. That revelation was delivered via another unfortunate encounter with Muriel Hormsby in the Olympia's lobby the following Thursday.

"I heard about you and that football player's son. Can't say that I blame you if he's half as much fun as he looks."

Instead of being appalled at the old dragon's audacity, Gavin was terrified. If Muriel Hormsby had heard about him and Dash, then it was likely that his father had as well. But Gavin remained outwardly unbothered and furrowed his brow as if he were only somewhat perturbed. "Madam, you have a habit of confusing my personal affairs for your own. I am begging you to read a book or find a hobby."

"I don't need a hobby, I have Calista," she said indignantly as she stepped into the elevator and gestured at the imperious poodle next to her. Its nose was pointed upward aloofly, as if the animal had more sense and shame than its master. "You could use better manners, boy," Muriel announced, leaving Gavin to stare in awe at her lack of self-awareness.

"Damn it!" He spat once the doors closed and went to speak to Walker.

"How bad is it?" Gavin asked once he and Walker were alone. Pierce had shown Gavin to the study with an excessive formality that had set his teeth on edge. Gavin suddenly missed his days of being a pitied, out-of-work accountant.

"Bad?" Walker asked, smirking as he reclined and propped his feet up on the corner of his desk. "If you mean the news about you and Dash, I have only heard good things. Everyone is over the moon, they're so happy for the two of you."

"No, no, no!" Gavin went to the decanters on the sideboard and swiped a tumbler off the tray. "Which one of these am I supposed to like?" He asked, looking over his shoulder at Walker.

"The taller square one in the front," Walker advised. "As you were saying." He gestured for Gavin to continue.

"I was hoping my father would die before the world found out about me and Dash," Gavin said as he poured, then cringed at how terrible that sounded.

"This is where I remind you that we won't let anything bad happen to you two," Walker said, reclining in his chair. "I know you'd rather handle it yourself and as quietly as possible, but you don't *have to*."

"I know," Gavin said, nodding and building up his courage before taking a large gulp. He waited until his left eye stopped twitching as the liquor burned its way down his throat and warmed his stomach. "That's the only card I have left and I was saving it for Dash and for an emergency. I was hoping it could be avoided for the sake of my own peace and privacy. But there's nothing worse I could do to hurt and humiliate my father than put my homosexuality on display for the whole world to gawk at."

"No one's forcing you to do anything and there's nothing wrong with living a quiet, private life. That's who you are, Gavin, and you don't owe your father your privacy and peace of mind," Walker said firmly.

"I don't care who knows or what anyone thinks as long as Dash never has a reason to regret loving me. I can't see how I won't be a disappointment in several...predictable ways, but I think I can learn and become the man Dash deserves if my father doesn't find some way to ruin our lives before he dies," Gavin said, taking a deep breath and another drink.

Walker laughed softly and shook his head. "We won't let that happen."

"No," Gavin gasped out. "I have a plan," he said as he raised the tumbler and pointed it at the window. "I'm going to email my father's attorneys and let them know that I would like to have a word with him."

"By yourself?" Walker asked, swinging his legs around and sitting up.

There was a quick tap at the door and Fin was wide-eyed as he sidestepped into the study. *"What?"* He made his way around and dropped onto the side of Walker's desk, facing Gavin. "What is this about a plan? It better include backup and that better include me," he said as he jammed his thumb into his chest. "Because your father is a monster."

"I have made it abundantly clear that he has our full support," Walker said as he stood and gave Fin's shoulders a knead and shushed in his ear. "But I believe Gavin has this under control."

"I do," Gavin said, feeling warmer and a bit bolder. "I will need your help if he calls my bluff, though. I'm going to demand that he stay out of *all* of our lives and allow me to live in peace with Dash. If I hear that he so much as mentions Dash's name I will make sure that *my name* is forever linked with his in every gay way possible. I will marry Dash and take his name and give him my name. And every year there will be a Gavin Selby-Griffin Is Gay Day parade that will put Macy's to shame. And the centerpiece of that parade will be a float dedicated to my all-consuming love for Dash and his spectacular ass." Gavin nodded firmly, then swallowed the last of his drink with a hard shiver.

"Yes!" Fin cheered as Walker clapped.

"I would gladly pay to make that happen," he said, making Fin laugh. He turned and Gavin was glad to see Fin so happy and content as he offered Walker his lips for a kiss. "Think of all the lights!"

"Spectacular," Walker said, stealing a quick kiss before nodding at Gavin. "You have our public support as well."

"Whatever you need. We're here for you," Fin said sincerely. "You're family, Gavin."

"Thank you," Gavin replied as he left the tumbler on the tray. "I appreciate that more than you know. And now, I will go back to being your accountant." He took the folder and bowed before making his exit.

He wasn't sure if it was the alcohol or having a plan, but Gavin was able to set aside his concerns and make quick work of the household accounts. On the way home and on a whim, Gavin stopped at a bakery for gingerbread cookies and braved a florist for a bouquet of flowers. He'd thought of nothing but Dash as he made his way across town, longing to see him smile and wanting to surprise him for a change. But it occurred to Gavin that he hadn't asked if Dash had plans for the evening until he was climbing his stoop. He juggled his briefcase, the flowers, and the box from the bakery to get his keys from his trousers, wondering how he'd ever be half as good as Dash or deserve him. He couldn't even remember to call him.

"I'm hopeless," he muttered at the lock. Gavin offered Norman a disgruntled greeting as he hurried through the lobby and around the corner to his door.

It opened before Gavin could push his key into the lock. "There you are!" Dash said as he waved Gavin inside.

Reid jumped out of the way, stuffing an arm into his overcoat. "You were late and we were getting worried. I thought I'd miss you," he explained and tucked a bakery box from Daily Provisions under an arm.

"Where are you going?" Gavin asked Reid.

"To Park Slope to see Brian, Sharon, and the girls. It's the eighth night and I've got donuts!" He said, patting the box.

Gavin's brows jumped as he recalled that it was the last night of Hanukkah. Reid did his best to celebrate the eighth night with his childhood friend every year and usually arrived with a box of sufganiyot. "Tell Brian and his family I wished them a happy Hanukkah," Gavin said and Dash nodded excitedly.

"I don't know Brian, but wish them chag urim sameach from me!"

Reid bowed his head, then pointed at Gavin. "I will, but what's all that?" He asked, grinning expectantly.

"Right!" Gavin gasped at the awkward bundle he was hugging. "I got you these." Gavin handed Dash the flowers and the bakery box, turning to hang up his overcoat and scarf and hiding his face until it stopped burning. "I wasn't sure if you'd be here or if you'd have plans, but it turns out you were here," he continued to ramble, then glanced at Reid. "I thought you were leaving."

"In a moment!" He scolded with a teasing wink at Dash. "This looks like it might be good."

"Not with you grinning at us like a demented clown. Go on," Gavin said, shooing Reid. "You'll scare Dash."

"No he won't!" Dash said, but his laugh was watery as he examined his flowers. "I love it here," Dash insisted as he opened the box, then looked at Reid and then at Gavin with big, glittering eyes. "Gingerbread! Thank you!" He offered the box so Reid could take a cookie but he declined. Dash shrugged and closed the lid. "I know you two probably get sick of me. But it's a little lonely at my place without Penny. I've never lived without her, really. My parents spend most of the year in Connecticut now and only come into the city for special occasions and TV appearances," he babbled.

Reid made a loud *pffft* sound and tossed a hand at him. "I wouldn't mind if you never left. You could even move in, for all I care," he added with a loaded look at Gavin.

He stared back at Reid, refusing to blink. "Shouldn't you be going?"

"Fine! Happy Hanukkah," Reid whispered as he opened the door and slowly backed out.

Gavin shook his head as it closed, leaving him alone with Dash. "Was that a threat?" He asked, then turned back to Dash and yelped when he was tackled.

"Thank you for the flowers and the gingerbread cookies!" was a strange way to warn someone before kissing them senseless.

Dash flung the arm with the flowers around Gavin's neck and it was delightful, the way Muriel Hormsby and all the other awful parts of the day melted away. Gavin angled his head, taking the kiss deeper as his hands slid around Dash's body. He boldly cupped Dash's ass, pulling him closer and dancing them into the back of the sofa.

The box dropped onto the cushions and a hand swept through Gavin's hair, creating a cascade of goosebumps down his spine. Gavin felt lighter with every twirl of his tongue around Dash's and he felt like laughing; he was so happy just holding him. He thought he could live a life without love. But now that he'd held Dash and kissed him, Gavin never wanted to let him go.

He took a chance, licking the corner of Dash's mouth and then his chin. "Good! Yes!" Dash pulled his head back and nodded frantically as he offered Gavin his neck. He whimpered when Gavin clumsily lapped and sucked, encouraging him with strangled gasps and pleas. "Yes! My ear!" Dash made a desperate sound as Gavin's tongue curled around it and he nibbled on the lobe. The leg around Gavin's hip locked tight as Dash writhed beneath him, mindless and panting as their erections pressed and rubbed between them.

Gavin could barely believe he was responsible, let alone involved, or that it was going so well. Because Dash did seem to be enjoying himself as he bucked and clung to Gavin. And at that moment it occurred to Gavin that it had been worth braving the crowds at the bakery and the florist and that the roughly $150 he'd spent on cookies and flowers had been one of the best investments of his life.

He was *alive* and there was so much warmth and pleasure radiating from his heart and spilling down his limbs, so hot and bright in contrast to the cold emptiness of his past encounters. Gavin understood that he had been missing out before, that the brief glimpses of sex he'd allowed himself had been nothing but shadows compared to the vibrant wonder and delight he experienced when he held Dash. And they were just kissing and dry-humping like teenagers!

It had cost Gavin nothing to hide and deny himself before, but there was no way he was giving Dash back now. He growled as the hand around Dash's ass tightened and the other twisted in his hair. Gavin claimed Dash's lips for a starving, seeking kiss. His tongue thrust brutally as he sucked and ground against Dash, hungry for more warmth, for more joy, for more of *them*. He moaned Dash's name and reveled in the taste of his breath, his lips, and his skin. Dash was insensate, clawing at the back of Gavin's coat. They were wild and free and Gavin's heart throbbed with happiness and he was crying when a bright flash of heat burst in his core, causing every nerve in his body to flicker and flare.

"Gavin!" Dash cried, wrenching his lips free to gasp for air as his body bucked and arched in Gavin's arms.

"My God!" Gavin laughed breathlessly and shook his head in disbelief. "I'm so glad you were here. I was so worried earlier and afraid that tomorrow would be a disaster. Then, I realized that you were all that mattered and that we would be alright as long as we had each other. But I was in such a rush to see you again, I forgot to ask if you had plans or if you even wanted to see me," Gavin admitted as he rubbed the end of his nose against Dash's.

"Of course, all I ever want is to be with you. But I had to be here tonight. I have to make sure you're ready for tomorrow."

"Why?" Gavin asked in alarm. "What have you heard?"

Dash's lips twisted and his eyes flicked upwards. "Tomorrow's Friday. You're making your big Santa debut. I kind of assumed that was the disaster you were referring to..." he said slowly.

"Oh." Gavin grimaced and looked around for a clock or a calendar. "Is that tomorrow?" he said as he clutched his stomach. It sank and he became queasy. "Now, I'm panicking again."

"Stop!" Dash pressed a loud kiss to Gavin's lips and turned him. "We're going to clean ourselves up and order a pizza and then we'll practice some normal, Santa-appropriate responses to typical kid questions."

"That would be helpful," Gavin agreed, already feeling more reassured.

"I even made a supercut of James's past Santa performances at the library. That way, you know exactly what to expect and can just copy him if you want. But no matter what, you'll be great and the kids are going to have an awesome time."

Gavin nodded slowly, not at all convinced about the great and awesome parts, but less certain that he'd blow it and ruin the entire evening for everyone present. "I'll just copy James," he said because imitating a tired man from Queens was infinitely easier than trying to pass himself off as Father Christmas.

Chapter Fourteen

The nice list burst into flaming smithereens as Dash watched Gavin Claus heft an impressively large toddler off his lap and into the arms of yet another adoring parent. As Dash had predicted, Gavin was charming in his own stiffly stoic way. His Santa was a taller, slightly more formal version of James's jolly old elf, but the children were spellbound as Gavin read *The Polar Express* to them.

Before storytime, Gavin had made a spectacular entrance, his bellowing laugh deep and melodic as he strode in with a sack of books slung over his shoulder. Gavin had clearly tapped into his musical training, the sound bounced off the walls, carrying over the kids' excited cheers. And Gavin never broke character, thanking everyone present for inviting him to share in the festivities and for being such good boys and girls. Gavin even told silly Santa jokes about his reindeer and traffic in the air as Dash and Ashley handed out books, cups of hot cocoa, and candy canes.

"Looks like someone's getting his bells jingled later," Ashley said, raising a brow at Dash over a red Solo cup as they looked on from the back of the room. Kids were lined up in their holiday pajamas, waiting for their turn to sit on Santa's lap.

Dash shushed and gave her a scandalized look. "We are at a family event." He kept a straight face for all of ten seconds before grinning mischievously. "We're taking it slow until he's ready, but it's already so hot and I can tell it's gonna be wild when we do *Scrooge*," he whispered before blowing on his cocoa and wiggling his brows at her.

"Ready?" She whispered back loudly, then shot Gavin Claus a disgruntled look. "What's he waiting for? You're both hot and hung like stockings."

"Ashley! And how do you know?" Dash was truly scandalized but she just shrugged.

"I don't, but that's how I'm picturing it."

"You're...not wrong," he admitted sheepishly.

She pumped a fist and did a little dance, waddling around in a circle. "It's a Christmas miracle!"

Dash laughed as he held out a hand, spotting her massive belly. "You've been watching the wrong kinds of Christmas movies and you'd better be careful or you're going to spill more than your cocoa. And I told you, we're taking it slow."

"Right. Why, exactly?" She was slightly winded as she braced her lower back.

"Look at him," Dash said, then winced. "But ignore the costume and your Santa fetish," he added pointedly, making her snort. "He's quiet and kind of conservative and *I like that.* But Gavin's never really explored his sexuality, even privately, because he's been stuck with only a foot out of the closet for most of his life."

"Stuck?" Ashley's neck swiveled. "Who hurt Tall, Stark, and Stuffy? I just wanna talk to them," she growled.

"Me too," Dash said with a heavy sigh. "But that's one of those things a man has to work out with his father and his therapist."

"That's probably a good call. He's come a long way, though, and I'm really happy for you." She wound her arm around Dash's and rested her head on his shoulder as they watched the adorable display at the other end of the room.

A pair of crying twin infants was placed on Santa's lap and Dash audibly swooned when Gavin bounced both knees and ho-ho-hoed tenderly, calming their siren-like wails. "But we are definitely frosting some cookies later," Dash promised, whistling appreciatively.

"And to all a good night," she replied dreamily.

It truly was a good night. The children and parents were thoroughly entertained and Gavin stayed an hour later than planned, refusing to get up until every child was able to take a picture with Santa. Several parents stopped to congratulate and thank Dash and Ashley for hosting such a wonderful event and spreading so much holiday cheer.

"You are certainly full of surprises," Ashley told Gavin when he emerged from the restroom with the Santa costume safely in its garment bag. He'd skipped his tie and Dash thought Gavin looked incredibly handsome with a light beard and his collar unbuttoned. His hair was disheveled from the fluffy white wig and there was a smudge of lipstick on his cheek from one of the elderly patrons, but Gavin was more relaxed and happier than Dash had ever seen him.

"I think it was the costume. One feels a certain responsibility when they put it on," Gavin murmured as he passed her the bag.

Ashley turned to Dash, looking slightly dizzy. "Get this man out of here and get to frosting," she ordered, startling Gavin.

"Haven't I done enough?" He asked Dash as he was led away.

"It's a *good* thing," Dash told him and decided it was probably safer if they took the long way home, heading toward 5th Avenue and Central Park instead of straight to Briarwood Terrace.

Gavin tried to run when he discovered they were going to the Wollman Rink until Dash promised they were only there to observe the ice skaters and enjoy a stroll through the park to see the lights and decorations.

"We'll save the ice-capades for another Christmas," Dash said, bumping his shoulder against Gavin's as they watched from the benches. "A sprained ankle or a wrist isn't my idea of romance. And I'd probably want to kiss you while we were out there and we're not ready for PDA yet," he said out of the side of his mouth, making Gavin chuckle as he shook his head.

"A trip to the ER would not be romantic," he agreed.

But Gavin still had a few surprises up his tweed sleeve. He captured Dash's hand as they were walking and Gavin kissed him in Central Park! It was completely unexpected and Dash didn't realize what Gavin was doing at first when he stopped them on the Bow Bridge.

"Someone might see us!" Dash warned breathlessly as Gavin gathered him in his arms.

Gavin simply shrugged and brushed his lips against Dash's. "Perhaps they could convince me that this is real. I don't care anymore and I'm done hiding because other people are afraid of my homosexuality."

As far as public displays of gay affection went, the kiss was brief and perfectly PG, but Gavin had completely swept Dash off his feet. "I love you, Gavin Selby, and I'd wait forever if I had to."

Gavin closed his eyes, rubbing his cheek against Dash's as if he was also trying to freeze the memory and make the moment last. "It was four years ago," he whispered softly. "You'd been to Briarwood Terrace with Penny a handful of times before, but it was the first time she brought you to brunch. You were wearing a pink Mr. Bubble T-shirt and a gray hoodie and I felt so *happy* when you walked into our apartment. And I wanted you so desperately, it scared me. I've never wanted anyone the way I wanted you," he said with a shaky laugh. "I didn't think that I'd ever have the nerve to tell you or that I'd ever get the chance."

"Four years?" Dash blinked back tears as he imagined how lonely that must have been for Gavin. His own crush had come on slowly and Dash had dated other people until the "teacup tantrum" caused him to enter into the unhealthier unrequited phase roughly two years earlier. But even then, Dash still made a few attempts at dating and had a couple of one-night stands before he noticed that Gavin felt *something* in return. "I wish I had known!"

"I couldn't let that happen," Gavin said. He held onto Dash's hands and he was a different man than the quiet, reserved Gavin from Briarwood Terrace. His eyes were heavy behind his glasses as they held Dash's and there was a beguiling easiness to his smile. "I wasn't strong or brave enough to stand up to him, then. And I don't think I would have taken the chance and fought for us. I never believed I was good enough or that something this beautiful was possible for me."

"That's not true," Dash argued, shaking his head stubbornly. "You've protected your friends for years and you wouldn't have let me help if I hadn't blackmailed you into being Santa and spending the holidays with me."

"I forgive you," Gavin said, shrugging a shoulder. "I would have found a way out if I really didn't want to do it, if I didn't want you. And now that I have you, I won't let anyone get in our way. We're going to be happy and nothing will stop me from loving you the way you deserve to be loved, Dash." The steam from their breaths plumed between them and Dash was in a fairytale as Gavin held onto his chin and kissed him. This time, his tongue swept across Dash's lips, tenderly stoking the flames that had been building since storytime until Gavin raised his head and let out a pained sigh. "I doubt I'll hear anything back until after the holidays, but I emailed my father's attorneys to request a meeting as soon as possible. I want him to know that I'm not afraid of him anymore and I won't let him hurt you," he stated firmly, causing Dash's heart to flip and burst.

Dash was ready to fight and he'd fight hard and dirty if he had to for Gavin. Even though Dash really didn't think they were in danger. "You didn't have to do that, but I'm not afraid of him. There's nothing your father can do to me and it's not like I'm helpless. My family will always have my back and they can be a little scary," Dash admitted, raising his hands. "I've been trying to tell you. I might be wholesome and my dad might be the NFL's favorite teddy bear, but my mom's side of the family is a little shady." He was joking, but the Mooneys' ties to the Irish Mob weren't that much of a secret. "I don't think he can make Reid fire me and I *volunteer* at the library... All that's left is this and I'm not letting go of *you*," he said, poking Gavin in the chest. "We've waited too long." He raised his left hand to check his wrist and groaned.

"What's wrong?" Gavin asked warily.

"I was trying to take it slow and kill a few hours when I brought us to the park to watch the skaters and see the lights," Dash explained. He pressed a kiss to Gavin's lips, apologizing as he lowered his arm.

"I don't understand."

"I want to go fast now," Dash said and pushed out a lip so Gavin understood that the evening was heading in a less climactic direction. "Ha!" He laughed at himself as he turned them back toward 5th Avenue and 79th Street. "But it's getting late and I don't have time for much more than a kiss after I drop you off before I have to book it back to my place. My pa—"

"Do you have to?" Gavin interrupted. He squeezed his eyes shut and begged Dash to continue.

"Mr. Selby!" Dash gasped dramatically, then hugged Gavin's hand against his chest when he tried to cover his face. "I would love to cross several things off our naughty list tonight but I need to get home and get some sleep because my parents are picking me up for breakfast in the morning. I had to work on Thanksgiving so they're calling in their rain check for some sightseeing and last-minute shopping. You could come home with me tonight and meet them," Dash offered carefully. He crossed his fingers but kept his expression neutral. He had a feeling they were also making the trip to do some snooping while they were sightseeing.

"No." Gavin shook his head. "Spend time with your parents. You don't get to see them often enough with every-thing you do for me and the agency and the library."

Dash waved dismissively. "They understand and they're happy as long as I'm happy. I was hoping it would be okay if I brought them by while everyone was at Briarwood Terrace for brunch."

"Of course," Gavin said immediately. "I'm sure they want to meet all of your friends and see who you work with."

"They do, but I think they'd like to meet you. Could I introduce you as my friend but also secretly *my* Santa?"

Another soft, drowsy smile tugged at Gavin's lips and he looked away bashfully as he nodded. "I think that would be acceptable."

"Acceptable?" Dash giggled as he gave Gavin another poke. "Get ready because my dad is going to hug you. He's going to hug everyone, but he's going to hug you even more and ask something inappropriate before my mom muzzles him," he warned.

"I might miss brunch."

"No, you won't," Dash said, pulling Gavin along. The night had been mild but it was starting to snow. "My parents are the best and you're going to love them. They've been dying to meet you for months and have already adopted you."

"Oh, well that's...lovely. I suppose I won't find a reason to be in the emergency room, then." Gavin mused and Dash decided they could pause for one more kiss under one of the lamps lighting the path.

"Be nice and we might try some things from the naughty list tomorrow night."

"That would be acceptable as well."

"Ha! I'll show you acceptable, mister."

This time, Dash made Gavin's toes curl.

Chapter Fifteen

Twenty-four hours later, Gavin was grateful for the cozy peace of Briarwood Terrace, his warm chair by the fire, and to be back in his own clothes. Being Dash's secret Santa had been a delight and surprisingly *fun*, and the entire evening had felt like something from a holiday fairytale, but Gavin was exhausted and needed more than a night to recover *before* the Griffins had dropped by for brunch that Saturday morning.

As Dash had warned, Swift Griffin hugged and thanked everyone for taking such good care of his "mini." That would have seemed like a ridiculous nickname given that Dash was rather tall and strapping himself. But Swift Griffin was even larger and more gregarious in person than he was on television.

And as Dash had also warned, Swift had spun Gavin around and given him a good shake. "Let me get a good look at you, son," he said, inspecting Gavin from head to toe before scooping him into a tight bear hug. "Welcome to the team. We better get some meat on your bones so Dash doesn't break you!"

"Dad!" Dash threw his hands up, exasperated.

Swift shrugged cluelessly. "What? He doesn't look like he weighs more than one-eighty."

Thankfully, Dash's mom interceded. "Go see Penny," she ordered Swift as she pointed him in the right direction. "They'll never come for Christmas if you keep embarrassing them," she said, sighing and offering Gavin an apologetic grimace. "Don't let him scare you, dear. Dash has told us so much and it's nice to finally welcome you to the family." She held her arms out, waiting for Gavin's permission before wrapping him in a gentle, perfume-scented hug.

Gavin swallowed the lump in his throat, nodding as he carefully returned her embrace. His mother had never hugged him and it was surreal, how soft and soothing it felt to put his arms around Hannah. As a child, he had often imagined what it would have been like to be held and kissed by his mother. Gavin had convinced himself he hadn't missed out on much as he got older, but this was actually quite lovely. "Thank you," he managed.

"You're shaking!" She leaned back and searched Gavin's face. "Are you alright?"

He coughed and nodded jerkily. "I'm fine. I...didn't really know my mother," he explained clumsily.

"You didn't know her? You poor thing," she said, pressing a hand over her heart. "Did she pass away?" She whispered.

"Yes..." Gavin confirmed. "When I was twenty-six, but she was busy with...other things when I was a child so I never saw her. My Uncle Henry raised me."

"You never saw her?" She echoed sadly. "Dash said your parents hadn't treated you well, but I had no idea."

Gavin chuckled wryly. "Dash was being generous and he's too kind to say anything bad about them, ma'am."

"You don't have to 'ma'am' me!" She gave his cheek a soft,

affectionate pat and cradled it. "You call me Hannah. Or Mom, whenever you're ready," she suggested tenderly.

"Thank you. I think I will. Soon," Gavin added, too touched and overcome to manage more.

The Griffins' immediate acceptance and obvious excitement about their son's new relationship was overwhelming in comparison to the state of fear Gavin had existed in, thanks to his father. And the contrast between Swift and Hannah's actions and Gavin's parents' at roughly the same points in their lives was striking. Gavin had been nineteen when he'd been ejected from Heathcote and Dash was in high school when he ejected himself from the game and ended his football career. But Dash was a shining testament to how unconditional love and support could save a struggling child and change their lives. Now, they were extending that loving support to Gavin.

That kind of warmth and generosity took Gavin's breath away, but he couldn't fathom why the Griffins approved of a stiff, semi-closeted accountant from a terrible family for their son. He had agreed to visit them in Connecticut for Christmas Eve with Dash. Gavin was ready to do damn near anything to stay in their good graces, even trek up to Connecticut for Christmas with the Griffins. Dash's parents lived in Greenwich, only an hour and a half outside of the city, but Gavin would walk to Switzerland if it made the Griffins happy and kept their approval.

There had also been the knowing grins and gentle congratulations from their friends. Dash had reminded everyone they had just begun to quietly date and not to overdo it for the sake of Gavin's nerves. But everyone was just too happy for them, so Gavin did his best to be gracious. The effort had left Gavin drained, though, so he was glad when everyone scattered shortly after Dash left with his parents, promising to return once they departed for Connecticut.

Maybe it was because of his stint as Gavin Claus, but he felt more centered in a charcoal tweed suit, red sweater vest, and plaid red tie. The ensemble was a touch formal and...traditional for a quiet evening at home, but that was just the sort of man Gavin was. He proudly noted that Dash liked his classic suits and enjoyed cozy evenings by the fire as he sipped from his *new* antique teacup.

That was not what Reid was dressed for when he strolled out of his room in a slim-fit sharkskin suit. It was definitely Italian and expensive and could mean only one thing. Reid confirmed Gavin's suspicions as he stroked his freshly shaved jaw while hunting for his keys in the living room. He'd anointed himself in his best aftershave and cologne, leaving a trail of exotic woods and spices in his wake.

Gavin watched Reid over the top of his paper. "Heading out for the evening, I see," he murmured and Reid was in rake mode as he flashed Gavin a grin.

"Dash should turn up soon and everyone else is in a Christmas tizzy tonight, so I thought I'd clean myself up and see what the city throws my way."

"The Baccarat?" Gavin guessed.

"Am I that obvious?"

"That's a new suit and it's too flashy for the Waldorf or the Peninsula."

Reid pointed at Gavin and winked. "They'll be packed with families and I'm in more of a 'champagne and cocaine' mood, instead of 'bourbon and cigars.'"

He never touched drugs—aside from a few hits off a joint if Penn was around—but Gavin understood exactly what sort of man Reid was in the mood for. Reid enjoyed men like they were supercars, preferring to ride them around a hotel suite for a few hours or a night. He was in the mood for high-end luxury and a touch of danger so he dressed like it and went where those über wealthy men liked to stay and play. Once he'd had his fill, Reid would return to his quiet, well-ordered life without any complications. At least, that was how Reid described his adventures and how confident he was in this "man of mystery" routine.

"Does it ever bother you, being mistaken for a high-priced gigolo?" Gavin asked, earning an amused chuckle from Reid.

"*I love it*," he said, his eyes lighting up with wicked anticipation.

"Don't you ever worry that you'll pull that with the wrong man and get in trouble?"

"It's only illegal if I take the money and it's not my fault if they *assume* I'm an escort. Plus, it keeps things simple and impersonal. No one's looking for romance when they bring a man like me back to their room and I get to enjoy a hot night in a five-star suite," Reid explained, gesturing at himself.

Gavin gave his head a tight shake. "Everyone looks up to you because you're so responsible and wise. If only they knew..."

"But you and I know better," Reid said, wagging a finger. "I'm an asshole to other men because other men are assholes. I like my life just the way it is and no one else needs to know what I do when I decide to take a night off."

"You're asking for trouble, fooling around with men like that," Gavin warned. "One of these days, you're going to get caught with someone's husband or a politician."

"No way. I don't ask a lot of questions because I don't want to know anything about them, but I do my best to avoid married men," Reid said, but Gavin clicked his teeth and went back to his paper.

"Do you really want to be known as some disgraced former prime minister's boy toy?"

Reid hissed as he pushed his hands into his pockets and

leaned against the front door like a Tom Ford ad. "Honestly... I might not mind, but my mom would kill me," he teased, then became serious. "I'll be alright. What about you, Gav? We go back and forth like this almost every time I go out, but you've been...stuck since college and you keep shrinking. I know it had something to do with the day your parents cut you off, but you've always shut it down whenever I tried to talk about it."

"I'm fine," Gavin bit out, shifting uncomfortably in his seat. He was pressed against the back, now wishing his chair had wheels and he could reverse it into the hall and make a getaway to his room.

"Are you? Because I can't remember the last time you complained about the trains or work. And you were quieter before Dash took matters into his own hands—if that's possible —and it was starting to scare me."

"Quieter? I don't know what you're talking about." Gavin pretended that was absurd as he scowled at his teacup. "Perhaps I have nothing to complain about or I've lost hope that the trains will improve or people at work will stop oversharing," he added flatly.

"Did I do something to embarrass you or make you too... uncomfortable to try dating? You know I was always here for—"

"Dear God, Reid. I'm *fine*. And as everyone now knows, I am finally dating Dash so I don't understand why you're even bringing this up."

"Because something's been holding you back with Dash and I was afraid it was me—or us—and that maybe you thought I'd judge you or get jealous," Reid said, cringing and mouthing an apology.

Gavin focused on the surface of his tea and breathing steadily until the surge of anger had passed. He wasn't angry with Reid, but with his father and himself for creating that wall between them. And Walker and Dash had been right, he'd done his friend a disservice by not trusting him and Gavin knew Reid would be bitterly disappointed if he ever learned the truth.

"You sound bored, Reid. Go find someone more interesting to psychoanalyze."

Reid sighed as he pushed away from the door and took his overcoat off the hook. "You know I'm here if you ever want to talk."

"Thank you. I'll keep that in mind," Gavin replied wearily.

"You know what I think?" Reid wound a soft pink Hermès scarf around his neck and paused mid-loop. His voice had risen; he was getting angry. "It got worse when Walker proposed to Fin and peaked with Riley and Giles and Penn and Morris."

That made Gavin angry with Reid. "I promise, I'm fine. But if I wasn't, it sure as hell wouldn't be because the people I care about the most in this world were happy," he stated loudly and set his cup and saucer on the table before standing and giving the front of his coat an indignant tug. He snorted and buttoned it. "Is it possible that you're projecting, or that you find yourself bored because you're running out of lives to meddle with now that we're the last two standing?"

"Wow." Reid leaned back. "Talk about cynical. Can't I be happy for the people I love the most and simply concerned about my best friend?"

"I was happy before this conversation turned to my personal affairs."

Reid's cheeks puffed out and he blinked at Gavin. "Personal affairs? We've known each other...just about our whole lives and we've lived together *for decades*. When have we ever had personal affairs or secrets aside from this?"

"Exactly. I've never had secrets, therefore I am not entitled to have any now or keep any of my affairs to myself," Gavin countered facetiously.

"Right." Reid nodded as he pulled a pair of black leather gloves from his pocket and slapped them against his palm. "You can take the boy out of Heathcote, but you can't take Heathcote out of the boy," he concluded while tugging them on. "You sound like your parents," he said, then held up a hand when Gavin opened his mouth to order him to take it back. "I'm sorry, but do you ever listen to yourself? And look at who you're talking to. Do you think I can't tell when you're lying and being evasive? I just can't figure out *why*, for the life of me. Nothing will ever come between us and there's *nothing* I wouldn't do for you."

"Enough, Reid," Gavin begged, his voice a ragged whisper.

Because it was all true. Gavin's father had been furious and disgusted by the entire chain of events that led to the creation of the Marshall Agency. And he got worse after Walker proposed and Giles Ashby publicly ruined Wolford for firing Fin over the video of him and Riley.

Edward had blamed Reid for "leading Gavin astray" despite the fact that Gavin knew from a very early age that he didn't want to grow up and marry Hillary Lauder. "I am fine," he insisted. "And I know you'd do anything for me." Reid would probably murder Gavin's father if he ever found out.

"So would Dash," Reid said suggestively and Gavin's face twisted as he swatted at the door.

"I don't know what Dash sees in me, but I'm not going to bore him by complaining about the past. Go on and enjoy your evening."

"You really are in the mood to fight," Reid said with a heavy sigh. "Thank goodness for Dash, because I was never getting through. He makes you happy in ways I didn't know you were capable of but you're still holding back and acting like a damaged spinster. I can't understand why because you told your parents to go to hell over twenty years ago." He didn't wait

153

for Gavin to deny it or offer his usual excuses. "Later," Reid said with a snappy, sarcastic salute before leaving.

"Later," Gavin said.

His eyes remained glued to the door until they began to burn. He wished he had Reid's confidence or his friend's temper because Gavin knew there would never be a 'later.' He would never be able to explain how he'd been damaged and how close Reid had come to the truth.

"It's nearly over," Gavin whispered, giving his head a shake.

He'd put his foot down and end his father's manipulations. He wasn't going to let his father have the last word or win that battle. Then, Gavin would put the past firmly behind him, focusing only on the future and Dash.

"I just wish this difficult, messy business was over and we could get to the future part. Being happy is lovely, but it's a lot more work than being lonely and miserable was," he grumbled and went to start another pot of tea. "And I wish Dash would hurry up and get here."

Chapter Sixteen

The mood had changed when Dash returned to Briarwood Terrace after saying goodbye to his parents at Bloomingdale's. Norman was on his way out and warned that Reid had stormed through the lobby, claiming that Gavin made the Grinch look like a Care Bear. The apartment was quiet and dark when Dash let himself in and leaned over the threshold. A fire crackled soothingly from the fireplace, casting the hearth in a warm glow, but all the other lights were out except the lamp over the stove.

Gavin was hugging his chest and scowling at the kettle when Dash hung up his coat and bag and tiptoed into the kitchen. "Everything okay? I heard there might have been a fight in here."

"It wasn't a fight. Reid was meddling and I told him to take it elsewhere. There was an...exchange and then he went out."

"Out?" Dash frowned as he picked the teapot up off the counter, gesturing for Gavin to let him take over. "Will he be back soon?"

K. Sterling

"Probably not until late tonight or morning. He went out... to scratch an itch."

"*Oh*. I thought you might have told him the truth." Dash turned on the water to give the pot a rinse. He felt that confrontation looming, both dreading and hoping for it. But to Dash, the secret was like a toxic boobytrap and he couldn't do anything to help Gavin and Reid out until one of them had tripped into it. "Glad to know Reid's human and has needs like the rest of us. Present company excluded," he teased as he shut off the water. He glanced over his shoulder and found Gavin standing behind him.

"I do have needs," he said quietly.

Dash set the pot down and turned, his nerves suddenly sparking and fizzing wildly. He attempted a casual shrug and braced his hands on the counter outside his hips. "Is there anything in particular that I can...help you with?"

"Maybe," Gavin croaked as he nodded. His eyes lingered on Dash's lips, making them tingle. "I would like to..." He cleared his throat and shuffled closer. "That is, I was wondering if maybe we might... Well... Try some things from your list." He squeezed his eyes shut, blushing and whispering a curse.

"And which list were you thinking about?" Dash turned off the burner and slid closer.

"It doesn't matter anymore," Gavin said, then shook his head. "It's all the same now. Things that used to be nice have started to feel naughty and things that used to shock me seem rather nice when you say them," Gavin explained in a shaky rush.

"Good. It's all the same to me, too, and I'm happy with letting you lead," Dash said as he caught Gavin's wrist, then his hand. Their fingers tangled and they were both shaking, but Gavin's nervous laugh made Dash's heart skip. And he held on as Dash backed out of the kitchen and into the hall, towing

156

Gavin with him. "We can go as slow as you want. I told you I'm not in a rush," he whispered softly, so as not to startle Gavin.

"No." Gavin shook his head and Dash halted, afraid he'd changed his mind.

"No to...this or slow?" He asked carefully.

Gavin pushed out a wavering breath and he reached for Dash's cheek. "I don't want to go slow and I *can't* lead." His thumb vibrated as it traced Dash's lip. "I'm too afraid that I'll lose control or that I won't be able to stop. I don't even know what I want or where to start," he said, his voice rising with panic.

Dash answered with a shushing kiss. "It's alright. I can lead but don't hide from me anymore. Tell me what you need or show me," Dash said firmly.

"I will try," Gavin vowed and nodded solemnly, his lips brushing against Dash's. "I told you, I've always done my best to be as disappointing as possible. I never paid attention before and I do regret that now."

"Stop it," Dash scolded, not hiding the flutter of frustration he felt as he captured Gavin's lips and kissed him. And Dash *kissed him.* He held onto Gavin's face and put his whole heart into it. Their tongues thrust and swirled hungrily and they were both breathless when Dash let them come up for air. "I knew the sex was going to be incredible that day you lost your teacup and I heard you swearing and slamming things in here."

"What?" Gavin shook his head in confusion. "That was your proof? I lost my composure because Reid couldn't get a loan."

"Right!" Dash said, pulling Gavin with him into the bedroom. "You *lost it* and there was so much pent-up rage and energy. You were wild and I wanted to grab hold of you and... ride all of that fury out of you. I thought about you tearing off my clothes and slamming me into the wall and it was so hot."

Gavin reared back, frowning. "But I would never do that."

Dash chuckled and hummed as he stretched toward Gavin's lips. "I know, I just thought you were Penny's cute, older friend before that. But after that day, all I could think about was you swearing at me and ripping my clothes off. I haven't stopped picturing you naked since then." He cheered encouragingly when Gavin's eyes widened and his blush deepened. Dash used his foot to slide the door shut behind them, not wanting to startle Gavin. He cleared his throat softly while winding his fist in Gavin's tie. "I think you might be a moaner and vocal, which is *the best thing ever* and I really hope you swear a lot during sex."

"I...don't know." Gavin shook his head slowly before his eyes strayed to the bed. He gulped loudly at it. "I've never tried it in a bedroom and I've always had to be quiet. I just wanted it to be over. But I never want it to be over with you and I don't know how to do any of the things you'll want to do," he rambled again and his wide, panic-filled eyes flicked to Dash's. "I've never—"

"Easy!" Dash crooned soothingly. He kissed Gavin's lips and along his jaw to his ear. "I just want to touch you and get off with you. There are all kinds of ways we can make that happen and they'll all be good." He pushed Gavin's coat over and down his shoulders, tossing it at an armchair in the corner. "I haven't tried *everything*, but I've liked everything I've tried and I'm not afraid to get weird and have fun."

"Weird?" Gavin squeaked and a rash spread up his neck. His skin grew warmer under Dash's lips as he licked along Gavin's collar. "Just how weird exactly..."

"That depends on how much lube you have." Dash tugged Gavin's tie loose. "I'm kidding, mostly. Relax and let yourself explore and enjoy this, please," he ordered gently, taking the reins so Gavin would stop overthinking.

"Thank you," he whispered, sounding relieved, and groaned in approval when Dash unbuttoned his collar. His chest heaved and Gavin became more and more restless with each button. Dash worked his way down Gavin's chest and he froze when his undershirt was untucked. Dash's hand slid beneath the hem and up Gavin's chest, causing it to shudder. "Yes!" Gavin nodded jerkily, licking his lips as he panted breathlessly. He shrugged out of his shirt and pulled his undershirt over his head. "More." He took Dash's hands and pressed them against his stomach and his chest and leaned into his touch.

"Okay." Dash kept his voice light and gentle, but he was a giddy mess on the inside. His hands spread and kneaded as they roamed Gavin's back and chest. Gavin was hard, his cock grinding against Dash's thigh with every frantic buck of his hips. He fumbled with Dash's sweater and muttered something about being an oaf. "Hold on." Dash leaned back to pull it over his head and his stomach was full of butterflies as he took in Gavin's swollen lips and pink cheeks. He was on the wiry side, but surprisingly toned for a man whose favorite pastimes were reading the paper, playing the clarinet, and chess. "Swimming?" Dash recalled and Gavin nodded.

"I used to go at least four times a week," he confirmed, looking down at himself warily. "Before you became my holiday 'helper,'" he added with a bashful, teasing grin.

"I wish I could get away with that," Dash said with a distracted sigh, more interested in the goosebumps that spread beneath his fingertips as they fanned across Gavin's skin. "I have to work out or some of those football injuries from high school creep up on me. And because Penny conned me into running another marathon with her."

"Running is barbaric."

"It is," Dash agreed, chuckling as he whisked his shirt off

and dropped it. "But we're running for cancer research this time."

"I'd rather write a check," Gavin said weakly as his gaze slid down Dash's chest. He looked like he was starving as his head tilted and he licked his lips. "I've never been with anyone who was younger than me. I don't know if I—" He started and Dash cut him off with another kiss.

"I promise, I'll let you know if you do something I don't like and I'll tell you when you do something that works and I want more. Okay?" Dash ducked and found Gavin's eyes and waited until he nodded. "And you'll do the same until neither of us can think straight."

"I'm already there but I like the sound of that," Gavin murmured. He reached and tentatively traced the fly of Dash's jeans. "May I?" He asked shakily.

Dash nodded, fighting the impulse to rip it open for him. He thrilled at the rapt wonder and desire etched on Gavin's face as he flicked the button free and slowly unzipped the fly.

"That's good. Keep going," Dash whispered, then bit into his lip and clenched his fists as Gavin petted his hard-on through his boxers.

Another nervous laugh huffed from Gavin and he cupped Dash's cheek with his other hand, pulling him close for a desperate, breathless kiss. "I don't want to stop. What do I do next?" He gripped and stroked as he moaned into Dash's mouth.

"Do you want to blow m—?"

"*Yes*," Gavin answered immediately, cutting Dash off. His blush deepened as he nodded. "I want to."

Heat rushed over Dash and he was suddenly lightheaded. For some reason, the idea had never occurred to Dash. His fantasies had usually involved him going down on Gavin. His cock ached, he was so hard when Gavin backed him into the bed.

Dash laughed as he dropped and toed off his shoes. "It's probably better if I'm lying down. I was feeling a little unsteady," he confessed, sliding out of his jeans as he scooted up the bed. He held out a hand, beckoning Gavin to join him.

"I'm glad it isn't just me," Gavin said as he set his knee on the bed, still wearing his shoes and trousers. His hand trembled as it rested on Dash's thigh, easing it aside as Gavin lowered. "You're the only person I've ever wanted to do this to."

"Oh?" Dash asked hoarsely, getting up on an elbow, then gasping when Gavin's tongue darted out. Instead of licking Dash's cock, Gavin's tongue teased his sac before swiping at the inside of an asscheek. There was a soft, pleased grunt from Gavin and he angled his head as he spread Dash's thighs wider. Lush heat washed over Dash's hole, making his eyes roll as he fell back and a wave of pleasure rolled up his spine. "Oh!" Dash's head lolled on the bed as he held onto a handful of Gavin's hair.

"Is this alright?" Gavin asked, the words feathering against Dash's puckered flesh only to be sucked away a moment later. The hot slide of Gavin's tongue, swirling and seeking as his hands wandered and clawed at Dash's body was glorious.

All he could do was nod and whimper a strangled *"More!"*

He was meant to be leading, but Dash let Gavin feast, exulting in his greedy moans and loud swears. His tongue lapped and drilled, winding Dash up until he was shaking and frantic.

"Fuck! Me!" Dash squeaked out when Gavin's lips wrapped tight around his shaft. Intense pleasure flared, merging with the gnawing ache in Dash's core, making him desperate. "Please tell me you have lube and a lot of it. I have a few packets in my bag by the door but I don't think they'll be enough."

"Bedside table," Gavin murmured against Dash's pelvis.

"Thank goodness! I didn't think you would," Dash said as he reached for the drawer.

Gavin's head popped up and he raised a brow, looking adorably disgruntled. "I'm not an animal, Dash. I do need it now and then, when I...think about you."

"And you thought this would be disappointing." Dash shook his head, snatching the tube of basic KY and wrinkling his nose at it. "Although, I will be in charge of buying lube from now on. We can do better than this."

"I took it from Reid's bathroom."

That made a lot more sense than Gavin browsing the sexual wellness aisle at a drugstore. "He probably keeps the good stuff by the bed," Dash guessed, pulling Gavin up and pushing him onto his back.

"The good stuff?" Gavin fixed his glasses so they weren't askew. "I wasn't aware..."

Dash giggled as he threw a leg over, straddling Gavin. "That's okay. You've got me now and I keep a nice variety in my toy box at home."

"You have a toy box?" Gavin's eyes were glued to Dash's hands as they worked between them, unzipping and tugging.

"I have *a lot* of toys," Dash informed him and they wiggled and shimmied until Gavin was able to kick his boxers and trousers away. "Think of all the fun we'll have, trying them out," he said, flicking the cap open. Gavin was spellbound as Dash squeezed a glob onto his palm, then reached behind him. He gripped Gavin's length, making him hiss and buck off the mattress as Dash coated it. "And let me know if this starts to feel disappointing at any time," Dash said haughtily, but he had to hold his breath when he lined up the head of Gavin's cock with his hole and slowly sank down. His schedule had been a bit hectic lately and it had been a while since Dash had played with his dildos, though, so his body needed a moment to adjust.

"Fuck, Dash!" Gavin sat up, throwing his arms around Dash as he kissed him wildly. He was crying and shaking as their lips and tongues fused, his nails digging into Dash's flesh as Gavin held them pressed together.

Once the stinging passed and he no longer felt unbearably tight, Dash was able to slide up and down on his knees and get a little friction going. "There we go," he attempted breezily, despite the incredible heat and pressure curling in his core. He was so full of Gavin and they were so close. Dash could taste every tea-scented huff of his breath and feel their hearts thrashing at the same frantic beat.

"D-Dash, I..." Gavin's jaw stretched and his breath hitched as he stared up at Dash. Tears had gathered in his glasses and the lenses were fogged so Dash carefully removed them and rested his forehead on Gavin's.

"Yes?" He asked, slowly sliding down and taking Gavin to the hilt.

"Oh, Dash... I..." Gavin's eyelids fluttered, his hands spasming around Dash's ass and his back. He lifted and pulled at Dash, urgent as he babbled and begged. "Please! I lovvv—*love* you and I— Oh, fuck, fuck, fuck, Dash!"

"I know!" Dash captured his face and kissed Gavin with all the tenderness he could muster because things were about to get *naughty*. "I love you too. Now, let me show you."

He pushed Gavin back onto the bed, moaning as he rocked forward and onto his knees. Dash was able to ride more of Gavin's length with every slide and set a faster pace. It wasn't long before his ass slapped against Gavin's pelvis, filling the room with swift claps, primal grunts, and ragged moans. They were so wet, covered in sweat, and dripping from Dash's hole as he rode harder and faster.

"Here!" Dash moved Gavin's hands to his cock and his chest. "Touch me!" He smothered a sob, nodding when Gavin tugged and tweaked a nipple as he bucked off the bed. Dash was mesmerized as he watched Gavin's hand twisting around his erection and his long, elegant fingers pinching and teasing *him*. He reached back, bracing a hand on Gavin's thigh and angling his hips, striking his prostate. "You're so deep! It's so good!" Dash panted.

"You're so, so good! Keep going!" Gavin had found Dash's rhythm, guided by decades of musical training, his hips bouncing with the mattress springs. "So good. So beautiful."

"Yours!" Dash held onto the hand around his shaft as he burst into bright light and his passage clenched tight around Gavin. Dash cried Gavin's name as his cum spilled over their fingers. "Yours," he said, offering Gavin a taste.

Gavin snatched Dash's wrist. "Mine." He sucked on Dash's fingers, arching off the bed and moaning ecstatically. Wet heat blossomed in Dash's passage and he gasped as another tremor of pleasure rippled through him.

"As often and as many times as you wish, Mr. Selby," Dash said with a sated purr once they were able to think straight again. He lowered and nuzzled his face all over Gavin's. "That was incredible."

"That was," Gavin concurred, sounding surprised as his hands settled tentatively on Dash's back and gently trailed up and down his spine. "In fact, I think I might like to try that again soon."

Chapter Seventeen

That...actually happened.

Gavin was baffled the following morning as he stared at Dash's prone, unconscious body. He was sprawled across Gavin's bed and sleeping peacefully. And most surprisingly, a wide grin was stretched across Dash's face as he hugged Gavin's pillow.

He was sated and content and somehow, Gavin was responsible. Gavin frowned at the bed from his vantage point by the bathroom door.

Baffled was an understatement. He was in a whole new realm of the confounding and the absurd. Yet all signs seemed to indicate that Gavin had participated in a raucous night of intercourse and *both* parties had enjoyed themselves immensely. Dash didn't look at all disappointed and while Gavin would remember every moment of the night in vivid detail, he was having a difficult time believing he hadn't dreamt the entire episode.

Finally getting to touch and taste Dash had been heaven and holding him as they nodded off had been a life-altering experience. Gavin had never felt as close or as happy as he did with Dash in his arms. The sex was a revelation and Gavin was anxious to try everything, but he was even more enthralled by the connection they shared before and afterward. He wanted *that* again and again just as much as he craved the taste of Dash's skin. But, more than that, Gavin didn't want to spend another night without Dash.

He realized there wouldn't be another night if he botched it all in the morning, so Gavin gave his robe's belt a firm tug and went to place himself at Reid's mercy. The absolute last thing Gavin wanted to do was discuss something personal and indelicate—especially at such an early hour—with Reid, but who else could Gavin turn to, really?

There were no other options so Gavin steeled himself when he tapped a knuckle on Reid's door. His lips twisted as he listened and waited. He tapped again, just a little louder. "I'm sorry to disturb you this early, but I have a...situation." He said, then frowned at the door when there was still no answer. "Reid?" Gavin gave the door another tap before easing it open and peeking at the bed. "Brilliant." It was empty and neatly made. "You're still out."

His spirits plummeted until Gavin heard the front door open and Reid whistling softly to himself. Gavin rushed down the hall and into the living room, surprising Reid. "You're up early," he noted and raised a brow at Gavin. "And you've emerged from your room unshaved and undressed. Are you sick?" He asked as he hung up his coat and reached for Gavin's forehead.

Gavin waved him off. "I'm fine. Very well, actually. But it would seem that I...um..." He squeezed an eye shut and braced himself. "I have company and I...need assistance," he managed and Reid, to his credit, remained very calm.

He nodded slowly and pressed his hands together. "Please

tell me it's Dash," he said quietly, earning a grimace from Gavin.

"Who else could it possibly be?"

"I was afraid another senior partner might have dropped by," Reid said. "You were in a mood when I left."

"*I was in a mood*," Gavin began, then spluttered when he remembered that he was in dire need of help. "It was Dash," he said slowly and took a deep breath when his heart began to race. "And I anticipate that he'll want to...again when he wakes up."

"That's a good thing!" Reid cheered as he grabbed Gavin's face and kissed his forehead loudly. "I am so proud and so happy for you and Dash."

"Would you—" Gavin pushed him away and gave the halves of his robe a tug, closing it tighter. "I am naked under this and I *have a problem*. I would like to engage in certain activities, but I don't know how to prepare myself," he added in a rushed mumble.

Reid was stuck and squinted back at Gavin before he snorted. "Do you need a condom?" He asked as he patted his pockets and spun. "I think I used them all, but I have some in my room and I can give you a quick lesson."

"Wait!" Gavin caught Reid's elbow and turned him. "I know how to purchase and put on a condom. We have decided to forgo them after discussing our statuses," he explained awkwardly. His face was on fire and he couldn't look Reid in the eyes. "I've never...bottomed," Gavin whispered to the wall. "And I would like to."

"Ah." Reid hummed thoughtfully, then gave Gavin a decisive nod. "Here's what we're going to do," he began as he put an arm around Gavin and turned them toward the kitchen. "I'm going to make us some coffee and you can ask me anything you want. Or we can just drink our coffee in peace and enjoy this gorgeous winter morning," he said as he waved at the windows on the other side of the kitchen.

"But I don't drink coffee," Gavin replied, making Reid smile.

"I know, but you're going to drink a cup and relax while nature takes its course. Once it does, you can use my bathroom and one of the kits under my sink. The directions are easy to follow and I'm a text away if you have any other questions."

He gave Gavin's shoulder a reassuring squeeze and it had worked. None of that sounded too complicated or uncomfortable and Reid was being delicate with Gavin's sensibilities. "Thank you," he said, bowing his head gratefully at Reid. "I'm sorry about last night."

"Me too. Want to talk about it?" Reid asked with a hopeful lift of his brows as he reached for the French press.

"Another time," Gavin lied gently as he went to his seat by the window and he did enjoy the view while Reid prepared their coffee. It was a chilly morning, though, and Gavin was grateful when Reid handed him a vintage Dean & DeLuca mug. They sat in companionable silence for several moments before Reid cleared his throat and smiled into his coffee.

"I can't tell you how *happy* this makes me."

"Don't get excited just yet," Gavin warned. "He might come to his senses or get bored once the...animal attraction wears off."

"Animal—?" Reid's hand clapped over his mouth to hold back a loud guffaw and he was insensate for several moments. "Animal attraction!" He giggled as he wiped his eyes. "Jesus, that may be the funniest thing you've ever said."

"I was being serious," Gavin replied flatly and Reid bit into a knuckle as he wheezed himself into another fit of giggles. "I'm not sure what comes over me when we're alone, but I'm sure it can't last and that Dash will be disappointed once he sees what I'm really like."

"You can't be! How could you possibly think that Dash—of all people—doesn't know exactly what kind of man you are?" Reid asked as he pointed at Gavin's room, then at him. "There is absolutely *no* mystery here. Dash is just wildly in love with you, for some reason," Reid teased and shook his head at Gavin. "And do give Dash a little more credit."

"I—" Gavin's head pulled back and he snorted at Reid. "I do."

"You do not. Everyone underestimates him, but I think Dash is an excellent judge of character. He has a far better idea of who he is and what he wants than most people I know."

"You're right, of course," Gavin said and chuckled as he sipped. "Sometimes, he knows me better than I know myself and I don't know why I ever doubted him."

"And have you figured out what *you* want?" Reid asked.

Gavin nodded quickly. "I could have gone the rest of my life without touching another man or being touched again, but I *need* Dash. I'll do whatever it takes to keep him."

"I don't think Dash is going anywhere," Reid replied, reclining with a satisfied sigh. "It makes my heart so happy to hear that, though. I'm so ready for us to settle down and get married." He beamed at the windows, brighter than the sun lighting the ancient leaded panes. "And Dash is perfect."

"Are you still drunk?" Gavin asked, earning a distant nod.

"A little. Why?"

"It's far too soon and that's bordering on dysfunctional."

Reid made a dismissive gesture and draped an arm over the back of his seat. "I'm going to have it all by living vicariously through you and everything's finally coming together." He raised his cup in salute, earning a hard eye roll from Gavin.

"I hope it isn't me that you've just cursed," he said as he

stood. "Those sound like unfortunate last words," he warned, then excused himself because the coffee was working.

Half an hour later, Gavin returned after a shower and a relatively easy cleanse with a disposable kit from under Reid's sink. He wasn't nervous until he heard Dash laughing with Reid.

Dash looked like Mr. Everything as he leaned against the refrigerator, grinning drowsily over a cup of coffee with perfectly messy hair and wearing nothing but boxers and Gavin's shirt. Dash had rolled up the cuffs so the sleeves wouldn't hang past his fingers but he'd left it unbuttoned, unlocking a deep desire Gavin didn't know he possessed. He would always want to see Dash in yesterday's shirt, laughing and looking thoroughly fucked in the morning.

"There you are," Dash said dreamily, pushing away from the fridge and holding out a hand.

Reid gasped as he checked his watch and stood. "Time for me to disappear. Going to take a long, hot shower and a great, big nap before I have to meet Mom and Dad for dinner. Believe me, I've earned it." He took his coffee with him, leaving Dash scratching his head.

"Do I want to know?"

"I would advise you to forget you saw anything. You could become an accessory or may have to testify in court," he said, hoping he was joking.

Dash laughed and shrugged, pulling Gavin into the hall. "He can keep his mysteries. I missed you when I woke up, but Reid explained that you needed to handle some things. Are you okay?" His head tilted in concern as he raised Gavin's hand and kissed his knuckles.

"Great," Gavin croaked. How could he be anything other than great with Dash Griffin looking at him like that while looking like that in one of Gavin's shirts? And Dash was getting turned on as well, judging by the large bulge tenting the front of his boxers. "Really great," Gavin said as he swatted his door shut behind him and peeled off his robe, letting it fall as he reached for Dash. "I missed you too." He groaned the words into the corner of Dash's neck, breathing him in as they fell onto the bed. It was true. Gavin longed to feel Dash in his arms every moment they were apart and now he craved the taste of Dash's lips, his skin, his ass, and his cum. He wanted to get lost in him and feel Dash deep in his soul. "I don't know what to do."

"Shhh!" Dash rolled them so he was on top, hovering over Gavin and covering his face in sweet, soft kisses. "Don't overthink it. Give me an idea of where you want to start and just let it happen like last night."

"Okay." Gavin nodded, liking that plan. "I'd like it to be just like last night but...reversed," he added clumsily.

"Say no more!" Dash whispered, then slid down Gavin's body and proceeded to make the room spin. He thought he heard a chorus and violins as Dash sucked, licked, and slowly fingered his ass. Gavin had touched himself there several times and it had never felt like *that*. He wasn't as gentle or as sensual as Dash, though. He took his time, winding Gavin up until he was delirious, thrashing on the bed and begging. Dash rolled onto his back, but he had to coax Gavin on top, promising it would be fine and really hot. "You can control how deep and fast we go until you're used to this," he said, carefully guiding the head of his cock to Gavin's hole and helping him ease back.

"Used to this?"

There was no way Gavin would ever get used to the heady pleasure skipping down his limbs and up his spine. He had felt a brief burning as he stretched around Dash. But it had quickly transformed into quivering warmth that spread through Gavin's core as he took more and more of Dash's thick length.

"Are you okay?" Dash choked out, his hands clasped tight around Gavin's waist as if he were holding him up and afraid to let go.

"Really good." Gavin nodded. "I was expecting it to hurt, but I think this is the best thing I've ever felt in my life," he mused, bracing his hands on Dash's chest and giving his hips a test roll. "Hah!" He shouted at the flash of throbbing pleasure deep in his ass.

"Thank God. Let me try something." Dash pulled Gavin close and rolled them so he was on top again. He hooked Gavin's leg around a hip and thrust hard, filling him with smooth, deep strokes. "How's that?"

"Yes! Dash, yes! Don't stop doing that!" Gavin clutched at Dash's hair and his ass, screaming as his legs began to shake and his feet curled. The throbbing pleasure radiated from his prostate and Gavin shattered when Dash licked, bit, and sucked hard on the side of his neck. Every nerve in his body flared with brilliant heat, and he was blinded as he sobbed Dash's name.

He heard Dash shout as he slammed forward and there was a warm, wet trickle in the cleft of Gavin's ass as they held onto each other and struggled to catch their breath. Dash was wheezing and giggled as he nibbled on Gavin's lip. "I almost forgot about the frosting," he said, then pushed off the bed with shaking arms.

"What?" Gavin asked and covered his face in shock and aroused awe as Dash licked every trace of cum off his chest, stomach, and ass.

Chapter Eighteen

I t was early Christmas Eve eve morning and Dash was quietly stirring in unit number 4 at Briarwood Terrace. He tiptoed into the kitchen to put on the kettle for Gavin's tea and the French press. Gavin was softly snoring, but Dash had waited until he heard the water running and Reid's electric toothbrush from the other bathroom to come out and make noise in the kitchen.

"Good morning!" Reid declared when he appeared and thanked Dash as he was passed a mug of steaming coffee.

"Good morning," Dash said cheerfully as he went to see what was in the fridge for breakfast while Reid strolled to his seat at the table.

"About yesterday... You know I am over the moon, but is there any chance you could do something about the volume? I wasn't expecting Gavin to be so loud," he said, smirking at Dash.

"Nope," Dash replied while checking the produce drawer. "It's his place and I'm his first boyfriend so he gets to be as loud as he wants."

"Fair enough," Reid conceded, his neck stretching so he could see what Dash was doing. "I couldn't find any decent fresh berries, but I have apples." He pointed at the bowl on the counter.

"How about some kind of spiced pancake?" Dash suggested, getting a thumbs up from Reid as he reclined again. He was a classic control freak if Dash had ever seen one. But Reid was getting better about allowing Dash to do more around the apartment and seemed particularly at ease this morning.

"This is why I know I can trust you," he said, raising his cup to Dash. "I love Gavin with my whole heart, but I have to think about what's best for all of us. You love everyone, but you'll always do what's best for Gavin. And I can trust you in my kitchen." But his eyes still trailed Dash as he gathered the ingredients for a batter.

"Thanks! That means a lot!" Dash said and they both turned when they heard a loud buzz from the intercom.

Reid went to the door and poked the button. "I don't know who you are, but it's 7:00 on a Monday. This better be serious," he said.

"Sorry, Reid," Norman replied over the speaker. "There's some man in a suit, he says he has something for Gavin. He looks like he's from the Matrix. Be careful."

"The Matrix?" Reid asked and glanced at Dash curiously when there was a knock on the door. Reid peeked through the hole and snorted as he opened it, revealing a tall bald man on the other side of the threshold. He was wearing a dark suit and glasses and offered Reid a bow.

"Mr. Selby?" He asked Reid.

"No, but you must be Mr. Anderson," Reid guessed as he pointed but the other man shook his head, frowning.

"Richard Nickerson. I'm an attorney with Davis & Ellis, on

behalf of Edward Selby," he stated, removing an envelope from inside his coat.

"Yikes!" Dash rushed from the kitchen and around Reid. "Can I have that?" He asked.

"Are *you* Mr. Gavin Selby?" Nickerson sounded dubious.

"I am," Gavin said, startling Dash and Reid as he stepped between them, tightening his robe around him and giving the belt a yank.

"Very good, sir," Nickerson said as he handed him the envelope. "Your father says he is willing to overlook your involvement with the Marshalls and will consider offering his blessing if you will come at once."

"His blessing?" Gavin snapped back, making Nickerson and Dash jump. "I didn't request a meeting to ask for his blessing. But I'll be there," he said, reaching for the door and swinging it shut in Nickerson's face. "Damn it." He tore open the envelope and Dash saw that there was just an address before Gavin crumpled it and headed into the kitchen.

"What are you going to do?" Dash asked as he followed.

"I'll have to go at once," Gavin said obviously. "I need to be back in time to prepare for the party and the performance."

"Hold on!" Reid said and snapped his fingers hard to get their attention. "What the fuck was that?" He demanded as he pointed at the door. "Why did that sound like a negotiation and what did he mean by your 'involvement with the Marshalls'?"

"It was nothing," Gavin replied with a shrug, turning to the counter for his teapot.

Dash bit down on his lips to hold in a startled gasp, stunned at how quickly Gavin had lied and how close they were to the precipice of the awful truth and a terrible fight. "Gavin!" He whispered, begging Gavin to do the right thing now and tell his friend the truth. Gavin shot him a hard look and Reid's brows rose when he caught it.

"I don't like this, whatever is happening right now," he announced, his voice rising.

Gavin held up a hand calmly. "It's not important and it's behind us," he said as his glance slid to Dash and was hopeful. "It's behind us and I'm going to tell my father to stay out of my life for whatever is left of his."

"Knock it off," Reid said as he set his hands on his hips. "He said the Marshalls. What's behind *us*?"

His anger rose between them as his eyes burned and his nostrils flared while Gavin remained composed, prepared to wait the storm out. Dash couldn't take it, his heart hurt worse as the moment stretched. "You have to tell him, Gavin."

"I'd rather not," he replied and Dash shook his head defiantly, his tiny mouse of a temper emerging from its safe hiding place.

"He deserves to know. He *should* know and it's not right and it isn't fair. He's your best friend and it's his job to take care of you too."

Gavin shook his head, his gaze locked with Dash's. "Reid has enough people to take care of."

Dash shook his head. "Please. I don't want to lie to him anymore. It feels terrible, Gavin."

There was a loud, sharp bark of laughter from Reid and he looked furious as he swept a hand through his hair. "Alright. I'll make this easier on you, Gavin. Tell me the truth *now* or I'll leave." He pinned Gavin with a hard stare, making it clear that he'd be walking out for good.

"Oh, God," Dash covered his mouth, suddenly sick. "Can we please just calm down and *talk* about this?"

"Fine!" Gavin threw his hands up, pacing toward the stove before swinging back around. "My father wasn't pleased about the agency and he wanted me to fix things when Giles fired

Wolford but I refused so he made Ernst & Waterhouse let me go last February," he summarized quickly.

"They let you go?" Reid appeared to be utterly dumbfounded. His stare swung to Dash for an explanation when Gavin shook his head again, refusing to answer or look at them.

Dash gave Gavin a moment to continue, then sighed in defeat as he turned to Reid. "Gavin's father had him blacklisted and he hasn't been able to find work anywhere except with his friends. He's been hiding at my library so you wouldn't find out."

Reid visibly reeled. "Why didn't you tell me?" His voice cracked and tears welled in his eyes as he went to Gavin.

"Because I didn't want you to have to choose between me and this agency. I think we both know what's more important," Gavin said quietly to the window.

"I don't think we do!" Reid growled angrily, but he pulled Gavin into his arms for a tight hug. "You should have told me so we could have figured this out together."

"There was nothing to figure out and I've landed on my feet," Gavin said as he set Reid away from him and attempted a brave smile. "The agency keeps me distracted and Cameron and Giles have thrown some work my way. And I'm managing Morris's portfolio."

"That's..." Reid's face twisted. "That's not enough. You handled corporate accounts with *billions* of dollars in assets and investments. That's child's play for you."

"This is *enough.* Now, if you'll excuse me, I have to get ready." Gavin said firmly before storming out of the kitchen and into his room. The door slammed behind him, leaving Reid stunned and Dash even more determined to have it all out in the open and heal the damage between them.

"It isn't enough and he's given up too much," Dash said. "Gavin's father has done everything in his power to end your friendship and Gavin has given *everything* to hold on and to protect us all."

"I had no idea!" Reid looked dumbfounded as he turned toward Gavin's room. "I knew his parents were mad because he wouldn't marry the Lauder girl, but I didn't think it had anything to do with me."

Dash scratched his head, wondering how anyone would assume that when it seemed pretty obvious to him. "But Gavin would have married her if he didn't have you. He wouldn't have been strong enough to stand up to his father."

"Gavin!" Reid groaned as he scrubbed his face. "I should have seen it! All these years, wondering if I was holding him back or he resented me for being a little bit of a slut. But it was right in front of my goddamn face! How could I be so stupid?"

"Because he didn't want you to see it," Dash said, giving Reid's shoulder a comforting squeeze. "And because Gavin *was* happy and didn't mind quietly holding up the wall and defending the kingdom while everyone he loved lived happily ever after. He didn't want to be the cause of a messy fight and to pull everyone into it."

"You're right. He's given up too much." Reid sniffed hard and it transformed into a sneer as his eyes narrowed. "His father will pay for this—maybe not here or at my hands, but in Hell for the rest of eternity. He's tried to push Gavin into the closet his whole life and I swear, he would have taken this place and every penny Gavin's uncle left him if he could."

"Why?" Dash stared down the hall at Gavin's door. "I can't make any sense of this, the more I learn about Gavin and his family. What kind of father would do that?"

That got a hard snort from Reid. "Edward Selby is a heartless son of an even more heartless son of a bitch. I thought he might back off when Gavin's grandfather died when we were in high school, but he got even greedier and more controlling. It was like he wanted *everything*, including Gavin. I was almost relieved when they cut Gavin off because I thought he was free. Part of me wondered if Gavin had started to regret that as we got older and that was why he's been so touchy about his father lately."

"No. He doesn't regret any of that. Gavin's been afraid of him finding out about me," Dash told Reid and laughed in disgust. "That's why he wanted a meeting. He says he wants to go alone, but I'm not afraid of his father. What can he do to me?"

"Good." Reid gripped Dash's arms. A calculating grin spread across his face. "We're going to help Gavin get revenge. Without stooping to Edward Selby's level," he added.

"Without stooping? Then, I'm definitely in!" Dash asked excitedly. He didn't care what he had to do or what it cost him, he would help Gavin no matter what. But he wasn't good at being devious or underhanded.

"We don't have to play dirty," Reid said. "Edward Selby's played every dirty trick in the book, and now, he's alone and miserable. And there's a special place waiting for him in Hell. But, before he goes, Edward's going to see that all of his dirty tricks and schemes have failed and Gavin has *everything* he tried to steal from him. Gavin's getting the life and the man of his dreams. We're going to prove that Gavin *won*," he said with a determined nod.

"That's perfect! What do you need me to do?" Dash asked, but Reid shook his head.

"Let me plot and handle all the details. You're the happily ever after and you'll have your work cut out for you with Gavin. He thinks he doesn't deserve Prince Charming and a fairytale ending, but that's what he's getting."

Dash gasped out a surprised, shaky laugh and his eyes watered. Reid finally *knew* and he was entrusting Dash with his best friend's happiness and his future. "Okay," he said, nodding jerkily. "I'll be his Prince Charming."

"You already are," Reid said reassuringly as he gave Dash's shoulder an affectionate punch. "You've spent years preparing for this and when you saw your chance, you swooped in and swept Gavin right off his feet. I want you to keep doing what you're doing and distract him with lots of sex and romance. Make him so blissfully happy he can't see straight. Don't let his feet touch the ground," Reid commanded and Dash's lips curved into a loopy grin as he began to plan.

"I can do that."

"I know you can. Keep him on cloud nine while we handle the rest. A happy life is the best revenge so we're going to show Edward how happy and *loved* Gavin is," Reid added with a wink before his eyes lit up, taking on a maniacal glow. "I'll get Agnes to help me, too. She's got more connections than the Selbys and this'll be right up her alley."

Dash grimaced, afraid he'd unleashed a monster. "You're probably right, but it's best if I know less in that case. This could still get sketchy or dangerous if you're teaming up with Agnes," Dash said and Reid hummed in agreement.

"Exactly. You focus on Gavin, lover boy, and we'll see that he gets his revenge."

Chapter Nineteen

Gavin recognized the Upper West Side address that Nickerson had given him. And he wasn't surprised when the doorman directed him to the elevator and instructed him to go all the way up to the penthouse. A butler was waiting when Gavin got out and was solemn as he took his overcoat.

"Your father is in his room," he informed Gavin quietly as he hung it on the hook and offered him a bow.

"I'm sorry. Do you think I know where that is?"

The older man flinched and paled. "My apologies, sir. This way," he said quickly. He blushed as he hurried down the hall to their right and through the maze of elegantly remodeled rooms and short hallways. "He's right through there," he whispered, pointing at the opened door at the end of the narrow hall.

It was just a few strides and Gavin was greeted by a loud, rattling bark-like cough when he leaned into the room. He was more impressed with the elegant slate blue velvet and silk upholstery, wallpaper, and curtains than he was moved by the sight of a nurse or the hospital bed with its bright white plastic and metal frame, the dozens of wires, blipping monitors, and its occupant.

"Get in here!" A thin, rasping voice commanded.

Gavin *almost* recognized the voice, but he barely knew the withered scarecrow swaddled in blankets and propped up with pillows before him. Edward Selby's blond hair had faded to pale ash and his skin was dry and sallow. Edward's sunken gray eyes followed Gavin as he posted at the foot of the bed.

"Sir," Gavin said simply, ducking his head and allowing his father to go first and hoping the deathbed might reveal a change of heart.

"I'll give your mother that, I never had to worry about where you came from. You're definitely a Selby," Edward noted as he flailed a hand, sounding almost proud, but Gavin found little comfort in this glimpse of his future. Granted, his father was approaching his forty-second year when Gavin was born so it wasn't the near future, at least. He still had plenty of time to live *well* and hopefully prevent such a lonely end.

"I am, indeed, a Selby. For my sins," Gavin added with a sigh for the nurse as she rose to untangle wires, signaling his impatience. Gavin felt very little as he stared back at a man who had lived a very long and supremely selfish life with almost no care or respect for his family or those around him. Edward was high on the valium slowly dripping into his veins if he thought Gavin would cry and apologize or beg for forgiveness.

"For *my* sins," Edward corrected. "I don't know where I went wrong with you, but you're still a Selby and you're the *last* Selby. It was too late to try for another when you humiliated us and Celia refused to put her body through it again," he added with a petulant sneer.

"The conception or the pregnancy?" Gavin asked, then

held up a hand because he truly shouldn't have asked. "I'm not here to negotiate and I'm not parting with any of my organs if that's what you're after."

His father chuckled to himself in amusement. "No, you'd let me rot first. I'm glad you know how to hold a grudge. You'll need a long memory and the vultures will pick you dry if you show them any weakness."

"I'm sorry. Vultures?" Gavin's head tilted in confusion. Only one of them looked like a carcass and it wasn't Gavin.

"Mark my words: they'll start circling as soon as it gets out that I'm gone. If they haven't already," Edward speculated.

"Let them. I've never cared and I'm not here for that. I've come to warn you. Stay out of my life and leave Dash out of this sick grudge you have against me."

Edward grunted and the humor faded from his eyes and his smirk. "You do have a knack for picking powerful friends and you chose well with the Mooney boy," he said, striking Gavin's temper like a match.

"I'd warn you not to threaten Dash or interfere in my life again, but it sounds like you already tried. You looked into Dash and realized he was untouchable because of his family. There's nothing you can do to him, but I can hurt *you*. I can make sure that the *only* thing the world remembers about the Selbys is that I was as gay as Christopher Street."

"I don't care about that anymore," Edward muttered, shooing away the past. Medical tape and IVs tugged at the blue-green veins and the dusty parchment-colored skin on the back of his hand, making each jagged gesture all the more difficult to watch. "I want to see what kind of man you are—what you've become," Edward declared, his gnarled fist smacking at the nurse's side. "Get me up!" He demanded. She jumped into motion and raised the incline behind Edward's pillows and gave them a fluff.

Gavin frowned down at him, keeping his hands calmly clasped behind his back. "I've already shown you exactly what sort of man I am. You've seen what I've become."

"Yes, yes..." His father's head bobbled and he gestured dismissively. "You're your own man and you don't need me or my money. Good for you. You won in the end because I have no other heir and I don't want my estate and my legacy frittered away. You might not give a damn about being a Selby, but at least I know you'll be sensible."

"I'd like to think I've always been sensible," Gavin replied, earning a hoarse, wheezing snicker from his father.

"You've been a fool. You would have had an empire if you had married the Lauder girl, but you pissed it away so you could pimp out nannies with Reid Marshall. At least it's paying off. I'll give you that. You have made some very impressive friends," he mused.

That got a chuckle out of Gavin. "*Reid* made some impressive friends," he corrected and smiled at Edward. "You would have ruined him and our agency if Walker Cameron III hadn't gotten involved. Then, you saw what Giles Ashby was capable of so you lashed out at me because I wouldn't save Wolford," Gavin reminded him.

"Oh, let it go!" Edward shouted, then began to cough and gag. The nurse hopped up and wiped at his mouth while Edward glared at Gavin. "Heathcote will be yours soon. I'm trusting you to manage the estate wisely."

"Are you?" Gavin didn't hide his surprise.

"You've never been stupid with money and you've kept your nose clean. You don't have a backbone or any ambition, but there's no denying that you know how money works."

"Thank you?"

"Did you hear that?" Edward asked his nurse. "It took more

than forty years and that's the closest I'll ever get to gratitude from him."

"Will that be all?" Gavin refused to engage or give his father one last chance to put him down.

"I worked hard to build on top of what was left to me and make my father proud. Try not to drag the family legacy through the mud after I'm gone, would you? That's all I ask," Edward said and attempted a nonchalant wave as if he had always been reasonable.

"I love Dash and I'm going to ask him to marry me. But aside from that, I have no plans to change how I live or behave," Gavin replied, holding up a finger. "Unless you back me into a corner again. All I have is my privacy but I'll blow it up just to spite you."

"I know you would," Edward said with an eye roll. "I'm done trying to make you see things my way and no one cares anymore. Everyone's gay out there." He gestured at the window to his right. "I just want to know that everything I've worked for and generations of Selby pride and honor won't die with me. I want your word that you won't sell Heathcote to one of those Bitcoin idiots or some asshole from TikTok."

"Ah. You're looking for security," Gavin said as he nodded and backed away from the bed, signaling that he was leaving. "Security is a powerful thing, isn't it?" He noted and smirked at his father's startled expression. "It can bring you great peace in your final hours. Or, when you're just learning who you are as a man."

"Hold on!" Edward argued, but Gavin shushed and shook his head.

"Don't worry. I won't sell Heathcote. You have my word."

Edward relaxed and nodded, watching Gavin closely. "You'll keep it and take care of it?" "I will," Gavin vowed, his conscience clear because he knew *exactly* what to do with Heathcote and couldn't wait to put Dash, Reid, and their friends to work. "If that's all, good evening and...goodbye," he said with a final bow, then turned on his heel and left the room. Gavin didn't know where his father was headed, but he hoped they'd never see each other again.

Chapter Twenty

Gavin was a changed man when he returned to Briarwood Terrace after his meeting with his father. His arms were overflowing with a garment bag, a large bouquet, a stack of pastry boxes, and bags hung from his fingers as he backed through the door.

"What's all this?" Dash asked as he and Reid hurried to help.

"Cookies and cupcakes for the party and I thought the flowers might brighten this place up," Gavin said with a scolding look at Reid. "And more decorations. All we have is that little potted tree in the kitchen and a few poinsettias."

Reid gasped indignantly. "You said anything else would be depressing because it was just you here on Christmas morning!"

"Since when do you listen to me?" Gavin replied flatly, winking at Dash and making him giggle. "It was just me before so it would have been depressing. You had a tree at your parents' place and spent your Christmas mornings with them.

But I have Dash now and I love Christmas," he informed them, holding up the garment bag. "I love it so much, I went back for this suit I've had my eye on. It's an *emerald* tweed." His eyes widened and he smiled mischievously. "I was afraid it was a little...loud, but I figured it's Christmas so why not!"

"Flashy," Reid said, fighting back a smirk. "But tell us how the meeting went!" He demanded.

"Fine," Gavin said with a dismissive shrug as he headed for his room with his new suit.

Dash and Reid exchanged baffled looks. "Fine?" They said as they followed on his heels.

He hummed absently. "My father has only a few days left and we've come to a truce. He's accepted that he can't stop me from being gay and will no longer interfere in my life and I won't sell Heathcote to some asshole from TikTok."

"Yay!" Dash clapped as he hopped. "You did it and it's finally over!"

"It is," Gavin said and a warm chuckle slipped from him as he studied the garment bag in his arms. "I'm going to live my life the way I want to from now on and nothing is going to stop me from being the happiest man in Manhattan."

"I love that," Dash sighed, as he pressed his hand over his heart to stop it from jumping out of his chest.

"Me too," Reid said, looking satisfied as he crossed his arms and grinned at Gavin. "Are you going to try that on for us or not? I'm waiting for a show."

"This?" Gavin shrugged again at the bag and nodded. "I suppose," he said as he turned and headed to his room.

They watched him go and Dash waited until the door closed to raise a brow at Reid. "Are we good to go?"

"Yup." Reid nodded, offering his fist for a bump. "I've already talked to Agnes and she's in."

"Good," Dash said, tapping his fist against Reid's while keeping an eye on Gavin's door. "What's the plan? We don't have a lot of time from the sound of things."

Reid laughed wickedly as he tapped his fingertips together. "Agnes...*knows* Edward's night nurse. It turns out Edward's a big fan of Hannity and Fox News and watches it while he's eating his dinner every night."

"Oh?" Dash asked, turning to Reid. "Why do I have a feeling Edward's dinner plans are going to be interrupted?" He said, enjoying the gleam in Reid's eyes as they widened.

"Because tonight, Gavin's going to have the best Christmas Eve eve of his life with his friends and family and Giles is going to make sure it's televised for one very special audience. Morris already has the intro music and graphics all ready to go."

"That's brilliant," Dash said and clapped softly.

"I thought so too," Reid replied, then became alert when Gavin's door opened and he leaned out.

"Could you come back here, Dash? There's a...thing I... need a hand with," Gavin mumbled at them before the door shut.

"Looks like you're up, lover boy," Reid said and gave Dash a suggestive nudge.

Dash had a feeling he knew what Gavin needed a hand with and already had a few ideas of his own as he puffed out his chest and strode down the hall to Gavin's room. "That's me and I've totally got this," he boasted. He knocked, then let out a shocked "Hey!" when he was yanked inside and thrown against the door.

"I told him that I love you," Gavin said, just before he attacked Dash's lips with starving licks and kisses. He had removed his more sensible gray coat, looking rakishly handsome with his tie tugged loose and his collar unbuttoned. And Dash was very interested in the hard-on straining against the front of Gavin's trousers.

"Hold on!" Dash begged as he ducked and weaved. He captured Gavin's face in his hands so they could focus for a moment before Dash visited the South Pole. "You told him?"

"I had to." Gavin stepped closer, resting his forehead on Dash's and breathing him in. "I wanted him to know before his miserable heart stopped beating that mine beats for Dash Griffin and only him. He thought he could crush my life until it was nothing, but I have you and you are *everything*, Dash. You're all that matters. *You* are my future and that is what he's reckoning with in his final moments. He failed because of you."

"All I'm hearing is that we won." Dash attacked Gavin's lips like *he* was starving. "I love you so much!"

"Enough to..." Gavin coughed and was blushing as he guided Dash's hand to the fly of his trousers. "I'm feeling rather...naughty at the moment."

Dash purred as he traced Gavin's lips with his tongue. "You read my mind," he panted, loosening Gavin's belt. He slipped the button free and savored Gavin's whimpering shudder as he pulled the zipper. "Want to see if I can read yours?" He pushed Gavin's trousers and proper white boxers down, making him gasp and nod frantically. Dash nipped on the end of Gavin's chin, making a sultry humming sound as he stroked Gavin's cock. "I think you want to see if I can swallow every inch of this again. And then, you want to come all over my face and lick it clean."

"Dash!" Gavin's hand closed over Dash's mouth and his eyes were watering, he looked so embarrassed.

"So, you weren't thinking that?" Dash asked once Gavin lowered his hand, earning a dry snort.

"I am now."

"Excellent!" Dash cheered, then canted toward Gavin conspiratorially. "That was kind of a setup. I can't read minds, but you want to give it a shot?"

"Are you sure you can do tha—?"

"Yes!" Dash slid down, dropping onto his knees and giving Gavin's shaft a long, appreciative lick and groaning loudly as he sucked on the head. "Don't be afraid to really go for it. It's Christmas, remember!"

"That is highly inappropriate."

Dash giggled against Gavin's sac. "Get into the spirit!" He whispered.

"For the love of God, *please* put it in your mouth," Gavin begged, but his voice cracked and his chest shook with laughter as he traced Dash's cheek.

"Honestly thought you'd never ask."

Dash opened wide and went to work. He encouraged Gavin with impatient moans, then made rapturous gurgling sounds when he braced his forearms on the door and bucked against Dash's face.

"Christ, Dash!" He cried when he finally let go, causing Dash's head to beat against the panels behind him. His throat stretched and there was an intense burn as Gavin's thick length pressed deeper with each thrust.

"Right against the door?" Reid called from the hallway. "I said I wanted a show, but that is not what I had in mind."

"Go away!" Gavin shouted back, never slowing his pace. Dash moaned in response because it was kind of hot, knowing Reid could hear his best friend falling apart. He sucked harder and louder and it had an instant effect on Gavin. "Oh, fuck!" He made a ragged sound as he rose on his toes, holding on tight to the back of Dash's head. Tears spilled from Dash's eyes as he watched Gavin go off like a rocket. Gavin's body jerked and jumped, shivering hard as he sobbed Dash's name and spilled deep in his throat. The pressure was intense and Dash saw stars for a moment before Gavin withdrew and pulled him to his feet. "Are you okay?"

"I don't think I've ever been better," Dash stated dizzily, laughing as they stumbled and he was hastily stripped and pushed onto the bed. It was rough and clumsy as Dash was mounted and rode fast and hard. But Gavin was beautiful without his inhibitions and utterly free of worry. He gave himself permission to revel in their connection and their bodies and take what he wanted, chanting and bouncing on Dash with wild abandon until they combusted.

After, they made out in the shower, kissing and teasing until they ran out of hot water. Dash kept his elf costume stashed in his backpack so it only took him a few minutes to get ready and was able to relax on Gavin's bed and enjoy the show. Dash found it endearing, watching Gavin sit in his shirt and boxers and meticulously polish his clarinet and test the reed before carefully packing it in its case to be transported to East 63rd Street for the evening's performance.

He was prepared for a private family performance with only his very nearest and dearest, but Gavin put as much care and attention into his shave and his hair to make sure they were as meticulous as his instrument. Gavin had no idea that everyone else was decorating, dressing, and practicing their hearts out in order to put on a good show for Edward Selby.

Dash fought back a giggle when Gavin unzipped the garment bag and boldly revealed his "green" suit. It was more of a dark hunter green with flecks of emerald, but Gavin looked breathtakingly handsome as he arranged a burgundy and gold plaid tie into an elegant knot and paired it with a matching paisley pocket square. And then, Dash had to fight back a watery gasp when Gavin produced the sprig of mistletoe from their first mistletoe kiss and tucked it into the buttonhole on his lapel.

"How do I look?" He asked, turning from the standing mirror.

"You look like the man of my dreams," Dash said sincerely, too moved and honored to crack a silly joke or say something naughty. "I should have dressed up," he complained, looking down at himself, but Gavin gave his head a quick shake and guided them toward the door.

"*You* look perfect and I'm planning to rip those tights off when we get back," he informed Dash dryly.

"It really is the most wonderful time of the year," Dash told Reid when they found him waiting in the living room.

"So I've heard," he said cheekily while pulling on his coat and gloves. "But we need to get going, the train's going to be packed."

"We won't be taking the train," Gavin said, looking offended as he held his large black clarinet case closer. Dash wondered if Gavin had been given the contrabass when he was a child because he was one of the few present at the time who would grow into it. "I've arranged for a limo."

Reid threw him a confused look. "It's not that far. I'd say we could walk if it wasn't going to be such a nasty night, but a limo is a little excessive," he said, earning a stubborn snort from Gavin.

"I won't be jostled or have to answer a hundred silly questions about the size of this case or where we're going with a slutty elf."

"Hey!" Dash protested. "There's nothing indecent about this," he said as he inspected his elf ensemble."

Gavin snorted dubiously. "I wasn't referring to the costume," he said and Reid made a knowing sound as he got the door.

"Neither of you have any elf-control from the sound of things," he said, his tongue pushing against the inside of his cheek as he nodded at Dash. "You keep those thoughts purely PG though until we get home. You're already pushing it with those tights," he said, causing Dash to blush.

Gavin grinned, hefting the clarinet case under his right arm. "I'm rather fond of the tights," he told Reid quietly as they waved at Norman and wished him a lovely Christmas Eve eve. "He has a really nice ass and thighs."

Reid sounded deeply relieved as he clutched his chest. "So you have noticed. I was truly beginning to worry about you, my friend. I didn't know how you could hold out for as long as you did with that much cake right in front of your face."

"Hey! I'm right here!" Dash said, looking back at them. Reid shrugged and gestured for him to turn back around.

"Yes, you are, and thank you for your service."

The three of them climbed into the limo a little after 5:00, sharing one of the seats so Gavin's clarinet could occupy the other. Less than ten minutes later, they emerged in front of Agnes and Penny's townhouse. Gavin rumbled about the weather and his hair while Dash and Reid exchanged excited grins and winks behind his back.

For Gavin, it would be a Christmas Eve eve like any of the others their close-knit gang had shared over the years. But thanks to Reid, it felt like they were about to attend a grand ball and Dash was walking in on Prince Charming's arm. Or, *he* was Prince Charming, according to Reid's plan for the evening.

"Let me get that!" Dash said, taking the case and sliding his other hand around Gavin's. He felt like the tallest elf in the city as the doorman let them in and everyone cheered and clapped at their arrival.

"Now, we can get this party started!" Morris announced as he recorded everything on his phone from the stairs.

"I'm fairly certain those words have never been uttered about a clarinetist before," Gavin mused as Agnes helped him out of his coat.

"Nonsense! You're the guest of honor," she declared, earning claps and whistles of agreement from Penn, Walker, and Riley. Even Giles had left the safety of the Olympia and 8B and was helping little Luna clap. Penn and Fin were with Milo, June, and the triplets along with Fin and Reid's parents, Evelyn Mosby, and Morris Sr. Everyone was there because Christmas Eve eve was mandatory and always a lively, lovely celebration. But the mood was even more rebelliously festive as Penn and Morris chanted "Gavin, Gavin, Gavin..." like he was about to kick a field goal.

Gavin was startled as he whipped around. "You're not making me dress up as Santa, are you?" He whispered to Agnes loudly. "These children know me and—"

"Do calm down," she scolded him, making everyone laugh. "You're our entertainment coordinator and the evening's emcee," she reminded Gavin, then slid Morris's phone a cocky smirk. "And it will be a night to remember."

"Perhaps you should calm down," Gavin replied with an eye roll, taking the case from Dash and going off to get set up in the living room.

"Did you get all of that?" Dash whispered and Morris held up a thumb.

"We've got a few more cameras recording and I have the perfect graphic ready so make sure you make good use of the mistletoe traps around the house," he explained quietly as they all watched Gavin set up in front of the Christmas tree from the foyer. "I'll be playing during the big number, but Reid will take over directing duties."

"Muahaha!" Reid said, rubbing his hands together in

delight. "He's our man of the night and the Briarwood magic will be televised!"

"Perfect!" Dash whispered, pumping a fist and there were several determined humphs and cheers from everyone around him. "Let's give Gavin Selby the best night of his life and show that bitter old man what he was missing."

Chapter Twenty-One

I t truly was a Christmas miracle.

The triplets had yet to bicker and nothing had exploded or been coated in glittering slime. Yet. Gavin was tempering his expectations as he turned on the little speaker and checked June's Bluetooth microphone to make sure it was working.

Instead of passing out gift cards—Starbucks for the adults and iTunes for the children—the "more thoughtful" gifts Dash had helped Gavin find at the various markets around the city were a tremendous hit. He had been very wrong in the past and the effort had been worth it, Gavin decided.

Agnes and Penny appeared to be quite moved by the lamp and June loved her monogrammed book tote. The triplets all squealed adoringly at their jewelry boxes and Walker seemed pleased with his bottle of King's County whiskey. Fin and Riley pulled on their matching sweaters immediately and were planning to wear them during their performance. Morris was *still* playing his handmade flute—which Gavin now regretted purchasing—and the Mosbys were thrilled with the framed antique map of Park Slope. And Penn and Giles had already snuck out to enjoy a few hits off the joints Dash helped Gavin select for them.

As always, the meal was a posh potluck that included a prime rib roast and vegan options for Penn and Penny with decadent desserts by the renowned Evelyn Mosby. It was a bit odd to Gavin, when he was elected to slice and serve the standing rib roast and give the toast. But he was feeling particularly moved and unusually loquacious thanks to Dash's Christmas cranberry punch.

"I'm usually not the most cheerful of people this time of year," he began with an apologetic wince. "Not that I'm cheerful any time of the year. Christmas has always been particularly difficult for me, but I've always looked forward to Christmas Eve eve because it was when I'd get to celebrate with all of you. You were the only reason Christmas had any meaning for me," he said, pausing as he turned to Dash. "Until this year. You dragged me out of Briarwood Terrace and gave me a whole new reason to love Christmas: you. Now, I can't wait until the holiday markets return so I can start shopping for gifts. And I want to learn how to ice skate so we can be one of those sappy couples who hold hands and kiss in the middle of the rink."

Reid leaned close to Morris and held up a hand so he could whisper behind it. "Should we call for an ambulance? I think he might be having a stroke."

"I'm fine," Gavin said, then shook his head. "Actually, I'm better than fine. I'm in love and every day feels like Christmas since Dash decided I needed some elf-help." He gave everyone a moment to boo and snicker before raising his glass. "To all of you for being the brightest part of my Christmas for so many years, and to Dash for giving me a new reason to celebrate."

"Hear! Hear!" Reid said as he held up his glass. "And to Gavin."

"To Gavin!" Everyone answered with enthusiastic cheers and Morris whistled like a rancher summoning cattle.

"Thank you..." Gavin frowned around the table as he sat, nodding when Dash offered to drop a spoonful of Penn's vegan macaroni and cheese onto his plate. "I think they're up to something," he whispered out of the side of his mouth.

"Who?" Dash laughed as he added a spoonful of sweet potatoes. "That was a beautiful toast."

"Thank you. I was thinking..." He looked to make sure everyone else was busy chatting and preoccupied and leaned closer to Dash. "I want to spend all of my days with you, at Briarwood Terrace."

"Okay..." Dash swallowed loudly. "What do you mean by that exactly? So I know how much screaming and crying would be appropriate in response," he explained shakily.

"Screaming and crying?" Gavin asked in alarm. "I had hoped you might come and live at Briarwood Terrace with me, but you don't have to if you don't want to," he added quickly, but Dash's hand clapped over his mouth when he let out a startled yelp.

"I do!" Dash yelled and Reid's fork and knife clattered onto his plate and Penny let out the loudest *"Woop!"* as she hopped out of her seat.

"Yes!" Reid shouted as he launched to his feet.

Penny turned, reaching over Agnes for him. "Oh, my God! They're getting married!"

"Wait!" Both Dash and Gavin cried, standing and waving for everyone to calm down.

Gavin was pale and wide-eyed as he gestured for Penny to calmly return to her seat. "We are not getting married. *Yet*," he said pointedly to her and Reid. "I've asked Dash to move in with us and he said yes to that. Not...the other thing. For goodness sake," he complained with a weary look at Dash. "Are you sure you want to be more involved with all of this? We're one whole obnoxious package, unfortunately."

Dash was crying as he nodded. "I have never been more sure of anything in my life, but you might want to reserve judgment yourself until after the holidays. You might feel differently after a couple of days with my family."

Gavin's eyes narrowed as he considered. "I survived a weekend in the Tuckers' hillbilly hideaway in the Catskills. I'm sure Christmas in Connecticut with the Griffins will be a cakewalk after that." He hadn't given much thought to what would happen after Christmas Eve eve, he'd been so distracted with his father and preparations for the party. Now, there was a rush of nerves and slight regret for agreeing to go. But his family was important to Dash and staying in Swift and Hannah's good graces mattered more than Gavin's nerves and discomfort.

"Just keep in mind that there could be an actual cakewalk involved, my parents are even bigger holiday nerds than I am," Dash warned.

"I don't mind," Gavin replied dismissively.

In truth, Dash's unabashed holiday joy had rubbed off on Gavin. He fully enjoyed his turn as the besotted boyfriend, pretending to be put out every time Dash insisted that they kiss under the many mistletoe traps around the townhouse. Dash was in his element, passing out sweets and party favors, keeping the punch flowing, and helping Morris at the turntables. But he blew Gavin away when he opened the talent show portion of their evening with a soulful acoustic guitar rendition of "All I Want For Christmas Is You." Dash dedicated it to *his* secret Santa, making Gavin blush while everyone else tittered and giggled obnoxiously. It was common knowledge that Dash played the guitar and sang well, but Gavin was moved to tears by Dash's performance, especially when the children all joined in at the end.

"I'm afraid the rest of the show might be a bit of a letdown after that," Gavin murmured shakily into the microphone when it was time for him to take over and introduce Fin and Riley. But their medley of holiday classics, including a consent-filled remake of "Baby It's Cold Outside" and a cheeky "Edward Got Run Over By A Reindeer" was a hit and had caused Gavin to guffaw into his punch. Because it was a Fin and Riley production, there was dramatic lighting, smoke, and rolling desk chairs were utilized for a jazzy sugar plum sequence.

June's performance was a success as well, her first since taking up piano lessons, she played a duet of "Have Yourself A Merry Little Christmas" with Beatrice that Gavin thought was delightful. Then, Reid sat at the keys and dedicated an unnecessarily moving "Thank You For Being A Friend" to Gavin and their Briarwood Terrace family. Everyone was brought to tears before Reid picked up the tempo and turned it into a singalong that was followed by Penny singing and *performing* "Run Run Rudolph" in reindeer makeup and antlers with Dash accompanying on guitar.

Neither Walker nor Agnes played instruments well or sang and he always swore he didn't have anything to contribute. But all Agnes had to do was put a drink in his hand and the two of them were comedy gold.

"Knock knock," she said over her champagne.

He gave the room a weary sigh and sipped. "Who's there?"

"Olive."

"Olive, who?" Walker asked as he slid a hand into his pocket, looking resigned.

"Olive the other reindeer!" Agnes sang and he let out a groan.

"How old are we, Aggie?"

She was undeterred. "Knock knock!"

"Who's there?"

"Ho ho," she bellowed, making him frown into his glass.

"Ho ho, who?" He asked in confusion, earning a snort from Agnes.

"Seriously, Walker. That's the worst Santa impression I've ever heard."

"You're the worst."

"Me?" Agnes asked indignantly. "If you were a reindeer, you'd be *rude*-olph."

He held up a hand. "And you'd be blitzed."

"Don't you mean Blitzen?" She asked and he shook his head.

"No. I'd never confuse anyone for a reindeer because unlike you, I don't spend my days lit like a Christmas tree."

"You awful thing."

"That would make you awful Thing 2," he countered with a shrug. "Are we finished? I need another drink," he muttered as he wandered off.

Everyone was in tears except for Fin. "This is just the way

they always act," he complained and threw a hand at them. "Riley and I started preparing for this six weeks ago."

"What can I say?" Agnes replied with an airy gesture. "We're just *gifted.*"

"Anyways," Gavin said loudly and checked the grandfather clock in the hall. "It's getting late and we still have the big finale."

"It's 7:45, you ninny," Morris said as he sat in front of the tree with his trumpet. "We can edit that out." He pointed at Reid and Gavin was about to ask what he was talking about, then decided he didn't care as long as it didn't interfere with the finale.

"Where is my violinist?" He asked as he searched the little people.

"Here!" Amelia waved her bow above her head as she raced around the tree and got in place on Morris's other side. Beatrice was giving her fingers a test wiggle at the piano and Penny was holding the sheet music for Dash as he got comfortable on the floor with his acoustic guitar.

For Gavin, this moment never failed to touch him deeply and it was why he was willing to wrangle the triplets and put up with Fin and Riley's nonsense. He had goosebumps as he took his place next to Morris, cherishing memories of them together at Saint Ann's as children. That's when he found the first piece of his family and every Christmas Eve eve the number of players and instruments grew in their little holiday orchestra.

He cleared his throat so his voice would work. "Shall we?" He asked, then quietly counted them in.

Of course, it was a singalong and this was *his* family so the tone turned rowdy rather quickly. The gentlemen with the deeper registers sang "five golden rings" when it was time, making the song more comical and everyone was laughing and shouting along at the top of their lungs by the time it was done. But every now and then, Gavin would catch Morris wiping a tear from the corner of his eye and they put down their instruments and shared a tight hug at the end.

"Merry Christmas! I love you so much, man," Morris whispered before clapping Gavin on the back and passing him the microphone.

"Thank you. I...love you too, Morris," he said stiffly, then coughed as he composed himself. "Now, if anyone was keeping track, that was 184 birds, 140 people, 40 rings, and 12 trees."

"Only an accountant would keep track of that," Reid shouted, making everyone chuckle and murmur in agreement, but Gavin just waved it off.

It never hurt to learn more about a holiday classic. "There is also some debate," he continued. "As to whether the golden rings were actually rings, or birds as well. So, that would give us...?" He looked around, waiting for someone to guess. There were only blinks and clueless shrugs so he rolled his eyes. "A total of 224 birds, 140 people, and 12 trees."

"And I thought this place was crowded," Walker said, raising his glass and signaling the end of the singalong and the evening's festivities.

"Let's get you home, Mister Christmas," Dash said once they were done saying their goodbyes and gathering their gifts, instruments, and plates piled with leftovers.

"I think I'll head out," Reid decided once they were outside and their limo arrived. "I'm all dressed up and it would be a shame to let this go to waste," he said as he gestured at his green velvet dinner jacket and tuxedo pants. "See you two in the morning." He offered them a salute, then strolled off toward the Baccarat again, if Gavin had to guess.

"That's probably for the best," Dash said as they got into

the back of the car. "I've got a special surprise for you back at the house and I have a feeling it might get loud again."

"Excellent," Gavin murmured, smiling in anticipation as he joined Dash and they settled in for the short drive. Before, "loud" would have intimidated Gavin, but he was in safe hands with Dash and so far, he loved everything they had tried together.

His nerves bubbled pleasantly as they let themselves into Briarwood Terrace and unit number 4. Normally, Gavin returned alone and had little to look forward to but his left-overs. This time, they quickly put their plates in the fridge and were laughing and kissing as they stumbled into Gavin's bedroom.

Their bedroom.

Gavin remembered that this was Dash's place now, too, and his days of spending Christmas alone were through. And Christmas wasn't over yet! He still had the rest of Christmas Eve eve and all the days up to New Year's to bask in the holiday glow with Dash.

He captured Dash's hands as they reached for Gavin's tie and collar. "Thank you for giving me this precious gift." He kissed Dash tenderly, doing his best to express the deep love and gratitude he felt. "I thought I was happy before and had all that I needed. Now, all I need is you. And I intend to spend every Christmas making you as happy as you've made me."

"You're already off to a strong start!" Dash's laugh was watery as he kissed Gavin and backed him toward the bed. "I can't wait to start some traditions of our own."

The thought dazzled Gavin as he fell back against the pillows, unbuttoning and unzipping as Dash nipped at his lips, ears, and neck. He was still in his elf costume and had produced a small bag from under his side of the bed. There was no telling what Dash had in store for them, but Gavin loved that he could count on more delightfully naughty surprises in the future.

But Gavin's heart lurched to a halt and his tummy flipped when Dash revealed a hot pink vibrator and a pump bottle of lube. "It's time to learn a new carol, Mister Christmas," he said and pressed a button, giving it a test buzz.

"Are you sure? That's rather...large," Gavin squeaked when it was passed to him for an inspection.

"You will be fine," Dash promised, then winced apologetically. "Your new trousers on the other hand..."

"What's wrong with my—?" Gavin asked in alarm just as Dash gripped the halves of the fly and ripped the crotch open.

"I owe you a new pair. I've been waiting to do this all night."

Gavin's boxers received the same treatment and he was stunned as he blinked down at his wrecked suit. "I don't mind," he decided, reaching for Dash and pulling him into a wildly joyful kiss.

"Good, because you're about to sing louder than you've ever sung before," Dash boasted as he wiggled his brows and lowered his head. His tongue flicked Gavin's nipple before he sucked and was rewarded with an appreciative groan.

"Whatever you want!" Gavin swept his hands through Dash's hair, reveling in the silky softness and the warmth of his body and his breath as it wafted over his skin. He exalted in the goosebumps and the heat, cherishing the magic of touching Dash and being touched by him. There was no way that Gavin could hold back when Dash's tongue washed up his ribs and into his armpit, making him gasp and moan. He wanted to sing as Dash slid lower and nuzzled his shaft and sac and parted his thighs, but all Gavin could muster were shredded pleas and sobs as his asscheeks were covered in greedy kisses. "Oh, fucking Christ!" His head lolled on the pillows as Dash sucked on his hole and drilled with his tongue. How was he ever supposed to be quiet when Dash was doing *that*?

"Hang onto your stockings," Dash whispered, sliding his tongue up Gavin's cock and giving the head a long, lazy suck. Slick fingers pushed into Gavin's hole, slowly twisting and stretching and setting him on fire.

"Fuck!" Gavin clawed at the duvet, holding on for dear life as Dash took him deep into his throat and sucked harder. A soft buzzing was all the warning Gavin had before the tip of the vibrator nudged into his ass. "Oh!" He looked down, fascinated and wildly aroused by the sight of Dash working the pink silicone cock in and out. The soft buzzing spread through his core and there was a pleasant warmth in his sac as pre-cum leaked from the head of his erection.

"Let's see how you like this..." Dash said, easing the vibrator deeper and angling it upwards.

"Dash!" Gavin cried when it hit his prostate and Dash's lips closed around his shaft, wrapping it in slick, sucking heat. He heard two soft clicks, dialing up the intensity of the vibration until Gavin's teeth rattled and his eyes rolled. "Yes! Don't stop!" His legs began to shake and his feet curled into tight fists as wave after wave of glittering delight swirled through Gavin. It radiated from his groin and grew brighter with each slide of Dash's lips and thrust of the vibrator. The pressure in his ass and sac built and built until Gavin's nerves burst and his soul leaped from his body. "Oh God, Dash!" For just a moment, he was as light as the flakes in a snow globe. He giggled deliriously as Dash rose and yanked down his yellow tights, freeing his cock and quickly coating it with lube.

"That was the sexiest thing I've ever seen," Dash panted, settling over Gavin, then filling him with slick, driving heat. "I'm about to come so hard." His hands closed around Gavin's ass as Dash rolled his hips and the room went up in flames.

Gavin came again, screaming Dash's name as a hot rush flooded his core.

"Dear Lord..." Gavin said dazedly when their breathing finally settled and the smoke cleared. "That was...incredible."

"Mmmm..." Dash agreed, running a finger through the cum on Gavin's chest and sucking it clean. "So incredible."

But a slight frown creased Gavin's brow as he traced the curve of one of Dash's asscheeks and gave it a possessive squeeze. "It's just that I had planned to rip *your* tights off tonight," he said, pouting slightly.

"Awww..." Dash moaned sympathetically as he pecked at Gavin's lips. "There's always next Christmas Eve eve," he said, giving Gavin something new and wondrous to look forward to next year.

Chapter Twenty-Two

Reid had materialized bright and early on Christmas Eve morning, much to Dash and Gavin's surprise. He was whistling cheerfully as he prepared coffee, tea, French toast, and bacon, the heavenly aromas luring them into pajamas and out of Gavin's room.

"Shouldn't you be at your parents'? You usually head to Park Slope after the party," Gavin observed as he was handed a cup of tea.

Reid laughed it off as he spun back around with the French press for Dash and filled his mug. "I had to come home and change. Couldn't turn up in last night's suit and reeking of scotch. And I have something I'd like to give Dash before I take off," he added with a gentle smile for Dash.

"But you already got me a gift! I love my new Converse!" They were black and had Dash's name and cool little flames embroidered on the sides.

"Good." Reid quickly plated their food and ordered them to take a seat. "I'm glad that Gavin's finally asked you to move in with us," Reid said as he sat and pulled his chair closer to

209

Dash's. A folder was on the table and Gavin looked curious as Reid flipped it open and pointed at a form.

"What are you talking about?" Dash laughed as he sat forward and read. "We *just* started dating."

"Maybe as far as the rest of the world is concerned, but it's been settled in my mind for ages," Reid said, ignoring Gavin's irritated huff. He held up a pen and smiled at Dash. "I want to make it official and make you a partner in the agency."

"A partner?" Dash's jaw fell as he quickly read the one-page contract.

"Let's be real, you're great with kids but your heart's not in childcare either," Reid said gently. "But you're dedicated to this agency, our nannies, and our clients. You've become my right hand and I don't think I could manage all of this without you now, we've grown so much in just a few short years." Reid waved the pen at Dash and gave him a hopeful look. "What do you say?"

"I..." Dash nodded and looked at Gavin. "What do you think?"

He used two fingers to slide the contract closer and scanned it. "I think it's all pretty straightforward and is warranted, considering all you do for us and the agency."

"Great!" Dash said weakly, feeling ridiculously over-whelmed. "I love everything about what I do here and it's felt like a dream, having someplace where I can just be me and help people and families like ours."

Reid gave Dash's hand an affectionate squeeze. "That's why you fit so well and why you're the partner I need to run this agency."

"Okay!" Dash signed without hesitation. The more he thought about taking a more active role and running the agency at Reid's side, the more excited and certain he felt.

"Excellent," Gavin stated, sliding his plate to the side. "If that's settled, there's something else I've been meaning to discuss with the two of you."

"Oh?" Reid's brow cocked as he swiped the contract and the file off the table and gave Gavin his undivided attention.

Dash turned and leaned in, ready to learn what their new adventure would be. "What's on your mind?"

"Heathcote," Gavin said simply, but Dash and Reid could only blink back at him. He snorted at Reid and shook his head. "I'm not burning it down. I'd like to turn it into a...shelter, of sorts, for queer high school and college students whose families have abandoned them. Young people who are in that in-between phase and still need support as they're finding their way in the world. I want to give them a place to stay and help them continue their education and find jobs so they can land safely on their feet."

"I'm in," Dash said, nodding as he snatched Gavin's hand. "Let's do it!"

"I love it," Reid stated with a decisive thump on the table as he rose and went to pace in the middle of the kitchen. "You and Walker can figure out how to fund all the scholarships and Dash and I can work on the application process and get that up and running," he said, planning out loud. "How many rooms at Heathcote?" He asked Gavin.

"Twelve... I think."

"I bet Agnes and her people can turn it into sixteen," Reid mused and rubbed his hands together. "We've got *a lot* of space to work with and put to good use. And Penny can help us find counselors and support staff because she already has great contacts within the foster care system. I'm sure she knows some queer former foster kids who would be a great fit to work at Heathcote."

Dash made a loud whooping sound and clapped. "I love our team so much! I really don't think there's anything we can't do," he boasted, feeling incredibly proud as he sat back because they were officially his team now, too.

"I think you might be right," Gavin murmured as he returned to his French toast. "I think I can leave you two to sort out the finer details. Let me know when it's time to talk about our finances."

"Yes, leave it all to us," Reid agreed, growing distant before turning and hurrying into the hallway. "I need to make some notes and find some phone numbers," he said as he left them.

"He'll have it up and running in a week," Dash predicted, earning a satisfied sigh from Gavin. "It's a brilliant idea."

Gavin shook his head. "No, it was more like a solution to a problem I didn't want to deal with," Gavin said to his paper. "I promised I wouldn't sell it, but I have no desire to ever step foot on the property again. A much wiser man than me suggested I give spite a try."

"Oh, spite! Nice!" Dash said excitedly, then gasped. "It was me! I told you to try spite!" He recalled and Gavin hummed and winked as he chewed.

"It was you and I'm finding it to be much more effective than suffering."

"You don't say..." Dash replied as he sipped his coffee. "Someone's back on the naughty list," he sang and whipped around in his seat when they heard the buzzer.

Reid looked at them as he came out of his room and went to answer it, but Dash and Gavin both shrugged. "Hello? It's Christmas Eve. What could possibly be this important?"

"It's Nickerson with Davis & Ellis," a dry voice replied. "I need to speak with Mr. Selby."

"Oh, no," Dash whispered as he stood and looked at Gavin.

He let out a heavy sigh as he set down his teacup and rose. "It's alright, Dash. I've made my peace with this," he said steadily, his head high as he went to greet Nickerson.

"Are you sure you're okay?" Reid asked, guarding the door. "I can tell him to come back after you've had some time."

"I don't need time. Let him in," Gavin said gently but firmly.

Dash was right behind Gavin when Reid opened the door and Mr. Nickerson bowed over the threshold. "Sir," Nickerson said solemnly to Gavin and offered Reid and Dash polite nods. "It is my unfortunate duty to inform you that your father passed away early this morning. Davis & Ellis offers you its deepest condolences and have sent me to deliver this," he said as he removed a thick envelope from inside his coat. "The entirety of the Selby estate, including Heathcote and the property in Bridgehampton, has been left to you. Davis & Ellis hopes you will remember that we are here for you in your time of mourning and await your instructions, sir," he said as he backed away.

Gavin nodded slowly as he processed. "Thank you. I will get back to you after New Year's," he replied and reached for the door.

"There is one thing, sir." Nickerson cleared his throat awkwardly. "Your father was unable to write to you himself, but he wanted you to know that he enjoyed the video and was glad to see that everything turned out so well for you. And that he was sorry it took him so long to see the error of his ways."

"Thank you!" Dash whispered to whichever Christmas ghost was responsible for Edward's change of heart. It would have taken a lot more than a video to pull off a miracle like this.

"I see..." Gavin replied, his brow furrowed as he turned to look at Dash and Reid. They both winced and shrugged sheepishly. Gavin gave his head a shake and regarded Nickerson. "Thank you for that. In regards to my wishes for the estate, Heathcote is no longer a private residence and is now in Mr. Marshall's and Mr. Griffin's control. From now on, you will refer to Heathcote as Briarwood House and forward all inquiries to them," he said and moved to close the door.

Nickerson offered Gavin a deferential nod. "Very well, sir. I will notify my superiors and see to that immediately. Is there anything else I can do to assist you?"

Gavin blinked at Nickerson, looking both irritated and confused before shaking his head. "That will be all for now. I'll be in touch after New Year's, once I've had a chance to get my head around this," he said, then allowed Reid to shut the door. The moment stretched as Gavin's eyelids flickered and his brow slowly rose as he regarded Reid. "Did you and Morris...?"

"It was a group effort," Reid replied with an apologetic cringe. "But it was mostly me and Morris with a little help from Agnes," he said and there was another long pause before Gavin smiled at him.

"Thank you. I'm going to finish my breakfast and get ready to go to Connecticut. I haven't had a chance to pack yet."

Reid and Dash stood back and watched in shared awe as Gavin returned to his seat by the window and draped his napkin over his lap. "What do you think?" Reid asked out of the side of his mouth.

"I think he's handling it well," Dash said.

"Good. Keep an eye on him and let me know if anything changes."

Dash snorted and held up a hand. "On it."

"Thanks, Dash," Reid said as he slapped it. "I knew I could count on you. Don't forget, you still have your mission," he added, heading back to his room.

"You don't have to tell me how to do my job," Dash said playfully, striding back to the kitchen to shower Gavin in love and support. The very last thing Gavin would want was to talk about his father or Heathcote so Dash went to the counter for the teapot. "You know, Riley and Giles are hosting New Year's at the Olympia but I was thinking we should swing by the Stonewall Inn for drinks and drag queens first. It won't get too busy until closer to midnight," he said, topping off Gavin's cup.

Gavin nodded and smiled. "I think I'd enjoy that. I've never been but I do admire drag queens."

"Our bravest soldiers," Dash said with a jaunty salute. He got a little emotional whenever he thought about drag queens and how strong they were. "Serving style, grace, and face despite ignorance and hate."

"Truly," Gavin murmured while stirring sugar into his tea. "We should all do more to support them."

"Amen," Dash said as he sat on the bench next to Gavin.

"Thank you," Gavin said softly, his hand curling around Dash's on the table. "All I want is to move forward with you and put that part of the past behind me."

"That sounds like a great idea," Dash said, nodding firmly. "And I know just how to start." He slid from his seat and held out his hand to Gavin. "There's something I'd like to show you in the bedroom."

Gavin's brows jumped and his eyes went to the clock over the stove. "Now? It's only been...six hours since we last... And we have to leave by 9:30 because you promised your mother we'd be there for lunch," he whispered, but Dash gestured dismissively.

"That's plenty of time and I don't think this is going to take long. I was planning to let you use the vibrator on me," he said, then laughed when Gavin nearly flipped over the table, he was in such a rush as he bundled Dash out of the kitchen and into the bedroom.

Chapter Twenty-Three

"That was the most beautiful thing I have ever seen."

There was no doubt in Gavin's mind as he licked the cum from Dash's stomach and chest. Watching Dash beg and undulate on the bed as Gavin slowly fucked him with the vibrator had been fascinating and incredibly erotic. He had a whole new understanding of sex as he explored Dash's body with his hands, his lips, and the vibrator. Instead of getting lost in the lust and heat, Gavin was able to facilitate Dash's pleasure and see his orgasm slowly building until he was quivering and begging for relief.

He came, praising Gavin and babbling words of love. And Dash had even sworn!

"I feel beautiful," Dash sighed dreamily, threading his fingers through Gavin's hair and pulling him up for a kiss. "Thank you."

"No. Thank you, thank you, thank you," Gavin whispered as he settled over Dash.

"What about you?"

A sly smile tilted Gavin's lips. "When I say it was the most beautiful thing I have ever seen..." He widened his eyes suggestively. "I barely had to touch myself." It required less than two strokes, Gavin had been so hard and so aroused as he sucked on Dash's sac and listened to him whimper.

"Really?" Dash chuckled as he rolled them. He rested his forehead on Gavin's, sighing heavily. "Are you okay? I don't want to bring you down, but a lot has happened this morning."

Gavin nodded slowly, sifting through his feelings. "I'm okay, perhaps a bit numb about my father because..." He frowned, not liking that he felt very little. "I didn't care about the money when he disowned me. I was nineteen and I would have found a way, even if Henry hadn't been there to save me. It was how little I *mattered* and how easy it was for him to snatch away my security and my very identity. As far as the rest of the world was concerned, I was no longer Edward Selby's son. I had a name, but it meant nothing and I had no family except Reid and Morris and Penn. And he tried to take them away from me too."

"I'm so sorry!" Dash said as he kissed Gavin.

"Shhh!" Gavin swept Dash's tears away and pecked at his lips. "I had to accept that I didn't have parents when my father kicked me out of Heathcote and *so many* letters to my mother went unanswered. There's nothing I can do with my father's apology because he waited too long to deliver it. I can't tell him it's too little too late or tell him I forgive him. He took that away from me too. So, it seems...pointless to dwell on his passing or what could have been. Especially when I have so many *good* things in my life to be grateful for." He chuckled softly, recalling various hilarious and touching moments from the party and regretting that he couldn't have seen his father's reaction. "Which he did get to see before he passed."

Dash hissed and winced apologetically. "You're not mad about that?"

"No." Gavin shook his head. "Frankly, I'm relieved that Reid handled it all as well as he did. That stunt with the video had all the hallmarks of a classic Reid Marshall comeuppance, but it could have been a lot worse. He had every right to take my father's behavior and my lack of honesty personally."

"He could have, but he loves you," Dash said simply. "And he knows you did it all to protect him, to protect all of us. That's the only reason you'd ever lie to Reid."

Gavin laughed in disbelief as he wound his arms around Dash. "Thank you for understanding me so well. And me and Reid, because I don't think anyone else could."

"I meant what I said, I think your friendship is beautiful and it's one of the things I love most about you. You're so loyal to Reid and you'd sacrifice literally everything to keep your friends happy. That's super sexy, to me, and there aren't a lot of people who could understand or appreciate me and Penny," Dash countered with a satisfied nod, earning a hard snort from Gavin.

"I regret to inform you that I am not one of them. I rarely understand what goes on in your delightfully wacky brains or how two people your age can have that much energy. But it's one of the things I love most about you," he added, kissing Dash with all the gratitude he could muster. With the exception of the part where his father died, it truly was the happiest Christmas of Gavin's life. Each moment with Dash felt like a gift and Gavin would cherish every memory. "In fact..." Gavin glanced at the closet and smiled. "Wait here for a moment," he said, easing out of Dash's arms and backing off the bed. "I want to give you one of your presents now, while it's just the two of us."

Dash's face and eyes lit up. "You got me a special gift too?" He rolled off the bed, snatching his pajama pants off the floor and hopping into them on the way to the door. "Be right back!"

He bolted from the room and Gavin chuckled softly to himself as he went to the closet and retrieved the blue velvet jewelry box from his luggage. Dash had one as well when he hurried back into the room and swung the door shut behind him.

It was black and a bit larger than a deck of cards and Dash blushed as he studied the box in his hands. "I thought about giving this to you at the party last night, but can you imagine if one of us had pulled out a jewelry box?" He asked, widening his eyes at Gavin.

"Dear Lord..." Gavin felt too hot and was getting a headache just thinking of the pandemonium that would ensue. "Could you please promise me that any...important questions will be asked privately. Or with just a *few* people present," he offered, whispering a silent prayer.

"You don't have to worry about that," Dash said with one of his heartstopping winks. "These were a... private, you and me thing so I decided to wait until we were alone," he said as he held it out to Gavin.

"That's why I waited too, but I love the mittens you gave me," Gavin insisted, passing his box to Dash. "You go first," he said and Dash nodded, but he stared at the blue velvet box. "What's wrong?" Gavin asked.

"Nothing!" Dash stepped closer so he could kiss Gavin. "I was so sure that you were the one and I *hoped* that we would be boyfriends by Christmas. But this still feels like a dream."

"If it is, I never want to wake up," Gavin stated. He had quietly yearned for Dash for so long, the last two weeks of Gavin's life had felt like a beautifully vivid fantasy. And it had all seemed impossible and Gavin was so frightened that he'd get caught, he still had a hard time believing this was *his* life and that Dash was truly his. "You make every day feel like a dream and I will cherish our first Christmas together."

Dash pressed a tearful, sniffling kiss to Gavin's lips. "Me

too. This has been one of the best Christmases ever." He took a deep breath and opened the box and Dash's lip began to wobble as he inspected the small platinum-dipped sprig of mistletoe.

"I broke off a piece from the one you gave me, from our kiss in the courtyard, and left it with Penn," Gavin explained. "I asked him to make some sort of keepsake out of it for me."

"It's beautiful!" Dash sniffled as he traced the stem, leaves, and berries. "It's the most beautiful gift anyone has ever given me and I'll treasure it as much as I treasure that kiss."

"It was a hell of a kiss," Gavin agreed bashfully, growing warm again at the memory. He gave himself a shake, then opened his box and gasped at the two sets of silver cufflinks. One was a set of teacups and the other a set of disposable coffee cups. "They're wonderful. I love them, Dash."

"I *knew* you would!" Dash said excitedly, pointing around the box's lid. "I saw the teacups and thought of you, but I also wanted you to have the little latte ones for when you feel like being a pumpkin spice guy."

"They're perfect," Gavin said, sincerely touched by the fine details and quality craftsmanship. They were just the right amount of "quirky" that Gavin enjoyed adding to his ensembles and they would remind him of their first Christmas together whenever he wore them. "And I will always want to be a pumpkin spice guy with you."

"Wow!" Dash sounded breathless as he offered his lips. "You're getting really good at this romantic Christmas business, Mr. Selby. I'm supposed to be sweeping you off of your feet."

"I always feel like I've been swept off my feet whenever you walk into the room," Gavin said, earning an adoring groan from Dash. He tried to tumble them back onto the bed but Gavin slipped free and wagged a finger at Dash. "We'll have to save the rest of this for later. I have a little over an hour to finish packing and get dressed."

"It's just two nights at my parents' place," Dash argued. "It's not *that* far and it's not like we're leaving civilization. We're going to Connecticut."

Gavin cast Dash a stern look as he headed for the closet. "I have never had a boyfriend or spent Christmas with his parents. I am venturing into the unknown in Connecticut and I would rather be over-prepared than underdressed."

"I suppose..." Dash said as he flopped onto the bed, hugging the jewelry box.

Ten minutes later, Gavin felt underdressed and slightly disoriented as he emerged from his closet in a hoodie, jeans, and sneakers.

"Whoa," Dash exclaimed as he scrambled off the bed for a closer look. "Where did you even get those?"

"This?" Gavin pulled the front of his Columbia hoodie away from his body and inspected it. "At school..." He answered warily. "I don't wear it very often, but I have a few for more casual occasions like car travel."

"But you're wearing jeans and Sambas!" Dash pointed at Gavin's black soccer sneakers, agog. "I didn't even know you owned shoes with rubber soles."

"Should I change?" Gavin asked, already turning back to his closet.

Dash grabbed Gavin and spun him. "No! You look perfect! In fact..." He tried to get his hands under the hoodie, but Gavin slapped them away.

"You said we'd be there by lunch and I'm already worried about the traffic."

"Come on. Give me half an hour," Dash begged, but Gavin turned him and launched him through the bedroom door.

"We need to leave in fifteen minutes. Get dressed and get your car and meet me out front."

"But it's Christmas Eve! And I have another present for you," Dash attempted rakishly but Gavin shook his head and pointed toward the front door.

"I'm forty-two, Dash. It's going to be a few hours before that trick will work on me."

"Fine. It's probably for the best," Dash conceded. "Dad's already got a dozen bad jokes loaded up and ready to go. He'd know we're late because of a last-minute 'gift exchange' and there's no way he'd miss an opportunity to embarrass me. Not when there are so many holiday double entendres to play with."

"Get. Ready. Dash," Gavin ordered as he pointed at Dash's bag hanging by the door. "Or I will leave you and go to Connecticut by myself."

"Alright! I'll be ready in ten," Dash said, sounding like he was ten-years-old as he trudged off.

There was an amused chuckle as Reid joined Gavin. He was appropriately dressed—to Gavin's relief—for a cozy family holiday in a flannel, a Henley, and jeans and was smiling and relaxed as he dropped his overnight bag on the sofa. "I can't tell you how much better this feels than leaving you alone for Christmas," he said, rubbing his hands together happily.

"Stop it. I was fine," Gavin murmured as he went to finish packing. "I never wanted you to feel sorry for me."

"Wait." Reid caught Gavin's elbow and turned him. "Before I take off, I want you to know that I love you and I won't forget how much you've sacrificed for all of us. And I know you have Dash now and you probably don't need me anymore, but I'm always going to be here to take care of you."

"I know," Gavin said, sighing wearily as he was pulled into a tight embrace. He closed his eyes, thanking fate for their friendship and giving him the strength to hang onto Reid no matter how hard his father tried to pull them apart. "I love you too," he said, clapping Reid on the back. "But I need to finish packing or we'll be late."

Reid laughed as he pushed Gavin away. "Fine. Go and enjoy Connecticut and let Hannah and Swift know that they're part of the family now, too. We're expecting them at the next Christmas Eve eve."

"Thank you," Gavin said warmly. "I'll let them know."

With that, Reid gathered his overnight bag and departed. Gavin lingered for a moment, taking stock and feeling absurdly blessed. Half of his heart was off to Park Slope and the other half was in the shower, singing "All I Want For Christmas Is Gavin."

"How is this my life?" He laughed as he wiped the tears from his cheeks.

He didn't think he needed more and Gavin didn't want anything to change before Dash started making his lists. Gavin didn't think it was possible to hold onto Reid and find room in his heart and his life to love anyone else, but his world was so much bigger and brighter now, thanks to Dash.

"I definitely need my poinsettia tie and the candy cane pocket square," Gavin murmured to himself as he went to finish packing. "I want to look extra festive."

Chapter Twenty-Four

Fifteen minutes later, they were on their way out of the city to Connecticut. Dash was thrilled because he was finally bringing someone home for the holidays for a family Christmas with his parents. But he was also worried this would be too much for Gavin, given the traumatic nature of his relationship with his parents and all that had happened that morning. He wondered if it would have been better to postpone and use the next year to slowly acclimate Gavin to the Griffins to avoid the parental culture shock.

Gavin surprised Dash, though, insisting he was ready and *wanted* to please Dash's parents. He studiously peppered Dash with questions, attempting to remember names and family connections like he was preparing to meet a prime minister or royalty.

"Should I avoid mentioning your mother's more...Irish connections?"

"You don't have to, but Mom will just pretend she didn't hear you or be extremely vague," Dash said with a shrug. "It's not that we don't want to talk about the mobsters in our family tree, we're just not proud of them and that part of our history because it's shameful and shouldn't be celebrated."

"Got it," Gavin said seriously as if he were keeping a mental checklist. "What about religion? Your mother is Catholic and your father is Protestant."

That made Dash laugh. "You're really overthinking this! But Dad converted for Mom. Wikipedia doesn't know because it would have been a bigger deal in Michigan back in the '80s so it's our 'dark' Griffin secret. Neither of them are really religious, though. My grandparents wanted my mom to have a proper Irish Catholic wedding and marry a Catholic boy and Dad was willing to do whatever it took to make them happy."

Gavin's head snapped toward Dash's. "That makes sense."

"Does it?"

"I'd convert but my parents were Catholic. I don't know if they ever went to Mass or stepped foot in a church for that matter, but you could tell them I'm Catholic," Gavin suggested helpfully.

"That's fine because you're about as Catholic as they are. We stopped going after my Grandma Jane passed away. But don't worry! You already met my parents and they love you."

"We met at brunch, once."

"I've told them *everything* about you. Like, about your dad and you and Reid," Dash whispered, wincing apologetically. "I didn't go into any detail, but I called my mom the morning after. After we did it again."

"Dear God, why?" Gavin choked out, looking ill.

"We're really close, me and my parents. Dad will make everything corny and Mom has a way of getting stuff out of you, you'll see."

Gavin cut his eyes at Dash and snorted. "I already have a pretty good idea."

"Yup. This apple did not fall far from the tree," Dash said

proudly. His pride was at a fever pitch when he took the exit into Greenwich. Everything looked picture-perfect like it did every year, but Dash was thrilled because this was *his* Hallmark moment. He was bringing someone home for the first time and Dash was expecting a thoroughly romantic and occasionally awkward family Christmas, but Gavin appeared to be along for the ride. "We'll come back tonight so you can see all the trees lit up," Dash said as he steered down Greenwich Avenue, pointing out his favorite shops. He felt like he was made of confetti and fairy lights and he had to be glowing. They were nearly home and he couldn't wait to get down to Christmas business. There were several presents in the back of the car for Gavin and his parents and Dash was looking forward to seeing all the lights at night as a family.

"This looks like something out of a fairytale," Gavin said as he turned in the passenger seat. "It's almost too clean."

Dash winced at the rearview mirror, noting the cars parked along the sidewalks. Most of them were Range Rovers and other high-end SUVs. In the spring and summer, there would be more convertibles. They were currently in a Range Rover but it was the car Dash had learned to drive in when he was sixteen. He was one of the few of his friends who had a car and a driver's license and the Range Rover came in handy when Penn and Penny wanted to head up to the cabin.

"Isn't Scarsdale pretty nice?" Dash was self-aware enough to feel self-conscious about how wealthy his family was.

Gavin made a dismissive sound, distracted by something outside his window. "It's been a long time since I've been, but it was a lot like this."

"A small apartment in an old townhouse in Manhattan sounds like heaven as far as I'm concerned."

"Good." Gavin's hand rose and his pinkie extended,

brushing against Dash's hand on the gear shifter. "I like watching you drive."

"Do you?" Confetti and snow should have shot out of Dash's mouth and ears, he felt like he'd swallowed a whole parade float. "We should take a road trip."

"A road trip?"

"Yeah! Just you and me and a bunch of audiobooks and snacks!" Dash stopped at the light and turned so he could pull Gavin's chin around for a kiss. "You would love Ann Arbor and we could be super pumpkin spice latte guys and play in the leaves. If you think I'm obnoxious now, wait until the leaves start changing."

"Don't your father's parents live in Ann Arbor?" Gavin asked suspiciously.

"They do!" Dash pretended he forgot for half a heartbeat, then nudged Gavin with his elbow. "They're really nice and way more low-key than Dad. And, oh my God!" He snatched Gavin's hand excitedly. "We have to go up to Marquette for the Northern Lights if we're being pumpkin spice guys. My grand-parents have a cabin up there and it'll take your breath away," he said and Gavin smiled and nodded.

"I'm starting to get used to that when I'm with you."

For a moment, Dash wished they were headed somewhere more private like the cabin in Marquette. "Hang onto that thought, okay? I really want to kiss you and keep kissing you until our clothes fall off, but it's going to be a few hours until we'll be alone like that."

"Okay," Gavin said, ducking his head and blushing.

"And if you want to repeat that part about getting used to being breathless around my parents, that would send them right over the moon and I'd be morally obligated to blow you later," he added.

Gavin's head bobbled jerkily. "Okay."

"In the meantime, brace yourself," Dash whispered as he turned onto the long drive that led to his parents' place.

"Why...?" Gavin asked, rocking in his seat to see through the trees and they both gasped when they saw the house and the front lawn.

The sprawling French chateau-inspired estate hadn't surprised Dash because that had been his home away from the city his whole life. Nor was he as shocked as Gavin to see so many decorations. It was the sight of Gavin's name in large, swirly red and green letters, painted on planks of distressed wood that read "Merry Christmas, Gavin!" and another said "Welcome To The Family!"

"Are...those real? Are those actual wooden signs?" Gavin sounded alarmed.

"They are, but don't panic."

"Don't panic..." Gavin's head slowly swiveled back around so he could mouth a silent "What the hell?" "Your parents have wooden signs as tall as me with my name painted on them, but I won't panic."

"I told her not to do too much," Dash groaned as he parked. "Look... Dad and I have done our best to hide it, but Mom's a compulsive crafter," he explained. "She's been on this sign kick for the last few years so you'll probably be getting one as a gift. Or four," Dash guessed.

Gavin blinked at the window. "A compulsive crafter? Why do you make it sound like she needs a support group?"

"I think she might," Dash admitted. "Her 'she shed' started out as a corner in her office, but Dad just had the whole basement turned into a craft...factory for Mom. You'll understand when you see all the signs."

"There are more?" Gavin asked, making Dash giggle as he nodded.

"These are just the beginning. My favorites are the

cheerful reminders in the bathrooms. 'Wash your hands, put down the seat, make sure you leave it neat!'"

"Shouldn't you wash your hands after you put down the seat?" Gavin asked and Dash winced.

"I wouldn't get caught up on order or readability. They're more...inspirational?" Dash attempted. "Mom's switched everything up for the holidays. But the rest of the year, the theme is rustic rainbows. Which is great, but also a little strange if you think about it because the aesthetic is basically 'Hey, look! Our son likes to have sex with boys too!'"

"It could be worse," Gavin said with a loaded look, then pointed at the sign in the flowerbed. "I don't understand that one. It's just three words and I don't know which order they go in because the middle word is bigger. Is it first or do we read it from top to bottom? Is it 'festive, fun family'? Or 'fun, festive family'?"

"Mom makes a lot of those and I like to think of them sort of like Venn diagrams of good things. "

"I see... And we've been spotted," Gavin said when Dash's parents came out and waved at them from the front door.

"Listen, they're going to be over the top about this. Clearly," Dash said, gesturing at the front lawn. "But they'll settle—"

"It's fine, Dash," Gavin said firmly, cutting him off. "*All* I want is for them to like me and it looks like they've already decided they do. Or, at least they're pretending they do and I think that's...*wonderful*."

Dash felt a little guilty for being embarrassed by his parents' enthusiasm but hoped they didn't overdo it and scare Gavin. "I think you're wonderful." Dash stretched over the center console for a kiss and Gavin leaned away.

"But they can see us!"

Dash laughed and grabbed the front of Gavin's hoodie. "Want to make my mom's Christmas?"

"By kissing her son?"

"I guarantee there's something in her she shed with a silhouette of two boys kissing on it and she's just waiting for a name to stencil next to mine."

"That's very odd," Gavin murmured, craning his neck and cautiously offering his lips.

Dash chuckled in agreement as he cradled Gavin's cheek and nibbled. "It's too late to back out now." He angled his head, taking the kiss deeper and giving his parents just a little more romance, and thought he heard his mom audibly swooning from the door.

Gavin looked dazed and his cheeks were pink when Dash released him to turn off the car. "I don't want to. I can pretend to be fun and festive," he said while checking his hair in the mirror.

"You look great and I want you to just be yourself. I love you and that's enough for them, but they're going to fall in love with you too." Dash booped Gavin's nose, then reached behind him to open his door. "Let's go!"

"There's my baby!" Hannah raced down the steps to meet Dash as he came around the car.

"You just saw me a few days ago," he said, bending at the waist so he could hug her when she ran to him.

"I'm always excited when my baby comes home." She held onto his face and searched his eyes. "You haven't been getting enough sleep, but we know what that's about."

"Mom!" Dash laughed as she kissed him, then turned and held out her arms as she went around to Gavin's side. "Welcome, Gavin!"

Dash's father had a huge grin and an even bigger hug ready for Dash. "Get over here, rocket!" He was waving and limping down the front steps to meet him. Swift let out an aching, but delighted groan as he pulled Dash into a tight embrace. "Now, it's Christmas," he declared, wrapping an arm around Dash's shoulders.

"Thank you, Mrs. Griffin," Gavin murmured when she complimented his luggage. He didn't need a large suitcase and a carry-on size toiletry bag for two nights, but Gavin was definitely prepared for *any* situation. All Dash had brought was his phone charger and gifts for Gavin and his parents. He still kept a whole wardrobe and toiletries in his suite.

"Please, I told you to call me Hannah or Mom," she insisted, hugging Gavin's arm and leading him into the house. "Dash told us about your father and we're so sorry. I understand if it's too soon or too difficult to talk about his passing, but we want you to know that you are loved and this is a safe place for you, Gavin."

Dash sighed and shook his head at Swift. "So much for easing him into it," he said, but Gavin nodded down at Hannah.

"I promise, I'm fine. But think I might like to call you... Mom," he managed and Dash and Hannah shared watery gasps.

"Oh, you sweet boy!" She sniffled up at Gavin. "Dash said you like tea so I put a pot on. Come and tell me all about your trip. Was the traffic bad coming out of the city?"

Forget the float, Dash was happy enough to power an entire parade as he watched them go. "Now, that is a Christmas miracle," he said to his father.

"We're so glad to have the two of you here with us. We can tell he's a good man. You're always happier when you talk about him and it's great to finally get to see you two together."

"Start getting used to it. I have a feeling Mom won't let me come up here without him," Dash predicted, making Swift laugh.

"She's way ahead of you, rocket. Your mom's in there trying

to wring a wedding date out of him. We hired a sleigh to take you two for a ride tonight and I told them to throw in a bottle of champagne just in case," he said with a suggestive brow wiggle.

"Oh, no!" Dash groaned. "It's way too soon! She'll freak him out," he said, taking off for the kitchen to rescue Gavin.

Chapter Twenty-Five

I t was his forty-second Christmas morning but it was the first time Gavin had woken up feeling a sense of anticipation and actual joy. Christmas Eve with the Griffins had been filled with so much laughter and warmth, Gavin's sides still ached and he'd awoken with a silly grin on his face. The surprise sleigh ride was a touch odd because Gavin couldn't flirt with or kiss Dash with a large man in a Santa hat sitting just a few feet away. But it was a lovely gesture on Swift and Hannah's part and the ride through the snowy woods at sunset was delightful. After, they strolled with Dash's parents, taking in the lights and singing along with carolers before heading back home for Christmas cookies, mulled wine, and an exhilarating game of holiday charades.

Dash's parents had attempted to smother Gavin with understanding and kindness throughout the evening. But instead of being mortified or overwhelmed, Gavin was grateful and determined to make the most of every moment with the Griffins. He was acutely aware of the fact that if it weren't for

Dash, he'd be spending Christmas alone at Briarwood Terrace with nothing but his tea and yesterday's paper for company. He simply refused to take all the warmth and generosity he'd been shown for granted.

Dash was still sleeping peacefully next to Gavin, hugging his pillow and smiling. A check of the clock on the bedside table revealed that it was only 6:30, too early for Gavin to wander the house in search of tea. Gavin decided to explore Dash's childhood bedroom while he waited, easing out of the bed and pulling on a pair of pajama pants.

According to Dash, very little had changed in the three-room suite, aside from the bed. It was upgraded to a king when he and Penny grew out of his bunk bed and she started staying in one of the guest rooms. Gavin smiled as he scanned the band and comic posters and the dozens of pictures of Dash and Penny and their many adventures.

There were so many of them as children and Gavin got oddly emotional at the photos of Fin and Riley as high schoolers, camping and performing in plays and musicals with Dash and Penny. Gavin and Reid had been in college and starting their careers and had missed out on many of those moments. Gavin hadn't been there to witness the early days of their friendship and it was magical to get this glimpse of them.

His eyes practically fell out of his head when he picked up a copy of *Sports Illustrated* with a young Dash on the cover. Gavin threw a stunned glance at the bed where Dash was now sprawled on his back and happily sleeping, then flipped open the magazine. Almost none of the bold headlines and glossy images made sense to Gavin as he searched the contents page for Dash's name and went to the article.

Gavin wandered over as he read and lowered onto the mattress, baffled at the description of a promising young quarterback whose historic football pedigree was undeniable the moment he stepped on the field. The author of the article described an arm and accuracy that could only come from a lineage like Griffin's and at 6'2" and just over 200 pounds, Dash was the total package.

At seventeen, he showed a maturity on the field that could only come from an athlete with football in his DNA and he would only get bigger, faster, smarter, and stronger once he got to Michigan. The article admitted that it was practically a foregone conclusion that Dash would be a Wolverine like his legendary father and grandfather before him. An anecdote stated that scouts from Michigan had been in the stands when Dash took the field as a tiny mite, the anticipation was so great around his entry into the game. Even at the age of six, Dash could throw long and clean and already showed impressive agility.

Gavin closed the magazine and studied the young man wearing a crown and hugging a helmet on the cover. He recognized the brilliant smile, but the shine was missing from Dash's eyes and Gavin could see that he wasn't comfortable. It was the same stressed smile that Dash had spread across his face whenever he was hiding Gavin's lies from Reid.

He wondered what Dash's life would have been like if he had stayed on the path his parents and society had chosen for him. Gavin imagined what *Dash* would look like if his coaches and trainers had pushed him to get bigger and stronger and what shape he would be in now, at thirty-two. Dash complained about his back and his knees occasionally and he'd left the game behind more than a decade ago. Swift, on the other hand, was a walking tragedy after his long and storied career. He creaked and cracked when he moved and every other sound out of him was a grunt or a stifled swear.

For Swift, the sacrifice had clearly been worth it. He was still in love with football and was proud of the life it had provided for his family. That was obvious to anyone who saw Swift on television or had the good fortune to meet him in person. But Gavin only had to look at Dash to know that Swift's love for his son eclipsed football and fame. Instead of pushing his son to sacrifice his body and his spirit, Swift had spared Dash and supported him unconditionally when he chose a different path.

Instead of being jealous or hating his own father more, Gavin was grateful to Swift and Hannah for seeing so much more in their son than his athletic talent and Wheaties box smile. And Swift and Hannah had proven what Gavin had long suspected, that it was possible to be privileged and powerful and still love and nurture your child. That there was nothing inherently disappointing or even defective about Gavin and that it had been his parents who were broken.

And Gavin finally understood how Dash could be so generous with his heart and why he was so driven to make the world better for the people around him. Dash had been given a gift that most young people—regardless of race, gender, or class—could only dream of. He had the unconditional love and acceptance of his parents and the freedom to be *anything* he wanted.

Most young men couldn't handle that much privilege and did ridiculous, useless things like release terrible rap albums or star in reality television shows. There were no cringey videos of Dash with his hair in braids and rapping and he rarely went to nightclubs because he had no desire to be hip or famous. All he wanted was to pay forward all the love and good fortune he'd been blessed with and Gavin felt profoundly honored that Dash had chosen him.

Gavin was bluffing when he told his father that he would make sure he was known for being nothing but extremely gay and devoted to Dash Griffin. But that was exactly what Gavin wanted as he returned the magazine to the stack and went to wake Dash. He slipped off his pajama pants before getting under the covers and gathering Dash in his arms.

"Morning," Dash slurred, winding his heavy limbs around Gavin and wiggling closer. He was hard and purred as he rocked his hips, rubbing his erection against Gavin's semi-hard cock.

"Just a moment," Gavin requested, even though his hand continued to glide around Dash's hip and kneaded an asscheek appreciatively. He angled his head and captured Dash's lips for a reverent, seeking kiss, thrilling at how easy it was to do that now and how naturally they fit together. "Marry me, Dash," he whispered as his arms tightened around Dash—bracing him—because Gavin's instincts warned that might be wise.

"Oh, my God! *What?*" Dash gasped and flailed, kicking the covers and tossing a pillow off the bed in his excitement. "Are you serious? Do you really mean it?"

"Shhh! Of course, I mean it," Gavin murmured as he patted and stroked soothingly. "Come here, please." He had managed to keep his voice even and smooth despite the wild thrashing of his heart. That wasn't a yes yet, technically, but it was pretty damn close and Dash's head bobbled rapidly and he was crying as he rolled Gavin onto his back and rose over him.

"I was going to wait until next Christmas and maybe ask you in the park," he said shakily.

"Ah. Would you rather we waited, then?" Gavin asked, then laughed when Dash's lips crushed his and he was smothered in loud, wet kisses.

"No, no, no, no, no!" Dash's head popped up as he paused

and his nose wrinkled as he considered. He slid Gavin a sheepish smile. "*Yes*, I want to marry you. But no, I don't want to wait. I'm ready if you're ready."

Gavin gave his racing heart and nerves a moment to settle. He felt like he was about to take a wild leap, but instead of being afraid, Gavin was *thrilled*. His heart was full and Gavin knew he had something precious with Dash that was worth so much more than a financial empire or a football dynasty. Their love was going to be his legacy and would inspire future generations of young people to live and love bravely.

"What if we had the wedding next Christmas?" He suggested, spreading his fingers through Dash's hair and pulling his lips closer. Gavin made a contented sound as he kissed Dash deeply. "I want the world to see us now and I want a whole year to flaunt my amazing fiancé."

"Flaunt?" Dash snorted and giggled against Gavin's lips. "You have never flaunted once in your life. And where would you do all this flaunting? You barely leave Briarwood Terrace."

"That's not true at all," Gavin said. "I've seen just about every store window and visited every holiday market in Manhattan over the last two weeks. I've followed you around Central Park and all the way up to Connecticut. But, from now on, instead of worrying and hiding while I'm with you, I want to celebrate every day—be it a Tuesday or a holiday—and make sure everyone knows just how lucky I am. I love you, Dash, and I want that to be my future and my legacy. I want the world to remember that Gavin Selby belonged to Dash Griffin and that they lived happily ever after."

"Okay," Dash replied in a broken whisper as he wiped the tears from Gavin's cheek. They were both crying. "I'll see what I can do about that," he said as he reached for the bedside table and the lube.

"I take it we're about to check something else off the naughty list," Gavin guessed, earning a sultry chuckle as Dash nibbled on his ear.

"But it's going to be so nice."

The End

Epilogue

O*ne year later...*

Gavin married Dash at Briarwood Terrace. There was no place more sacred to Gavin and he wanted his Uncle Henry to be with him when he said his vows. None of Gavin's extraordinary life would have been possible if it hadn't been for Henry.

He had been a quiet, sensible man who bothered no one and preferred the company of his books and his tea to leaving his apartment. And Gavin suspected—rather gratefully—that he'd taken after Henry more than his parents. It was Henry who had shaped Gavin's fashion sensibilities—and explained his sexual preference—when he said that a good suit could hide a great many faults *and* lead you to temptation. Henry was fanatical about fine tailoring and carried himself with under-stated elegance, always dressed in a tasteful suit or housecoat. Gavin was certain Henry approved and was smiling down on them when the back courtyard at Briarwood Terrace was chosen as the wedding venue.

A dozen Christmas trees, yards of pine-scented garland, an explosion of pink and white poinsettias, thousands of string lights, and bolts of fluffy white fleece hid the fence and the raised gardens, transforming the small courtyard into a romantic winter wonderland. A beautiful arch with an intricate snowflake trellis that had been built by Penn stood at the end of a glittery white aisle and a ball of mistletoe hung above the grooms' heads.

They were a bit daring with their tuxedos, choosing navy with silver and pink ties and pocket squares. Gavin thought Dash looked devastatingly handsome when they met under the mistletoe. His parents and Penny were with Dash and Gavin had asked his brothers and best friends, Reid and Morris, to stand with him. The wedding was small and attended only by close friends and family, but it was still unnerving for Gavin to be the center of so much attention and celebration.

Henry had come to the rescue again when Gavin was fretting over his vows. And he was there to settle Gavin's nerves when it was time to share them with Dash and their guests. "I believe that Reid and Morris are the only people here who knew my Uncle Henry," Gavin began, looking around, but no one aside from Reid nodded and there was a sad sigh from Morris. "He was a quiet, generous, gentle man and whatever good qualities I possess are because I try to be a credit to his memory. He took me in when I was six and gave me a home here at Briarwood Terrace. We never discussed his homosexuality because..." Gavin cringed, his soul curdling at the thought. "Because it wasn't any of my business and because he lived in a different world and *had to* live quietly. I think he recognized that I was like him in that way as well, long before I understood, and knew what challenges I'd face. He did everything in his power to shelter and nurture me and through this place I've been able to grow a beautiful life and a loving family. And when my father tried to take it away, I fought to protect the Marshall Agency and keep it here at Briarwood Terrace because it's what Henry would have wanted me to do." Gavin blinked back tears so he could see Dash's eyes and chuckled softly. "Not just because he would have believed in this agency, but because that was the only way a cranky homebody like me would find a decent man."

There were murmurs and titters of agreement and Dash shushed everyone. "I think this is the part where I come in!"

"It is," Gavin confirmed, his heart beating faster as he was bombarded by memories of Dash laughing as he came through the front door, filling the apartment with love and warmth. "The perfect man came into my already lovely life, but it took me a while to build up the courage," he admitted. "I've come to realize that Henry didn't leave me Briarwood Terrace and protect me from my father and the world he knew so I could live just like him. He left me this place and protected me so I could have the life he *couldn't*. Henry would have wanted me to find an extraordinary man and love him freely and completely. But I don't think he could have imagined anyone as beautiful as you, Dash." Gavin raised Dash's knuckles and kissed them.

"I love you so much!" Dash whispered, sniffling loudly.

"One day, you came up with a nice list and turned my world upside down in the most beautiful ways," Gavin continued shakily. "I was already secretly in love with you, but you gave me hope and made me believe in magic. Most importantly, you believed in *us*, and you gave me a reason to stand up for myself. I didn't believe that I deserved anyone as good as you or that happily ever after was possible for me. But I have *everything* now and thanks to you, I'm going to fill this place with the kind of love Henry could only dream of. I love you, and have only ever loved you, Dash, and I will spend the rest of my life trying to make you as happy as you've made me." Their hands were shaking as he slipped a simple platinum ring on Dash's finger. But Gavin was no longer nervous, he was bursting with pride and in awe of the gratitude he felt for Dash and the life Henry had left him.

"Goodness, and I thought we'd done something special with a teacup," Dash joked when it was his turn. He had come armed with a blue handkerchief from Swift and dabbed at his eyes before taking Gavin's hands again. "I've been asked more than a few times why I was so sure about you and why I was willing to wait for so long. But a few years was nothing, when I had already waited a lifetime to find you," he paused and shushed when Gavin made a dubious sound. "It's true," Dash said, looking back and smiling at Penny and his parents. "I've been surrounded by love my whole life, but I've been waiting for my soulmate. And one day, while we were having brunch, I realized it was you. You were the one I'd been looking for and all the other questions I had about who I wanted to be and what I wanted the future to look like had been answered. What was a few more years when I had found the love of a lifetime?"

"How can I ever deserve you?" Gavin worried out loud.

"Stop it!" Dash laughed as he stole a quick kiss. "You're going to make me forget the rest. I didn't regret a moment of those years because I got to see *you* and learn who I was giving my heart to. And when the time came and we finally happened, you were even more caring and loyal than I was expecting. You blew me away with your unconditional love for your friends and I saw how far you were willing to go to protect them and there was no doubt in my mind that you were the one I was meant to spend my life with. Falling in love has already been a dream come true, and I can't think of anything that would make me happier than to share this beautiful life and family with you."

Dash put a matching ring on Gavin's finger and they were pronounced married, to loudly rapturous applause. They kissed, both crying and blushing as they were swept up in cheerful, tearful hugs. The rest of the evening felt like a fairytale, dancing with Dash beneath the stars and string lights.

Gavin would cherish the night, being surrounded by the people who meant the most to him. Fin and Walker were there with the triplets as were Giles, Riley, Milo, and Luna. Agnes, June, Penn, Cadence, Evelyn, and Morris Sr. were there. Ashley, James, and Carolyn were also invited to share in the celebration and Norman had even made it and had brought his wife, Lucy. But for Gavin, the most magical part of the evening had been when he was dancing with Dash and looked around to find that everyone except the band had left.

"How did that happen?" He asked with a delighted gasp.

Dash smiled knowingly, sliding an arm around Gavin's shoulders and pulling him closer. "I heard they had a surprise planned for us. They know your idea of a perfect party is one that requires you to talk to as few people as possible and ends promptly at 9:00."

"And your idea of a perfect party is when it's just you and me," Gavin murmured as he rested his forehead on Dash's.

"Exactly," Dash said happily. "All that's left is to get us out of these suits, but I'm giving Reid a little more time to clear everyone out and find someplace else to stay tonight. I warned him that this could get loud."

"I'm certain Reid has plans. You saw how tight his suit was. And at his age," Gavin complained, clicking his teeth.

Dash swatted Gavin's shoulder. "There was nothing wrong with his suit. I thought he looked sharp."

"He looked fine. You on the other hand..." Gavin turned

them so Dash's back was away from the band and gave his ass a possessive squeeze. "I believe it's customary to eat cake on one's wedding night," he whispered, causing Dash to giggle.

"Mr. Selby-Griffin!" He said dramatically and Gavin shrugged, maintaining his hold on Dash's backside.

"You're the one who made the winter wedding punch, Mr. Griffin-Selby, and you're the one who kept refilling my cup." The sound of their names together made Gavin feel drunker and like he was floating as he kissed Dash.

"And my plan is all coming together," Dash chuckled. "Seriously, what are we going to do about Reid? Don't you think it's his turn to be some man's Prince Charming and find his fairytale?"

A laugh exploded from Gavin and he had to hang onto Dash until he could control himself. "Reid? Prince—?" He wiped his eyes and giggled. "Reid will never be any man's Prince Charming, nor does he want to be."

"That's not nice! Reid can be charming...when he wants to," Dash added hesitantly, but Gavin gave him a dry look.

"Reid is one of the very best people I have ever met. He is selfless, brave, forthright, and the most loyal person I know. But he is *not* charming and he certainly doesn't want to be charmed by any prince. And you better not let him hear you talking like that," Gavin warned, shaking his head. "I don't think we should *do* anything about Reid."

"You don't?" Dash looked skeptical as he leaned back in Gavin's arms. "You're fine with whatever it is he's doing when he sneaks off," he verified and Gavin humphed.

"Reid is a grown man," he said, then smirked confidently. "I've tried warning him, and I have a feeling he's about to run out of luck. A man can't play those kinds of games without winning stupid prizes and I've been expecting the consequences of one of Reid's little misadventures to find its way back to us," he predicted.

"Why? What do you know?" Dash asked, but Gavin shook his head.

"Nothing at all, thank goodness. We've never shared those kinds of personal details and I truly believe that's why our friendship has lasted as long as it has. Oversharing can be a terrible burden when one learns things they don't want to know. But Reid has no one else to look after, now, and he's going to feel like a fifth wheel wherever he goes. That's a recipe for disaster because Reid *needs* someone to look after and a problem to fix or else he self-destructs."

"Oh, no!"

"He'll be fine. He has us," Gavin said dismissively. "And it'll serve Reid right, meddling and setting us all up while he cosplays as a boy toy at the Baccarat on the weekends."

"Really?" Dash sounded shocked as he stared over Gavin's shoulder at the kitchen windows. "No wonder he thinks everything is perfect just the way it is."

"And we've seen what happens around here when a man thinks his life is perfect just the way it is."

"Yes, we have," Dash chuckled as he wound his hand in Gavin's tie and towed him toward the door. "I pity the man because he'll have his hands full with Reid, but it'll be worth it."

"I'm not so sure," Gavin said, smiling as Dash reached for the door. "He's going to have to put up with all of us and that's enough to send even the bravest man screaming."

"Stop it," Dash scolded as they danced through the door and into a quiet, dimly lit apartment. "I love our chaotic family and every minute here at Briarwood Terrace has been magical."

"Only because of you, Dash. We were happy and doing fine, but you saved me and you helped heal a wound that had been festering for a long time. You brought your big, beautiful heart and changed everything and I will never be able to repay you for the joy you've brought me," Gavin said, tipping Dash's chin back for another kiss.

A soft laugh escaped Dash as their lips clung. "I have everything I've ever wanted now that I have you. But I have a list of ideas you could try if you're in the mood for something naughty," he teased and Gavin nodded, smiling as he backed them through the kitchen to their bedroom.

"I think I'd like to take a look at that list. I might have a few suggestions of my own..."

The End

His Secret Santa

Chapter 1

Another year later...

There was absolutely *nothing* better than winter in New York City as far as Gavin Selby-Griffin was concerned. The decorations, the store window displays, the twinkling lights, the parades, the holiday music... Gavin loved all the music! New and classic holiday tunes played in every store, bar, and restaurant and there were carolers in the parks and on street corners. But the possibilities were endless if you were planning a romantic Christmas Eve with the world's most perfect man and holiday fan.

Gavin had planned, and planned, and planned, and all that was left was for Dash to leave Briarwood Terrace. He was currently chatting with Reid in the kitchen about an impending snowstorm and last-minute gifts. Dash would be headed out soon for a few errands and Reid was leaving to spend Christmas Eve in Park Slope with his parents.

As soon as they were gone, Gavin would spring into action and was looking forward to his first turn as Secret Santa. It was

Chapter 1

also their first Christmas Eve *alone* at Briarwood Terrace and it had to be every bit as magical as Dash had made the holidays for Gavin.

Dash's parents were going to be on television, hosting a night of musical performances in Bryant Park. They wouldn't be finished until late so Swift and Hannah were staying in the city and coming to Briarwood Terrace for breakfast Christmas morning.

The very idea of Swift and Hannah spending Christmas with them at Briarwood Terrace overwhelmed Gavin in the most wonderful way. Especially when he imagined what his Uncle Henry would think about Hannah and Swift and how much he would have loved hosting them for Christmas. Gavin still had a hard time believing he was married and had in-laws. And they were simply the loveliest people Gavin had ever met. He was deeply grateful to have them in his life. So grateful that he might have gone a touch overboard with the decorations and food...

There was a giant tree in the lobby. Dash swore it was as tall as the one in Rockefeller Plaza. It was not. But it was as tall as the staircase and decorated with jump ropes and toys. Gavin *loved it* because it looked like Santa's workshop had exploded in Briarwood Terrace. Pedestrians could smell the pine garland from blocks away, Gavin had draped yards and yards of it inside and outside the building.

The tree inside unit number 4 was almost as impressive and practically took up half of the living room. Gavin was seated in his chair next to it and calmly sipping his tea, despite feeling the very opposite of calm. So far, the holidays and Christmas Eve eve had been a delightfully festive whirlwind, but Gavin had barely had a moment alone with Dash. He was looking forward to remedying that while Reid was away for two nights and intended to cherish every minute.

252

Chapter 1

"I think I'll take off," Reid announced as he headed to the door and got his coat and scarf off the hook.

Gavin set down his tea and rose. "Give your parents my love and we'll see you on Boxing Day."

"Isn't that a weird holiday?" Dash asked, scratching his head as he followed Reid and reached for his peacoat. "It used to be a day of charity and sharing with the less fortunate in the UK. But now it's like another Black Friday."

"It would be nice if there was more charity and sharing these days," Reid said as he knotted his scarf and Gavin hummed thoughtfully.

"Perhaps we could take it upon ourselves," he murmured despite already having a plan for that as well. No one in their group had claimed the day and Gavin was going to start a joyful new tradition. *After* he had his quiet Christmas Eve with Dash. "Have a Merry Christmas, Reid," Gavin said, opening his arms and pulling him into a tight embrace.

"You too." Reid held on for a moment, then clapped Gavin on the back. "I love you and I left something for you under the tree." He winked at Gavin as he reached for Dash. "It's for both of you. Merry Christmas, kiddo."

"Merry Christmas, Reid!" Dash scooped him into a hug and Reid laughed as he was spun.

"Alright, I'll see you two later," he said with a tap of his brow, then grabbed his overnight bag on the way out.

Dash sighed happily as Reid left. "Isn't he *the best*? Are you sure you don't want to tag along?" He asked, turning to Gavin. "I'm hitting the market for a few more gifts and then I'm swinging by Bryant Park to have lunch with Mom and Dad while they're in hair and makeup. After that, I'm heading to East 63rd to drop off those Christmas friendship bracelets from Milo," he explained cheerfully, but Gavin shook his head.

Gavin had "forgotten" to deliver said bracelets after his last

Chapter 1

visit to the Olympia but had promised they would make it to June, Penny, and Agnes before Christmas for the express purpose of getting Dash out of Briarwood Terrace. "Think I'll stay and clean my clarinet. It's covered in little fingerprints from last night," he mused with a dismissive wave, earning an amused hum as Dash leaned close and pecked at Gavin's lips.

"We can't have that!" He teased. "It's probably for the best. The wind's extra prickly today and it's supposed to snow like crazy later."

Gavin shook his head, winding Dash's scarf around his neck and giving it a gentle tug before tucking it in. "I'll go ahead and put the kettle on," he decided.

"Want me to do it before I go?" Dash offered, but Gavin shushed him.

"Go and give your parents my love. Tell them I'm looking forward to my sleigh ride with Swift," he said, chuckling as he got the door for Dash.

After Dash and Gavin's first couples' sleigh ride in Greenwich, Hannah and Swift decided to make it a tradition. Having learned that the experience wasn't ideal for romance, Swift had hired two sleighs and was making it a race. Gavin had been chosen to be Swift's sidekick and Hannah would be on Team Dash.

"I can't wait! You're going to love the matching pajamas Mom got for you and Dad."

"Matching—?" Gavin started, but Dash gasped as he checked his watch.

"Look at the time! I better get going!"

"No one said anything about matching pajamas," Gavin said, frowning. "There had better not be fuzzy slippers and it will go directly in the fire if it is any sort of onesie," he warned.

"Gotta run and no it won't!" Dash grabbed Gavin's face

and kissed him until all thoughts of hideous and humiliating pajamas had faded. "Love you," Dash whispered.

"I love you too," Gavin said dreamily. It still didn't seem real that Dash was his and that this was Gavin's wonderful life. "Have fun and I'll see you soon."

"Okay. Message me if you need anything while I'm out," Dash said and pouted loudly as he pulled his lips away from Gavin's. "I'll miss you," he said, backing through the door and into the hall.

"I'll miss you too," Gavin said with a wave, leaning and watching until the door closed. He rolled his eyes at the soft, swooning sigh that slipped from him. "Time to get to work. It's going to take a lot to tickle the world's sweetest elf."

Chapter 2

"What happened?" Dash turned in Briarwood Terrace's foyer, confused and a touch concerned.

Almost everything looked like it had when he left, but all the toys were missing from the giant Christmas tree. It was still stunning with its rainbow-colored ribbons, glittery snowflakes, and shiny baubles, but all the jump ropes, teddy bears, dolls, and firetrucks were gone. Norman wasn't there, obviously, so Dash hurried around the corner to see if Gavin knew the toys had been taken.

But Dash's steps halted when he spotted the two laundry carts by their front door. "Um..." They were filled with the dolls, bears, jump ropes, and trucks from the tree. He let himself into unit number 4, juggling his bags, then almost dropped them when he saw all the children's books on the floor. There was a trail of them leading from the door, past the sofa and the kitchen, and down the hall. "What in the..." His voice cracked and Dash's mouth watered as he sniffed. He could smell freshly baked cookies and Dean Martin was crooning softly about a white Christmas. "Gavin?" Dash called, setting

Chapter 2

down his bags and picking up the first book. "*Little Blue Truck's Christmas?*" He read excitedly, then bent to pick up the next. His eyes widened when he saw the candles, the elegantly set table, and the little tree in the corner of the kitchen. It was covered in red roses and wrapped in gold ribbon. "Gavin?" He attempted again, but it was a weak croak as Dash scooped another book into his now precarious pile.

"In here," Gavin called back from the bedroom.

"Good." Dash nodded as he navigated around the corner with his arms full of awesomeness. "I don't know what all of this is about, but it will involve sex. Lots and lots of sex," he promised, using his foot to push the door wider and pausing to look over the stack. "Oh!" He squeaked.

"It's our new Boxing Day tradition," Gavin said, holding out a glass of pink champagne. He looked so handsome and festive in a red flannel robe and a Santa hat, Dash's knees felt weak as he carefully set the books on the dresser.

"Boxing Day?" He asked shakily as he went to Gavin. "What's this?" He poked at one of the cranberries floating on the champagne's fizzing surface

"They're candied and I added a splash of cranberry juice to make it pink," Gavin explained, raising his glass and encouraging Dash to take a sip.

"That's lovely!" Dash said, looking around. "What's happening on Boxing Day?"

Gavin held up a finger, taking a long drink while gesturing for Dash to do the same. He waited until they both had a chance to enjoy their beverages, then took Dash's and relocated them to the bedside table. "I thought that we could start our own Boxing Day tradition here at Briarwood Terrace by taking all the toys and books to some of the foster homes around the city. You and Penny already know the appropriate people to contact to make that happen so—"

Chapter 2

"Totally called it. Sex time!" Dash shouted as he tackled Gavin onto the bed. He was crying as he attacked Gavin's lips and squirmed out of his sneakers and clothes. "This is the most wonderful thing anyone has ever done for me. I can't wait to tell Penny about what we're doing with all those toys and books."

"You didn't think I bought all those teddy bears and dolls for myself, did you?" Gavin chuckled, but it was strained as Dash licked along his jaw and nibbled an earlobe.

"I assumed it was all getting donated. I didn't know you already had such an amazing plan. This is so, so awesome. And everything in the kitchen looks perfect!"

Dash had already prepared most of their sides and it wouldn't take him long to cook their steaks. They had decided to forgo a large roast, ham, or turkey since it was just the two of them and Dash had purchased gorgeous filet mignons. But Gavin had managed to make their cozy, quiet evening in even more romantic and magical than Dash was expecting. And he was already expecting it to be lovely because it was just him and Gavin.

"You're perfect, Dash," Gavin said, tracing Dash's cheek. "You make every day feel like Christmas and I have so much joy in my life now, thanks to you. I want to share that with as many people as I can on Boxing Day."

"Then that's what we're going to do!" Dash kissed Gavin with his whole heart and rolled them so he was on top. "What's under here?" He asked, tugging the belt around Gavin's waist free and parting the halves. "Hello, Mr. Christmas!" He gasped in approval at Gavin's *red* flannel briefs. Gavin insisted that while he enjoyed Dash's brighter-colored briefs, bikinis, and jockstraps, anything other than white cotton would be garish *on him*. But it was the gift tag that Gavin had secured to his chest, just over his heart, that brought fresh tears to Dash's eyes.

Chapter 2

Dash thought that *he* was the master of holiday romance, but Gavin had swept him off his feet. "I'm really going to have to step up my game next year," he said, earning a dry snort from Gavin.

"I can't think of anything that needs 'stepping up' but no one will ever accuse you of phoning it in when it comes to holidays and being romantic."

"That's because it's extra fun and sexy having someone to celebrate with now," Dash purred, nuzzling his face in the hair in the center of Gavin's chest. He used his teeth to easily tug the gift tag free and flicked at Gavin's nipple with his tongue, making him buck off the bed. He licked and sucked his way down Gavin's body, enjoying his stifled swears and whimpers.

"Yes!" Gavin nodded frantically when Dash ripped the briefs open.

"Wow!" Dash did a double take. "You put a golden ring on it," he said, then slid down to get a closer look.

"It's not actual gold. It's silicone," Gavin mumbled before letting out a loud groan. Dash had traced around it with his tongue and sucked on the base of Gavin's shaft, just beneath the ring. "I thought it would be more...festive, but it's kind of tight."

"I *love* it."

Gavin loved it too, moaning and undulating on the bed as Dash licked and sucked every inch of his cock, his sac, and his ass. "Yes, Dash! Don't stop!" He begged when Dash took him deep into his throat and slid two fingers into Gavin's clenching heat.

"Not until we're both frosted and covered in sprinkles," Dash said, lapping at the end of Gavin's erection. He was so hard and he tasted so good. And he was *so* tight. It took Dash just a moment to coat his shaft with lube and line the head of his cock up with Gavin's hole. He rolled his hips and they both let out ecstatic moans as Dash filled him with a smooth, driving thrust.

"Oh, fuck!" Gavin's eyes rolled as Dash stroked lube onto his hard-on and ground against his prostate. "Could you...?" He licked his lips as his head thrashed. His glasses had been knocked off and his eyes were glazed and unfocused as he reached for Dash. "Could you...ride me?" He finally choked out.

"Like the Polar Express," Dash said with a saucy wink.

"You can stop *that* at any time," Gavin attempted wearily. But his snort turned into a gasp and neither of them was laughing as Dash rose over him and rearranged their legs so he was straddling Gavin. He slowly lowered, taking Gavin to the hilt and giving himself a moment to adjust, then swung forward and captured his lips for a quick, taunting kiss.

"Make me!" He whispered, rocking back and slamming his ass against Gavin's groin. "Even though we both know you love all my corny Christmas puns."

Gavin chuckled, flipping Dash onto his back and driving hard. "Most of them."

Chapter 2

"All of them!" Dash countered as he hooked a leg around Gavin's hip and an arm around his neck, pulling him closer and deeper.

"You're right," Gavin panted against Dash's lips, then kissed him. He was ravenous and desperate as hips pumped and his tongue swirled wildly around Dash's. "I love every single pun and corny joke. I love it all," he said, breathlessly babbling as his fingers tangled in Dash's hair and the other hand gripped his ass possessively.

"Me too." That was all Dash could manage. He was so full of Gavin and they were so close. Dash had never loved anyone as much as he loved Gavin and he felt so thoroughly cherished as they chanted and cried each other's names.

"*Love. You!*" Gavin shouted as he came and pulled Dash right over the edge with him.

For just a moment, the world was bright and soft like the inside of a snow globe that had just been shaken. His nerves hummed and flickered and Dash felt like he was floating back to earth and reality. But in Dash's case, reality was *almost* as glorious as getting off with Gavin. He was drifting from one dream to another as Gavin licked his way up Dash's body to his lips.

"Let's put on our pajamas, eat dessert before dinner, then open our gifts so we can sleep in tomorrow morning," he suggested in his low rumble, making Dash's heart flutter. "I want to see what Reid left us. I hope it isn't better than the watch I slipped into his bag. We said we weren't exchanging gifts unless they were small and I couldn't think of anything else he'd like that was small."

Reid had already hinted to Dash that the tenant in the unit directly above number 4 would be out of town indefinitely and that it might be nice if they had a little more room. "I think he's going to love the watch and I think you're going to...enjoy Reid's gift. If it's what I think it is."

"Wonderful," Gavin stated and bounded from the bed. "I snuck in a gingerbread cake from Evelyn's shop and I can't wait for you to try the cookies. She taught me how to make them."

Dash rose on his knees and pointed at Gavin. "Hold on. Are you telling me you learned how to make cookies?"

"I asked her while we were at Penn and Morris's a few months ago." Gavin shrugged nonchalantly, but a blush spread across his cheeks. "I've been stopping by the bakery for lessons when you're with your parents or Penny."

"Okay..." Dash reeled at how sexy *and* sweet that was. "We both need some time to recover, but I can't eat too many cookies after dinner. They'll have to wait until after we've demolished the naughty list."

Gavin smiled sheepishly as he fixed his glasses. "There's also a pint of Christmas cookie ice cream hiding in the freezer."

"Christmas cookie ice cream..." Dash's eyes widened when he had an epiphany. "What if I made a Christmas cookie sandwich with the Christmas cookies and the Christmas cookie ice cream?"

"That's a lot of sugar, but if anyone can handle that much sweetness, it's you," Gavin said with a bow, reaching for his robe on the dresser.

"Not so fast," Dash said, reconsidering and shuffling their plans for the evening. The sexiest thing he'd be in the mood for after stuffing himself with dinner and desserts was a nap. But he had a sweet, secretly sexy husband and was looking forward to starting some private traditions of their own. "I think you'd better get back in this bed. I've got a few more ideas for our naughty list."

A Letter From K. Sterling

Dear Reader,

Thank you so much for your time and for reading *The Nanny With The Nice List*. I hope you had fun falling in love with Dash and Gavin! Before you go, I'd appreciate it if you'd consider leaving a review. Your review would really help me and help other readers find their way to us. And I promise, I read and appreciate every single one of them. Even the negative reviews. I want your honest feedback so I know how to steal your heart.

Please help me out by leaving a review!

Once again, thank you from the very bottom of my heart. I love you for sharing your time with us and hope we'll see you again soon.

Love and happy reading,
K.

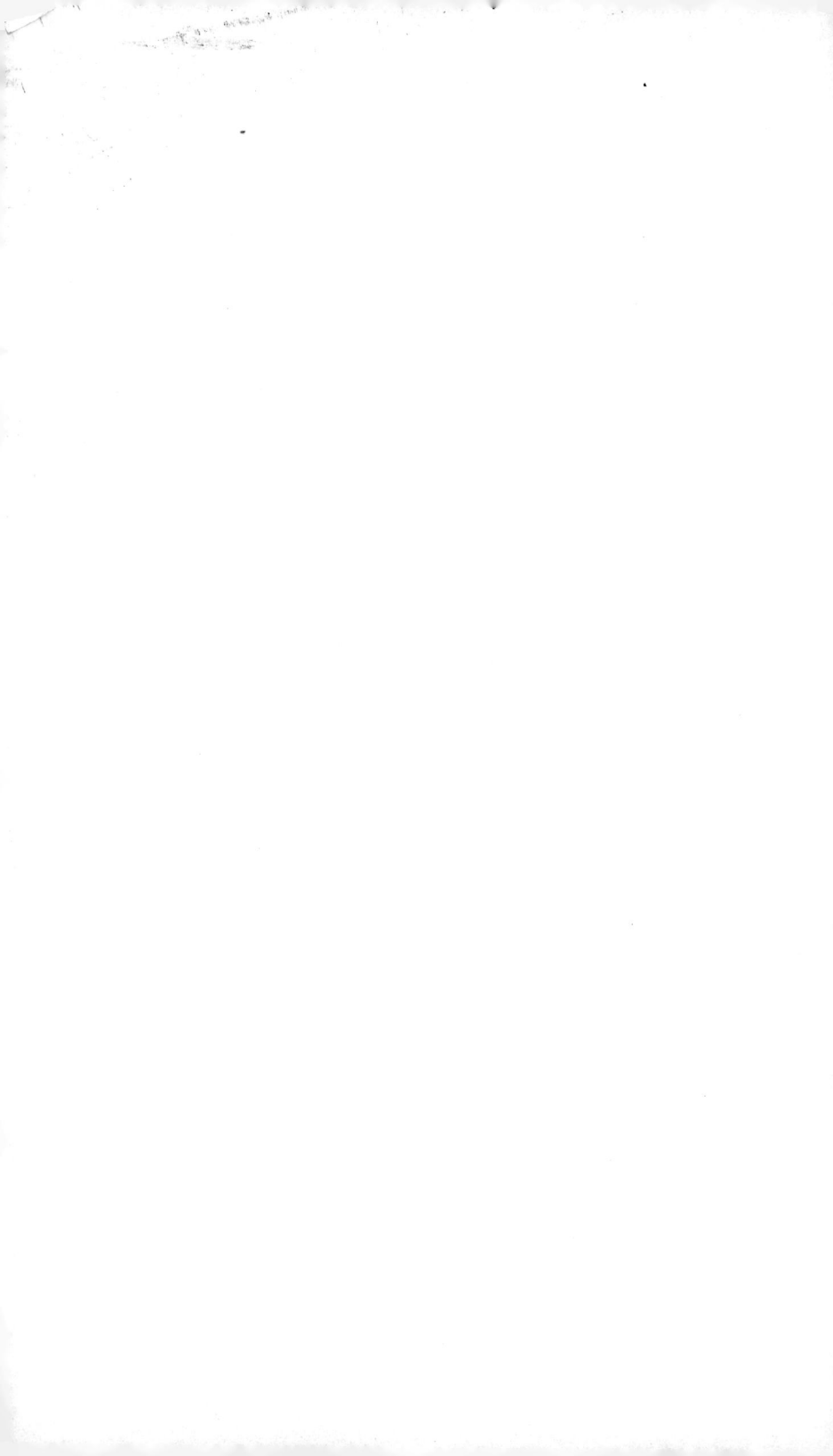

Coming Soon: One Night With The Nanny

Reid Marshall meets his match when the sexy consequences of his secrets comes to Briarwood Terrace looking for help with an angsty teenage daughter.

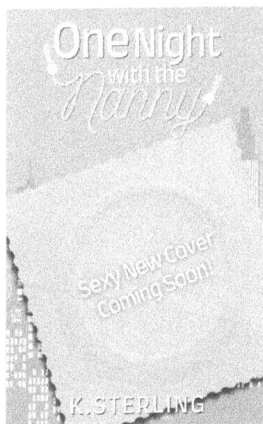

PreOrder NOW on Amazon!

About the Author

K. Sterling writes like a demon and is mother to Alex, Zoe, Stella, and numerous gay superheroes. She's also a history nerd, a *Lord of the Rings* fan, and a former counterintelligence agent. She has self-published dozens of M/M romance novels including the popular *Boys of Lake Cliff* series and *Beautiful Animal*. K. Sterling is known for fast-paced romantic thrillers and touching gay romcoms. There might be goosebumps and some gore but there's always true love and lots of laughter.

Milton Keynes UK
Ingram Content Group UK Ltd.
UKHW022027190824
1311UKWH00074B/1766

9 798866 903474